THE SERPENT KING

JEFF ZENTNER

THE SERPENT KING

A NOVEL

TUNDRA BOOKS

Library and Archives Canada Cataloguing in Publication

Zentner, Jeff, author
The serpent king / by Jeffrey Zentner.

ISBN 978-1-77049-883-9 (bound)

I. Title.

PZ7.1.Z46Se 2016   j813'.6   C2015-901070-5

Published simultaneously in the United States of America by
Crown Books for Young Readers

The text was set in New Baskerville
Jacket photographs: (bridge/figures) rolfo/Rolf Brenner/Getty Images;
(clouds) Shutterstock.com
Jacket design by Alison Impey

Printed and bound in the United States of America

www.penguinrandomhouse.ca

1 2 3 4 5   20 19 18 17 16

For Tennessee Luke Zentner,

my beautiful boy.

My heart.

1

DILL

There were things Dillard Wayne Early Jr. dreaded more than the start of school at Forrestville High. Not many, but a few. Thinking about the future was one of them. Dill didn't enjoy doing that. He didn't much care for talking about religion with his mother. That never left him feeling happy or saved. He loathed the flash of recognition that usually passed across people's faces when they learned his name. That rarely resulted in a conversation he enjoyed.

And he *really* didn't enjoy visiting his father, Pastor Dillard Early Sr., at Riverbend Prison. His trip to Nashville that day wasn't to visit his father, but he still had a nagging sense of unformed dread and he didn't know why. It might have been because school was starting the next day, but this felt different somehow than in years past.

It would have been worse except for the excitement of seeing Lydia. The worst days spent with her were better than the best days spent without her.

Dill stopped strumming his guitar, leaned forward, and wrote in the dollar-store composition book open on the floor in front of him. The decrepit window air conditioner wheezed, losing the battle against the mugginess of his living room.

The thudding of a wasp at the window caught his attention over the laboring of the air conditioner. He rose from the ripped sofa and walked to the window, which he jimmied until it screeched open.

Dill swatted the wasp toward the crack. "You don't want to stay in here," he murmured. "This house is no place to die. Go on. Get."

It alighted on the sill, considered the house one more time, and flew free. Dill shut the window, almost having to hang from it to close it all the way.

His mother walked in wearing her motel maid's uniform. She looked tired. She always did, which made her seem much older than her thirty-five years. "What were you doing with the window open and the AC on? Electricity's not free."

Dill turned. "Wasp."

"Why you all dressed to leave? You going somewhere?"

"Nashville." *Please don't ask the question I know you're going to ask.*

"Visiting your father?" She sounded both hopeful and accusatory.

"No." Dill looked away.

His mother stepped toward him and sought his eyes. "Why not?"

Dill avoided her glare. "Because. That's not why we're going."

"Who's we?"

"Me. Lydia. Travis. Same as always."

She put a hand on her hip. "Why you going, then?"

"School clothes."

"Your clothes are fine."

"No they're not. They're getting too small." Dill lifted his skinny arms, his T-shirt exposing his lean stomach.

"With what money?" His mother's brow—already more lined than most women's her age—furrowed.

"Just my tips from helping people to their cars with their groceries."

"Free trip to Nashville. You should visit your father."

You better go visit your father or else, you mean. Dill set his jaw and looked at her. "I don't want to. I hate it there."

She folded her arms. "It's not meant to be fun. That's why it's prison. Think he enjoys it?"

Probably more than I enjoy it. Dill shrugged and gazed back out the window. "Doubt it."

"I don't ask for much, Dillard. It would make me happy. And it would make him happy."

Dill sighed and said nothing. *You ask for plenty without ever actually asking for it.*

"You owe him. You're the only one with enough free time."

She would hang it over his head. If he didn't visit, she would make it hurt worse for longer than if he gave in. The dread in Dill's stomach intensified. "Maybe. If we have time."

As his mother was about to try to drag a firmer commitment from him, a bestickered Toyota Prius zoomed up his road and screeched to a stop in front of his house with a honk. *Thank you, God.*

"I gotta go," Dill said. "Have a good day at work." He hugged his mother goodbye.

"Dillard—"

But he was out the door before she had the chance. He felt burdened as he stepped into the bright summer morning, shielding his eyes against the sun. The humidity mounted an assault even at nine-twenty in the morning—like a hot, wet towel wrapped around his face. He glanced at the peeling white Calvary Baptist Church up the street from his house. He squinted to read the sign out of habit. NO JESUS, NO PEACE. KNOW JESUS, KNOW PEACE.

What if you know Jesus but have no peace? Does that mean the sign is wrong, or does that mean you don't know Jesus quite as well as you think? Dill hadn't been raised to consider either a particularly good outcome.

He opened the car door and got in. The frigid air conditioning made his pores shrink.

"Hey, Lydia."

She grabbed a worn copy of *The Secret History* off the passenger seat before Dill sat on it, and tossed it in the back-seat. "Sorry I'm late."

"You're not sorry."

"Of course I'm not. But I have to pretend. Social contractual obligations and whatnot."

You could set your clock by Lydia's being twenty minutes late. And it was no use trying to trick her by telling her to meet you at a time twenty minutes before you really wanted to meet. That only made her forty minutes late. She had a sixth sense.

Lydia leaned over and hugged Dill. "You're already sweaty and it's still morning. Boys are so gross."

The black frames of her glasses creaked against his cheekbone. Her tousled smoky-blue hair—the color of a faded November sky streaked with clouds—smelled like honey, fig, and vetiver. He breathed it in. It made his head swim in a pleasant way. She had dressed for Nashville in a vintage sleeveless red gingham blouse with black high-waisted denim shorts and vintage cowboy boots. He loved the way she dressed—every twist and turn, and there were many.

Dill buckled his seat belt the instant before her acceleration pressed him into his seat. "Sorry. I don't have access to AC that makes August feel like December." He sometimes went days without feeling air as cool as in Lydia's car except for when he opened the refrigerator.

She reached out and turned the air conditioning down a couple of clicks. "I think my car should fight global warming in every possible way."

Dill angled one of the vents toward his face. "You ever think about how weird it is that Earth is hurtling through the black vacuum of space, where it's like a thousand below zero, and meanwhile we're down here sweating?"

"I often think about how weird it is that Earth is hurtling through the black vacuum of space and meanwhile you're down here being a total weirdo."

"So, where are we going in Nashville? Opry Mills Mall or something?"

Lydia glared at him and looked back at the road. She extended her hand toward him, still looking forward. "Excuse me, I thought we'd been best friends since ninth grade, but apparently we've never even met. Lydia Blankenship. You are?"

Dill took advantage of the opportunity to take her hand. "Dillard Early. Maybe you've heard of my father by the same name."

It had thoroughly scandalized Forrestville, Tennessee, when Pastor Early of the Church of Christ's Disciples with Signs of Belief went to the state penitentiary—and not for the reasons anyone expected. Everyone assumed he'd get in trouble someday for the twenty-seven or so rattlesnakes and copperheads his congregants passed around each Sunday. No one knew with certainty what law they were breaking, but it seemed unlawful somehow. And the Tennessee Department of Wildlife did take custody of the snakes after his arrest. Or people thought perhaps he'd run afoul of the law by inducing his flock to drink diluted battery acid and strychnine, another favored worship activity. But no, he went to Riverbend Prison for a different sort of poison: possession of more than one hundred images depicting a minor engaged in sexual activity.

Lydia tilted her head and squinted. "Dillard Early, huh? The name rings a bell. Anyway, yes, we're driving an hour and a half to Nashville to go to Opry Mills Mall and buy you the same sweatshop garbage that Tyson Reed, Logan Walker, Hunter Henry, their intolerable girlfriends, and all of their horrible friends will also be wearing on the first day of senior year."

"I ask a simple question—"

She raised a finger. "A stupid question."

"A stupid question."

"Thank you."

Dill's eyes fell on Lydia's hands at the steering wheel. They were slender, with long, graceful fingers; vermilion-colored nails; and lots of rings. The rest of her wasn't ungraceful but her fingers were affirmatively and aggressively graceful. He relished watching her drive. And type. And do everything she did with her hands.

"Did you call Travis to tell him you were running late?"

"Did I call *you* to tell you I was running late?" She took a turn fast, squealing her tires.

"No."

"Think it'll come as a surprise to him that I'm running late?"

"Nope."

The August air was a steamy haze. Dill could already hear the bugs, whatever they were called. The ones that made a pulsing, rattling drone on a sweltering morning, signaling that the day would only grow hotter. Not cicadas, he didn't think. Rattlebugs. That seemed as good a name as any.

"What am I working with today?" Lydia asked. Dill gave her a blank stare. She held up her hand and rubbed her fingers together. "Come on, buddy, keep up here."

"Oh. Fifty bucks. Can you work with that?"

She snorted. "Of course I can work with that."

"Okay, but no dressing me weird."

Lydia extended her hand to him again—more forcefully, as though karate chopping a board. "No, but *seriously*. Have we met? What was your name again?"

Dill grasped her hand again. Any excuse. "You're in a mood today."

"I'm in the mood to receive a little credit. Not much. Don't spoil me."

"Wouldn't dream of it."

"In the last two years of school shopping, have I ever made you look ridiculous?"

"No. I mean, I still caught hell for stuff, but I'm sure that would've happened no matter what I wore."

"It would. Because we go to school with people who wouldn't recognize great style if it bit them right on their ass. I have a vision for you, planted in rustic Americana. Western shirts with pearl snaps. Denim. Classic, masculine, iconic lines. While everyone else at Forrestville High tries

desperately to appear as though they don't live in Forrestville, we'll embrace and own your rural Southernness,
continuing in the vein of 1970s Townes Van Zandt meets
Whiskeytown-era Ryan Adams."

"You've planned this." Dill savored the idea of Lydia
thinking about him. Even if only as a glorified mannequin.

"Would you expect less?"

Dill breathed in the fragrance of her car. Vanilla car
freshener mixed with french fries, jasmine-orange-ginger
lotion, and heated makeup. They were almost to Travis's
house. He lived close to Dill. They stopped at an inter-
section, and Lydia took a selfie with her cell phone and
handed it to Dill.

"Get me from your angle."

"You sure? Your fans might start thinking you have
friends."

"Hardy har. Do it and let me worry about that."

A couple of blocks later, they pulled up to the Bohannon house. It was white and rundown with a weathered tin
roof and wood stacked on the front porch. Travis's father
perspired in the gravel driveway, changing out the spark
plugs on his pickup that had the name of the family business, *Bohannon Lumber*, stenciled on the side. He cast Dill
and Lydia a briny glare, cupped his hand to his mouth, and
yelled, "Travis, you got company," saving Lydia the trouble
of honking.

"Pappy Bohannon looks to be in a bit of a mood himself," Lydia said.

"To hear Travis tell it, Pappy Bohannon is in a permanent mood. It's called being a giant asshole, and it's incurable."

A moment or two passed before Travis came loping outside. Ambling, perhaps. Whatever bears do. All six feet, six inches, and 250 pounds of him. His shaggy, curly red hair and patchy red teenager beard were wet from the shower. He wore his signature black work boots, black Wranglers, and baggy black dress shirt buttoned all the way up. Around his neck, he wore a necklace with a chintzy pewter dragon gripping a purple crystal ball—a memento from some Renaissance festival. He always wore it. He carried a dog-eared paperback from the Bloodfall series, something else he was seldom without.

Halfway to the car, he stopped, raised a finger, and spun and ran back to the house, almost tripping over his feet. Lydia hunched over, her hands on the wheel, watching him.

"Oh no. The staff," she murmured. "He forgot the staff."

Dill groaned and did a facepalm. "Yep. The staff."

"The oaken staff," Lydia said in a grandiose, medieval voice.

"The magic staff of kings and lords and wizards and . . . elves or whatever."

Travis returned, clutching his staff, symbols and faces carved on it with clumsy hands. His father glanced up with a pained expression, shook his head, and resumed work. Travis opened the car door.

"Hey, guys."

"The staff? Really?" Lydia said.

"I bring it on journeys. 'Sides, what if we need it to protect ourselves? Nashville is dangerous."

"Yeah," Lydia said, "but it's not dangerous because of all the staff-wielding brigands. They have guns now. Gun beats staff in gun-staff-scissors."

"I highly doubt we'll get in a staff fight in Nashville," Dill said.

"I like it. It makes me feel good to have it."

Lydia rolled her eyes and put the car into gear. "Bless your heart. Okay, boys. Let's do this. The last time we ever go school shopping together, thank the sweet Lord."

And with that pronouncement, Dill realized that the dread in his stomach wouldn't be going away any time soon. Maybe never. The final indignity? He doubted he'd even get a good song out of it.

2

lydia

The Nashville skyline loomed in the distance. Lydia liked Nashville. Vanderbilt was on her college list. Not high on the list, but there. Thinking about colleges put her in a good mood, as did being in a big city. All in all, she felt a lot happier than she had the day before the start of any school year in her life. She could only imagine what she'd be feeling the day before next school year—freshman year of college.

As they entered the outskirts of Nashville, Dill stared out the window. Lydia had given him her camera and assigned him to be expedition photographer, but he forgot to take pictures. He had his normal faraway affect and distinct air of melancholy. Today seemed different somehow, though. Lydia knew that visits to Nashville were a bittersweet affair for him because of his father, and she'd consciously tried to pick a route that would differ from the one he took to visit the prison. She spent a fair amount of time on Google Maps plotting, but to no avail. There were only so many routes from Forrestville to Nashville.

Maybe Dill was looking at the homes they passed. Houses as cramped and dilapidated as his didn't seem to exist even in the parts of Nashville with cramped and dilapidated houses, at least along the path they took. Maybe he was thinking about the music that flowed in the city's veins. Or maybe something else entirely occupied his mind. That was always a possibility with him.

"Hey," she said gently.

He started and turned. "Hey what?"

"Nothing. Just hey. You're being so quiet."

"Don't have much to say today. Thinking."

They crossed over the river into East Nashville and drove past coffee shops and restaurants until they pulled up to a restored Craftsman-style bungalow. A hand-painted sign out front said ATTIC. Lydia parked. Travis reached for his staff.

Lydia raised a finger in warning. "Do not."

They walked in, but not before she had Dill take a picture of her standing next to the sign, and another of her leaning on the wide porch.

The shop smelled of old leather, wool, and denim. An air conditioner purred, pumping out cool air with a whiff of clean mildew. Fleetwood Mac played over hidden speakers.

The wood floor creaked under them. A pretty, bohemian-looking strawberry blonde in her twenties sat behind a glass counter display full of handmade jewelry, staring intently at her laptop screen. She looked up as they approached.

"Okay, I love your look. How hot are you, seriously?" she said to Lydia.

Lydia curtsied. "Why thank you, madam shopkeeper. How hot are *you*, seriously?"

Lydia gave Dill a look that said *Try to get this kind of treatment at stupid Opry Mills Mall.*

"Are you guys looking for anything in particular today?"

Lydia grabbed Dill by the arm and pushed him in front of her.

"Clothes. Duds. Britches. That will fit this guy and make women swoon across Tennessee's Cumberland Plateau region."

Dill averted his eyes. "Let's maybe focus on the fitting part for now, Lydia," he said through clenched teeth.

The woman gasped. "My parents almost named me Lydia. They went with April."

"Lead the way, Miss April," Lydia said. "I see you have an excellent and well-curated selection."

Dill went in and out of the dressing room while Travis sat on a creaky wooden chair and read, lost to the world. Lydia was in her element, seldom happier than when playing dress-up with Dill, her own little fashion charity project.

Lydia handed Dill another shirt. "We need some clothes-trying-on-montage music—'Let's Hear It for the Boy' or something. And at one point you come out of the dressing room wearing a gorilla costume or something, and I shake my head immediately."

Dill pulled on the shirt, buttoned it up, and studied himself in the mirror. "You watch way too many movies from the eighties."

Eventually they had a stack of shirts, jeans, a denim jacket lined with sheepskin, and a pair of boots.

"I love vintage shopping with you, Dill. You have the body of a seventies rock star. Everything looks good on you." *Mental note: in college, any boyfriends should have Dill's body. It's a fun body to dress. Actually, it would also probably be a fun body to—well . . . anyway, it's a fun body to dress.*

"I can't afford all this," Dill said under his breath.

Lydia patted his cheek. "Calm down."

April rang them up. Thirty dollars for three shirts. Thirty dollars for the jacket. Forty dollars for the boots. Twenty dollars for two pairs of jeans. One hundred twenty dollars total.

Lydia leaned on the counter. "Okay, April. Here's the deal. I'd love it if you'd sell us all this for fifty bucks, and I'm prepared to make it worth your while."

April gave Lydia a sympathetic head tilt. "Aw, sweetie. I wish I could. Tell you what. I'll do one hundred, the friend price, because I wish we were best friends."

Lydia leaned over the counter and motioned at the laptop. "May I?"

"Sure."

Lydia typed *Dollywould* into the browser and waited for it to load. She turned the computer toward April.

"Ever been here?"

April squinted at the screen. "Yeah . . . looks familiar. I'm pretty sure I have. Was there an article on here about the best vintage stores in Tennessee?"

"Yep."

April scrolled through. "Okay, yeah, I've been here before. That was a great article."

"Thank you."

"Wait, you wrote that?"

"That and every other article on *Dollywould*. I run it."

April's jaw dropped slightly. "No way. Are you serious?"

"Yep."

"What are you—maybe eighteen?"

"Seventeen."

"Where were you when *I* was in high school?"

"Forrestville, Tennessee, wishing I were you. How do you advertise?"

"Word of mouth, mostly. I don't have much of a marketing budget. I'll run the occasional ad in the *Nashville Scene* when I've had a good month."

"How about I prominently feature your store on *Dollywould* in exchange for you cutting us a break on this?"

April drummed her fingers on the countertop and thought for a second. "I don't know."

Lydia whipped out her phone and typed while April mulled. She set her phone on the counter, stepped back, and folded her arms with a broad grin. Her phone buzzed and beeped.

"What's that? What'd you do?" April asked.

"Thought I'd give you a taste. Are you on Twitter?"

"I have an account for the store."

"I tweeted to tell my 102,678 followers that I'm currently standing in the best vintage store in the state of Tennessee and that they should come check it out."

"Wow. Thanks, I—"

Lydia raised a finger and picked up her phone. "Hang on. Let's see what we're getting. Okay, we've got seventy-five favorites, fifty-three retweets. *Thanks for the tip, will def check it out . . . Always trust your taste . . . Need to make a trip to Nashville, maybe we can meet up and do some shopping . . .*"

"What if—"

Lydia raised her finger again. "Oooh, here's a good one. This is from Sandra Chen-Liebowitz. That name probably doesn't ring a bell, but she's an associate features editor at *Cosmo.* Let's see what she has to say: *Great tip, actually working on Nashville feature as we speak. Thanks!* So you maybe made the pages of *Cosmo.* Convinced?"

April regarded Lydia for a second and threw up her hands with a little laugh. "Okay. Okay. You win."

"*We* win."

"So, you're basically the coolest girl in school, I guess?"

Lydia laughed. Dill and Travis joined her. "Oh my. Yes, I'm the coolest. Now, most *popular*? Let's just say that being Internet famous carries little cachet among my classmates."

"It kind of carries negative cachet," Dill said.

"What he said. Not much high school cachet to be had

in being a female who has, you know, vocal opinions about anything."

"Well, I'm impressed," April said.

"Fantastic. Now, while you're ringing up my friend, I'll be figuring out how best to spend three hundred dollars here."

"How about you?" April said to Travis. "I'm not sure we have much that fits someone as tall as you, but we might."

Travis blushed and looked up with a crooked smile. "Oh, no thanks, ma'am. I mostly wear the same thing every day so I can think about other stuff."

April and Lydia shared a look. Lydia shook her head. April's face registered understanding.

• • •

Lydia had no trouble whatsoever spending her clothing allowance. Before they left, she had Dill take about fifty pictures of her wearing her new outfits in various combinations. And she had him take about twenty more of her and April. She and April exchanged phone numbers and promised to stay in touch.

They began sweating immediately upon walking outside. It was at least ninety-five degrees. The late-afternoon sun blazed. The cicadas' hum throbbed like a heartbeat on an ultrasound.

Lydia motioned for everyone to huddle up. "Let's get some pictures of all of us together. Last school shopping trip to Nashville."

Dill forced a smile. "Come on, dude, you can do better than that," Lydia said. He tried again. No better.

"Hey, Lydia, could you take a couple of pictures of me with my staff?"

Lydia was exuberant over the coup she'd scored for Dill, her own clothing finds, and her stylish older new friend. Still, she feigned great annoyance, for consistency's sake. "Oh *all right*. Go on. Fetch thy staff."

Travis bounded to the car and grabbed it. He returned and assumed a grim, contemplative stance. "Okay."

Lydia took several pictures. Travis changed poses: leaning on his staff, holding the staff at the ready to strike. "Make sure you can see my dragon necklace in them."

"Dude. I'm not a beginner at making sure cute accessories feature prominently in photos."

When she finished, Travis came up beside her to look at her work, a wide, childlike grin lighting up his face. He smelled of sweat and the musty odor of clothes that had been left too long in the washing machine before going into the dryer.

"I look good in these," he murmured. "Like Raynar Northbrook from Bloodfall."

Dill craned to take a peek. "Oh, those have Raynar Northbrook written all over them." His teasing went over Travis's head.

Lydia clapped. "Gentlemen. I'm hungry. Let's go to Panera."

"Panera's too fancy. I want to go to Krystal's," Travis said.

"(A), it's 'Krystal,' singular and nonpossessive. And (b), no."

"Come on, you got to pick the music on the way."

"There's a Krystal in Forrestville. There's no Panera. We didn't drive all this way to eat at dumb Krystal and get the same diarrhea we could get in Forrestville."

"Let's let Dill decide. He can be the tiebreaker."

Dill had been staring into the distance. "I'm . . . not hungry. I'll eat at home."

"Doesn't matter," Travis said. "You can still vote."

"A vote for Krystal is a vote for walking home," Lydia said.

"I vote for Panera then," Dill said, with a more genuine smile.

They ended up getting Krystal for Travis.

3

DILL

Dill had hoped that when he asked if they could make a stop at the prison on the way out of town, after eating, Lydia would say that she had to get home for some reason and couldn't possibly wait for him to visit his father. But no.

Riverbend Prison was in a deceptively beautiful, pastoral part of Nashville. Rolling hills and a lush carpet of trees surrounded blocky beige buildings with slit windows.

"I won't be too long, y'all. You know I hate it here," Dill said, getting out of the car.

Lydia tapped away at her phone. "No worries, dude. I can work on my back-to-school blog post."

Travis held up his book.

"You guys are supposed to tell me how important it is for you to get home," Dill said.

"Oh, right," Lydia said, not looking up. "Okay, Dill, hurry it up in there or, like, I'll be grounded or get spanked or something."

"Yeah, hurry it up, Dill," Travis said. "I really want to get home and hang out with my cool dad instead of reading my favorite book."

Dill gave them an uneasy smile and flipped them the bird. He took a deep breath and walked toward the main building. He went through security and signed in. Guards took him to the visiting area. It didn't look like the visiting areas on TV. There weren't clear dividers and telephone handsets. There was a big room full of round tables, each with two or three chairs, and some vending machines. It resembled his school cafeteria, and he was as excited to be there as he would be at his school cafeteria. It was stuffy and just cool enough to remind you that the building had air conditioning, but some budget or moral constraint kept it from being used to make things very comfortable. Several guards kept vigil around the room.

Dill was the only visitor there. He sat at the table and drummed his fingers. He couldn't stop bouncing his legs. *Just get through this.*

He turned and stood as a door opened and a guard led in Dillard Early Sr.

Dill's father was tall and gaunt, rawboned. He had deep-set dark eyes; a handlebar mustache; and long, greasy black hair streaked with gray and tied in a ponytail. Every time Dill saw him, he appeared harder. More cunning. More feral and serpentine. Prison was whittling him down, carving away what little softness and gentleness he had. He was almost exactly ten years older than Dill's mother, but he looked twenty years older.

He wore dark-blue denim pants and a light-blue scrub shirt with a number stenciled on the breast and TDOC stenciled on the back.

His father sauntered up. He had a predatory, wary walk. "Hello, Junior." Dill hated being called Junior. They stood and faced each other for a second. They weren't allowed to hug or touch in any way. Dill could smell him across the table. He didn't smell bad, exactly, but unmistakably human. Primal. Like skin and hair that weren't washed as often as free people's.

They sat down. Dill's father set his hands on the table. He had MARK tattooed across one set of knuckles and 1618 tattooed across the other. The tattoos were a new development. *And not a good one. Not a promising sign to see him moving in the direction of more weirdness.*

Dill tried to sound casual. "Hi, Dad. You got some tattoos, looks like."

His father glanced at his hands, as though learning a new piece of information. "Yes, I did. They won't let me practice my signs ministry in here, so I wear my faith on my skin. They can't take that from me."

Looks like you're doing fine in here. When his father had gone to prison, everyone supposed he'd have a hard time, considering what his conviction was for. But they underestimated his father's charisma. Apparently if you can convince people to pick up rattlesnakes and copperheads and drink poison, you can convince people to protect you from what his father called "the Sodomites."

They sat and regarded each other for several awkward seconds.

"So . . . how are you doing?" Dill asked.

"I'm living one day at a time, praise Jesus."

"Are you . . . getting enough to eat?" Prison small talk was hard. Not even the weather was a topic of mutual interest.

"My needs are met. How are you and your mother?"

"Surviving. Working hard."

His intense eyes glittered with a strange light that made Dill feel dark inside. "I'm glad to hear that. Work hard. Pay off our debts, so I can rebuild my ministry when my time here is done. Perhaps you can join me if you've grown mighty in faith by then."

Dill squirmed. "Yeah, maybe. Anyway, school starts tomorrow."

His father rested his elbows on the table and interlaced his fingers as if he were praying. "It's about that time of year, isn't it? And how will you spend this year in school? Will you be a soldier for Christ and spread the good news of salvation and its signs to your peers? Will you do the work I cannot?"

Dill shifted again in his seat and looked away. He didn't like making eye contact with his father. His father had the kind of eyes that made people do things they knew could hurt them. "I—I mean, I don't think my classmates really care that much what I have to say." *Perfect. A reminder of how unpopular I am combined with a reminder of how much I disappoint my dad, all rolled into one package. Visiting prison sure is fun.*

His father scooted in, his eyes boring into Dill, a conspiratorial hush to his voice. "Then don't *say*. *Sing*. Lift that voice God's given you. Use those hands that God blessed with music. Spread the gospel through song. Young people love music."

Dill stifled a bitter laugh. "Yeah . . . but not music about picking up snakes and stuff. That kind of music isn't that popular."

"The Spirit will move in them the way it moved in our congregation when you sang and played. And when I get out, our congregation will have grown tenfold."

How about I just try to survive the school year? How about I don't do anything to add to the ridicule? "Look, Dad, your— our . . . situation . . . makes it hard for me to talk to my classmates about stuff like this. They don't really want to hear it, you know?"

His father snorted. "So we surrender to Lucifer's device to ruin our signs ministry? We hand him victory without argument?"

"No, I—I don't—" The surrealness of being made to feel unworthy by a *prison inmate* set in, preventing Dill from finishing his thought.

"Remember how you would write psalms and sing them with the praise band? Remember that?"

"Yeah. I guess. Yeah."

Dill's father sat back in his seat, looking off, shaking his head slightly. "Those songs were beautiful." He stared back at Dill. "Sing one for me."

"You mean—like right here? Now?" Dill looked for any sign that his father was joking. That would be an exceedingly rare occurrence, but still.

"Yes. The one you wrote. 'And Christ Will Make Us Free.'"

"I don't have my guitar or anything. Plus, wouldn't it be . . . weird?" Dill nodded at the bored-looking guards talking among themselves.

His father turned and glanced at the guards. He turned back with a gleam in his eye. "Do you think they think we're not weird?"

That's a fair point. Dill blushed. Might as well rip off the Band-Aid. He quickly and quietly sang the requested number a capella. Out of the corner of his eye, he saw the guards stop conversing to listen.

"More," his father said, applauding. "A new one."

"I . . . haven't really written any new ones for a while."

"You've given up music?"

"Not exactly. I just write . . . different stuff now."

His father's face darkened. "Different stuff. God did not pour out music on your tongue so that you could sing the praises of men and whoredom."

"I don't write songs about whoredom. I don't have even one song about whoredom."

His father pointed at him. "Remember this. Christ is the

way. The only way. Your path to salvation. And your music is your path to Christ. My path to Christ was the manifestation of faith signs. We lose our path to Christ; we lose our path to salvation. We lose our eternal reward. Got it?"

"Yeah. I got it." Talking to his father made Dill feel like he was talking to a sentient brick wall that somehow knew about Jesus. "Okay, well, I have to go."

His father's face darkened further. "You just got here. Surely you didn't come all this way just to spend a few minutes and go back home."

"No. I hitched a ride with some friends who had to do some school shopping. They're waiting out in the parking lot and it's really hot. They were nice to let me come here for a few minutes."

Dill's father exhaled through his nose and stood. "Well, I guess you'd better go to them, then. Goodbye, Junior. Give your mother my love and tell her I'll write soon."

Dill stood. "I will."

"Tell her I've been getting her letters."

"Okay."

"When will I see you again?"

"I don't know exactly."

"Then I'll see you when God wills it. Go with Jesus, son." Dill's father raised his two fists and put them together side by side. Mark 16:18. Then he turned and walked away.

• • •

Dill released a long exhale as he left the building, as though he'd held his breath for the entire time he was inside to

keep from inhaling whatever virulence the men imprisoned there harbored. He felt only slightly better without
the dread of visiting his father. Now he just carried the
original dread from that morning.

He reached the car. Lydia was saying something to Travis about how many calories a dragon would have to eat per
day to be able to breathe fire. Her argument did not seem
to be persuading him.

She looked up as Dill approached. "Oh thank God." She
started the car. "So, how's your dad?"

"Weird," Dill said. "He's really weird."

"Is—" Travis started to ask.

"I don't really feel like talking about it."

"Okay, jeez."

"I'm sorry, I'm not trying to be rude," Dill said. "Just . . .
let's go home."

They were mostly silent on the return trip. Travis read his
book. Lydia switched to a Nick Cave & the Bad Seeds/Gun
Club mix and tapped the steering wheel to the rhythm,
still radiating good cheer. *And why shouldn't she. She's had a
great day.*

Dill gazed out the window at the trees that lined both
sides of the highway, the occasional handmade roadside
cross, marking where someone had met their end, punctuating the unbroken wall of green. Three vultures circled
something in the distance, soaring on updrafts. He tried
to savor the remaining moments of the drive.

Last time school shopping together. The death of a little piece of my life. And I didn't even get to enjoy it completely because of my crazy dad. Who keeps slowly getting crazier.

Out of the corner of his eye, he watched Lydia drive. The edges of her mouth. The way they turned up in a near-perpetual smirk. How her lips moved almost imperceptibly as she unconsciously sang along with the music.

Remember this. Write it on a handmade cross and plant it in your heart to mark this ending.

When they pulled into Forrestville, the shadows were long and the light looked like it was streaming through a pitcher of sweet tea. They dropped Travis off first.

Travis hopped out and bent down to look in the car, his hand on the roof. "Another year, y'all. See you tomorrow?"

"Unfortunately," Dill said.

Travis ambled up the front walk. He turned and waved again when he reached his porch, staff held high.

Lydia sped off.

"I'm in no hurry to get home," Dill said.

"Habit."

"Want to go to Bertram Park and watch trains until it gets dark?"

"I'd love to hang, but I really need to start putting some time into the blog for the next few months. I'll be leading with it in my college apps, so there needs to be good content."

"Come on."

"Look, that'd be fun in its usual somewhat boring way, but no."

They pulled up to Dill's house. He sat for a moment, not reaching for the door handle, before turning to Lydia. "You gonna be too busy for us this year?"

Lydia's face took a defiant cast. Her eyes hardened, her exuberant air evaporating. "Sorry, I wasn't paying attention—what were we doing for the last several hours? Oh, right."

"That's not what I mean. Not today. I mean in general. Is that how this year's going to be?"

"Um, no dude. Same question. Is this how this year will go? You not understanding and being weird when I need to do the stuff I need to do?"

"No."

"Well, we're not off to a great start."

"I get it. You'll be busy. Whatever."

"But you'll just be really silent and taciturn about it and maybe somewhat of a dick."

"I have a lot on my mind."

"I'm serious, Dill. Please don't be gross when I'm busy."

"I'm not being gross."

"Yeah, you are a little."

"Sorry."

They regarded each other for a moment as though giving the opportunity for airing additional demands or grievances. Lydia's face softened. "On a different topic, half of my salad from Panera isn't much of a dinner."

"I'm fine."

"You sure?"

"Yeah."

"Okay. I better go. Buds?" She reached over and hugged him goodbye.

Dill breathed in her smell once more, gathering it along with his new clothes. "Thanks for doing this. I didn't mean to come off as unappreciative."

"Good, because I made you something." She pulled from the center console a CD with "Joy Division/New Order" written on it in black Sharpie. "This is what we were listening to on the drive to Nashville. I knew you'd want a copy."

Dill tapped the CD. "You were right. Thanks."

"And you should know that 'Love Will Tear Us Apart' is my favorite song on Earth."

"Noted."

"Tomorrow, seven-fifteen."

He gave her a thumbs-up. "I'll be ready."

Dill got out and walked up to his house. He climbed the cracked, eroding concrete steps to his front door and had his hand on the doorknob before thinking better of it. No use sitting in a gloomy house until it got dark. He laid his bags of clothes and CD on the steps, then sat and stared at the church sign.

No peace, no peace. No peace, no peace.

4

TRAVIS

It cheered Raynar Northbrook's spirit every time he returned from the hunt to see the battlements of Northhome. He wanted nothing more than to sit beside a roaring fire and let his weariness melt away with a flagon of summer mead, trading tales of conquest of lands and beautiful women with his captain of the guard. Until he looked down from his highest battlement and saw the ranks of Rand Allastair's army of fell men and Accursed approaching to lay siege to his walls, he meant to enjoy life. . . .

Travis walked in to see his father finishing off a can of Budweiser, his feet on the coffee table, watching the Braves play the Cardinals. A plate covered in congealing chicken wing bones sat on his lap. His eyes were red and bleary.

His father didn't look up from the TV. "Where were you?"

"In Nashville, school shopping for Lydia and Dill. I told you."

His father belched, crumpled the can, added it to a large pile, and drew a new can from a dwindling pile. "You get yourself some new clothes? So you don't look like Dracula?" He popped open the beer.

"No. I like my clothes."

His father chuckled. "And why on Earth wouldn't you. Reading all that shit about wizards and fairies."

"Clint, honey, please don't curse," Travis's mom—timid and red-haired like him—called from the kitchen. How Travis ever came from such a tiny woman was a mystery. Actually, how Travis came from his father was also a decent mystery.

"My house. I'll damn well curse," his father called back.

"Well I wish you wouldn't. Travis, are you hungry for supper?"

"No ma'am." Travis started for his room.

"Hang on. Ain't done talking with you yet."

Travis turned.

"First day of school," his father said.

"Yep."

"I ever tell you I was quarterback my senior year? Threw the winning pass against Athens High in the semis. Matt was quarterback too."

"You had mentioned that before. Couple of times." Travis felt a sharp pang at the mention of his deceased brother. Matt had always sat down with him the night before school started and given him a little pep talk. Told him how to talk to girls. To stick up for himself. To be a leader and not a follower. Travis already didn't care for this new sort of pep talk.

"You plan on spending senior year with your dick in your hand?" his father asked.

"No sir. In my pants like normal."

"You being cute?"

"No sir." Travis inched toward his room.

His father wasn't done. "What do you plan to do?"

"Shop classes. Try to get good grades. Graduate. Learn, I guess."

His father smirked. "You gonna kick some beaner ass again this year?"

"I wasn't planning on it," Travis said. "Alex's left me alone."

During junior year, Alex Jimenez cornered Dill in the cafeteria and began playing the "slapping game" with him. The game was simple: Alex slapped at Dill until hopefully he provoked Dill to retaliate, so that he had an excuse to beat Dill's ass. As the only Latino in their class, Alex wasn't much higher in the social hierarchy than Dill, but winning a fight usually moved you up a rung.

Travis walked up as Dill dodged another slap and told Alex to stop. Alex turned his attention to Travis. Winning a fight against someone much bigger than you? That would really cement his status. Travis didn't do much to defend himself until Alex landed a hard slap across Travis's eye.

Then Travis boiled over. He picked up Alex by his soccer jersey and half-pushed, half-threw him a solid seven or eight feet. When Alex landed, he turned his ankle, causing him to fall and crack his head against the edge of one of the cafeteria tables. Blood gushed. He went into seizures.

That was Travis's make-or-break moment. Had he said something like "What now, bitch?" and spit on Alex, he would have advanced in the school hierarchy. Instead, he tried to go to Alex to help him, but the crowd kept him away. He paced and ran his fingers through his hair, sobbing and telling anyone who would listen that he was sorry. EMTs showed up. His clear remorse proved his salvation from a full twenty-day suspension. The school administrators knew that if someone could win a fight and still come out the loser, it was by revealing such gentleness. The contempt that earned him would be punishment enough. And when the video hit YouTube, captioned "BIG DUDE TAKES DOWN BULLY AND CRYS LIEK A LITTLE BITCH LOL," it confirmed the administration's suspicions.

But Travis's father never saw the video (which school administrators got removed in a day by threatening to expel the poster). He didn't see Travis begging Alex to forgive him as Alex convulsed, his eyes rolled back, blood pooling all over the white linoleum. He didn't see when Travis, fresh off his suspension, took a container of his mom's banana pudding—his favorite treat—and found Alex sitting alone in the cafeteria with his ankle cast resting on a chair. Travis offered him the banana pudding. Alex didn't say anything; he wouldn't even look at Travis. Slapped away the container as Travis tried to give it to him.

Travis's father knew only that his son had kicked some Mexican ass and that the parents, who didn't speak English, seemed to be afraid to go to the cops or even to ask him to pay their son's medical bills. And so went one of the few times Travis had ever made him proud.

"Speaking of using your size for something worthwhile, I ran into Coach the other day at the Walmart," his father said. "Said you don't even have to have played the other years to go out for football."

"Good to know."

"I said you don't run so fast or catch so good, but you're a big piece of meat he could put in the defensive line." His father took a gulp of beer and belched.

"That's true. I am a big piece of meat."

"You going to try out for the team? Make me proud? Maybe we'll see you with a girl other than Denny Blankenship's dyke daughter?"

"I guess I'll see."

His father gave a disdainful snort. "You guess you'll see." He leaned forward and spun the plate of wing bones onto the coffee table. "And then what? After you graduate? Join the Marines like Matt?"

Another pang, sharper still. *Because that turned out well for Matt.* "I haven't thought about it. Keep working at the lumberyard I guess."

"You might ought to think about enlisting. Make a man of you. We could hire to fill your position easy."

"I'll think about it." There was silence as his father returned his attention to the game. Travis stood for a second, watching him, the TV reflected in his father's eyes. He hoped that if he waited for a second or two more, his father would offer some words of encouragement or wisdom for the start of school; that he would say something that let Travis know he believed in him. Like Matt used to do.

Just a stifled burp. Travis started once more toward his room.

"Tell you a story," his father said, not taking his eyes off the TV. Travis's heart leapt with hope.

His father sipped his beer. "Was dropping off this load of two-by-fours where they was adding on to a church. Anyway, this church had a little pond out front and there was these little ducks and a big-ass turkey, all hanging out together, happy as you please."

Travis forced a laugh. Best to humor him when he was in storytelling mode. "Yeah, that's pretty funny." Not the words of encouragement he hoped for, but better than nothing. Maybe.

His father fixed his glassy eyes on him. Then back on the TV. "Anyhow, that's what you remind me of, hanging out with that son of the Pervert Preacher and your dyke friend. That big-ass turkey, thinking he's a duck."

Travis stood there and let the barb sink in, feeling deflated. He waited for his father to say *just kidding* or explain why he thought turkeys were great. Maybe at least wish him luck at school tomorrow. Nothing. Just the reflection of the TV in his eyes. So much for words of encouragement. There went a damn fine day.

He went into his room and shut the door, resting his staff behind it. He sat down at his cheap, Walmart pressed-board desk and turned on his nine-year-old laptop—a hand-me-down from his brother Matt. The fan whined as he navigated his way to the Bloodfall forums. He typed in his username, *Southern_Northbrook,* and settled into a spirited debate about the forthcoming *Deathstorm,* the sixth and final book in the Bloodfall series, due out in March of the following year.

He tilted back in his chair and surveyed his legion of digital friends—invented names, profile pictures of cartoon characters or frowning cats. He was glad to have them. As he scrolled through the forums, clicking on threads, a little pop-up window appeared at the top of his screen. A direct message. His heart galloped. He opened it. It was from exactly whom he hoped: *autumnlands.* He didn't know much about *autumnlands,* just that she was around his age and that she lived near Birmingham, Alabama. They had just started direct messaging a week ago, after Travis had come to her defense in a heated argument over whether The Accursed were undead humans or something else entirely.

autumnlands: Hey what's up?

Southern_Northbrook: Nothing much just hanging out. What's up with you?

autumnlands: Just hanging out too. Loved your theory about Norrell Bayne being the real son of Torren Winterend.

Travis bounced in his chair and typed. **I wish I was the real son of Torren Winterend because he's probably way cooler than my dad LOL.**

autumnlands: Ugh I totally know what you mean. My dad acts so douchey sometimes. He's literally on my case all the time about stupid stuff.

Southern_Northbrook: Yeah my dad was just blabbing about me going out for football when school starts tomorrow. I hate football. Compared me to my brother. I hate it when he does that.

autumnlands: My parents are always comparing me to my perfect younger sister. It's the worst. And your school hasn't started yet??? No fair mine started last week!!!!

Southern_Northbrook: Maybe you should move here LOL.

Travis blushed as soon as he hit "send."

autumnlands: Ok I will but you have to promise to sit with me at lunch.

Travis felt warm all over. He was starting to compose his reply when a knock startled him. He prayed it wasn't his father. Not that his father felt like he had to knock to go anywhere he wanted in the house. "Come in," he called.

His mom entered, holding a brown paper bag. She closed the door behind her.

"Hey, sweetie. I was at the grocery today and I picked you up a little something as a back-to-school present." She handed Travis the paper bag. "It's not much."

He opened the bag. It contained a paperback entitled *The Rebel Knight*. On the cover was a chiseled, grim-looking man with long, black hair; a five o'clock shadow; and a tunic open to reveal bronzed pecs. He had a sword in one hand and a shield in the other. Travis had a pretty good idea of the sort of book he was holding.

"Oh man, thanks, Mom!" he said, as convincingly as he could. "This looks awesome!"

Travis's mom looked pleased. "I know how you like to read about knights and things like that. I thought maybe you hadn't read that one."

"No," he said softly, leafing through the book. "I haven't read this one."

"Your dad means well," she said.

Travis stared at the book, hefting it in his hands. "I wish he was better at meaning well."

"Me too sometimes. Anyway. I'll let you get back to what you were doing." She leaned forward, hugged him, and kissed his cheek. "Have a great first day of school tomorrow. I love you."

"I love you too, Mom."

After she left and closed the door behind her, Travis shook his head and tossed the book on his bed. This wasn't the first time. In fact, Travis had a respectable collection of steamy medieval romance novels under his bed. But he couldn't bear to tell her.

Another message from *autumnlands* popped up. Ok I guess you won't sit with me at lunch. Boo.

Southern_Northbrook: No no of course I'd sit with you at lunch LOL. Sorry my mom came in and I was talking to her.

autumnlands: Yay! Because I usually eat lunch alone. I don't have very many friends at my dumb school. No one likes Bloodfall.

Southern_Northbrook: I totally know what you mean. I have two awesome friends but even they don't get Bloodfall.

autumnlands: If we're going to sit together at lunch I guess I better learn your real name. Mine's Amelia.

Southern_Northbrook: I like the name Amelia. My name's Travis.

autumnlands: Good to meet you Travis.

Southern_Northbrook: Good to meet you Amelia.

His heart beat the syllables of her name. *A-mel-ia.* While she was composing her reply, Travis got up, paced around quickly, picked up his staff, and twirled it around his head as best he could in the confined space of his room, watching himself in the mirror.

5

DILL

Dill hated going back into his house after hanging out with Lydia. It was like waking up from a euphoric dream. His house was still and suffocating when he opened the door. He set his CD on the kitchen table and considered the possibilities for dinner. They weren't promising. He improvised a casserole with a couple of dented cans of green beans, a couple of dented cans of cream of mushroom soup, and a block of expired cheese—all freebies from his job bagging groceries and stocking shelves at Floyd's Foods.

He threw the sad concoction in the oven, went and plugged in the air conditioner, and began playing his guitar, working on a new song that no one would ever hear. One about endings. One about people leaving you behind.

At around 8:45, Dill heard his mother clatter up the

driveway in their 1992 Chevy Cavalier and come in the house. She exuded fatigue.

"How was work?"

"I'm tired. I had to turn away about twenty kids your age trying to buy beer."

She flopped down with a soft groan in their battered recliner and rubbed her face.

"Did you take your pills for your back?" Dill asked.

"Ran out. Can't refill until payday."

Dill returned to the kitchen and checked on the casserole.

"Dinner's done," he called out to the living room.

Dill's mother sucked in her breath and rose from the recliner, holding her mid-back, taking a moment to straighten, and grunting with pain. She entered the kitchen and sat at the table. She picked up Dill's CD.

"What's Joy Division and New Order?"

Shit. Dill had a peculiar genius, honed over his years of friendship with Lydia, at turning any band into a Christian band on the spot. Arcade Fire? Refers to the fires of hell that those who forsake Christ in favor of video games will experience. Fleet Foxes? Refers to the Bible story in which Samson captured foxes, tied torches to their tails, and let them burn the fields of the Philistines. Radiohead? Refers to how human minds have to be living conduits to the Holy Spirit, akin to radio antennas.

"Oh . . . New Order . . . refers to the new order that Christ will create when he returns to Earth and reigns . . .

Joy Division . . . refers to the division in joy between people who've been saved and people who haven't. They're Christian bands."

Either his explanation satisfied his mother or she was too tired to quarrel. Probably the former, since she never seemed to be too tired to fight with him.

Dill pulled the casserole dish from the oven. It smelled okay and it was hot and cheesy. They weren't picky in the Early house. He took a quarter loaf of stale white bread from the top of the refrigerator, to help soak up the casserole. Grabbing a couple of plates and spoons from the drying rack beside the sink, he set the table and dished them both up some food.

They ate quietly. "How was Nashville?" his mother finally asked.

"Fine. Lydia helped me get some good clothes for cheap."

His mother dabbed at her mouth with a napkin. "I wish you had more Christian friends from church."

"Travis is from church."

"I wonder about him. Dressed in black all the time with that demon necklace."

"Dragon."

"Same thing. Read Revelation again."

Dill got up to refill their water glasses.

"And Lydia's not from church," his mom said.

"Yeah, but I told you that she's Episcopalian or Presbyterian or something. She's Christian."

Dill's mom snorted. "Love to see an Episcopalian take up the serpent or speak in tongues. Signs follow the faithful."

"I can't choose my friends according to who's willing to pick up a copperhead."

"Sure you can. It's that you won't."

"Kind of hard now anyway, since the only snakehandling pastor around got locked up."

Dill's mom gave him a sharp look. "Don't make light."

"Trust me. I'm not. I visited him while I was there."

Dill's mom gave him another look, with a different sort of sharpness. "You might've mentioned that sooner. How was he?"

Dill stuffed a bite in his mouth and chewed slowly while he considered how to answer. "All right, I guess. I don't know. Fine for prison? Looks like he's made some friends because he had some tattoos on his knuckles."

Dill's mother wrinkled her forehead. "Really. Tattoos? Of what?"

"Mark sixteen eighteen. Across each of his eight knuckles."

Dill's mother stared at her plate. "He's always been able to hear God's voice. I haven't understood everything your father's done, but I trust that God's willed it." She mopped up the last bit of her casserole with a heel of dry bread.

I wouldn't be so sure about God wanting Dad to do everything he's done in his life. Somehow I sort of doubt that. Dill took their plates to the sink and put them in to soak. He opened a drawer, careful to not pull it off its track (it could be finicky), and pulled out a sheet of plastic wrap that they used, washed, and reused. He wrapped up the casserole and put it in the fridge.

"You better get some sleep if you're going to start school tomorrow," his mom said.

"Why do you say 'if'?"

"Because I'm not making you. You know that."

"I guess I didn't think you were serious when you said that."

"I was. I'd just as soon you went full time at Floyd's. They like you there. Make you a manager and you'd be earning thirty-five thousand a year before you knew it. That's real money."

"What about graduating?" *I can't believe I'm actually defending school to my mom.*

"You can read. Write. Add. Subtract. You got a line to a good job. What do you need a piece of paper for? I care that you learn your scripture, that's all."

Dill scrubbed the dishes. "Lydia's about to apply to every one of the best colleges in America; meanwhile, my mom is telling me to become a high school dropout."

"Lydia's dad is a dentist and her mom works too, and they don't have our debts. No use comparing yourself to her."

"No use is right."

"Your dad didn't graduate from high school. And I quit high school to marry him."

Dill put down the dish he was washing, turned, and gave his mother an incredulous look. "You can't possibly believe that'll convince me."

"Someday you'll learn that you're no better than your own name."

Someday? "Yeah, well, maybe I'll learn it in school this year. They seem pretty determined to teach me that. Good night."

Dill put the dish in the cracked white plastic drying rack and went to his room. He lifted up his door by the knob, on its broken hinge, and shut it. He sat down on his twin bed, the only piece of furniture in his room besides a Goodwill dresser, and the lumpy mattress groaned under his weight. He popped his new CD into his hand-me-down CD player from Lydia. He put in his earbuds and reclined with his hands behind his head.

Sometimes music worked on the loneliness. Other times, when he felt as if he were sitting at the bottom of a dry well, looking up at the sky, it didn't work at all. Today marked the beginning of the end for him, but only the beginning of the beginning for Lydia. He sighed.

No song would fix that.

6

lydia

When Lydia got home, her dad and mom were lounging on the couch, watching TV. Her mom had a glass of red wine and sat with her feet tucked under Lydia's dad's leg. A pizza box rested on the reclaimed-wood coffee table in front of them. Lydia's dad had a fetish for industrial antiques. He had filled their meticulously restored Victorian house with them. The Restoration Hardware catalog was his pornography.

"Hey, kid," her dad said. "Have fun in Nashville?"

Lydia held up her bags.

"I have my answer. How'd Al Gore treat you?"

"The real Al Gore who lives in Nashville? We didn't run into him."

"Your car, Al Gore. Ran okay?" Lydia had inherited Al Gore (the first Prius in Forrestville) from her dad.

"Treated us fine." Lydia kicked off her boots, flopped onto the couch on the other side of her dad, and tucked her feet up under his leg.

"Are you hungry? We've got some Pizza Garden left there," her mom said.

"We need a real pizza place in this town," Lydia said.

"One more year and you'll be in some amazing big city with more pizza places than you could ever possibly try," her mom said.

"Yeah," Lydia said, "but another year is a long time to eat subpar pizza."

"You're such an elitist," her dad said. "Pizza Garden is fine. How bad can pizza ever really be?"

"'Elitist' is synonymous with 'has discerning taste,' but I'll concede that Pizza Garden more or less gets the job done, as long as you avoid ham and pineapple."

"That's true of any pizza place, though," her dad said. "Go on. Have some."

"I shouldn't."

"You should."

"I'm too lazy to get up."

Her dad leaned over, grabbed the pizza box, and handed it to her.

"Shall I feed it to you as well, milady?"

"Shut up." She took a slice.

Lydia's mom sniffed. "Come on, Lydia."

Lydia took off her glasses and wiped away a smudge. "I wish I could sit here and eat and nerd out with you two, but

I need to work on my blog tonight. My audience awaits a back-to-school post."

"Suit yourself," her dad said. "But first, why don't you go look at what's on the kitchen counter. The senior-year fairy dropped by while you were out. We tried to tell her that you've been bad by telling your dad to shut up, but she wouldn't listen."

Lydia rolled her eyes playfully, got up, and walked to the kitchen. A brand-new Mac laptop, wrapped up with a red bow, sat on the counter. She clapped her hands to her mouth and squealed. Any lingering unease from her fight with Dill disappeared in a blink. She ran into the living room and hugged her parents, almost causing her mom to spill wine on the couch.

"The last thing you need is your computer crashing on you in the middle of a college application or writing your admission essay," her dad said.

"I love you guys. Even despite your penchant for inferior pizza."

• • •

Lydia bounded upstairs. Her dad always joked bitterly about how she'd annexed the top floor. Her parents occupied one bedroom. She occupied another. The other two bedrooms were Lydia's wardrobe room—filled with wheeled clothing racks—and her sewing/project room.

Lydia sat in her bedroom at her stark, modern desk, bought on an Ikea run to Atlanta. While she waited for her new laptop to boot up, she scanned through the photos on her phone, posting the best shots to Instagram and Twitter.

Her phone beeped. A text from Dahlia Winter. *Ugh first day of school?*

Dahlia was her best Internet friend. Actually, they'd become close real-life friends after Lydia had spent two weeks that summer at Dahlia's family's beach house in Nantucket. Returning to Forrestville after that wasn't easy. The experience had confirmed to Lydia that they'd make good roommates at NYU, which both of them had chosen as their top pick for college. Lydia had her fingers crossed to get in. Of course Dahlia would get in. Dahlia's mother, Vivian Winter, was the infamously icy editor-in-chief of *Chic Magazine*. Dahlia could waltz into any school she liked, but she wanted to be near the heart of the fashion industry and she had a thing for slumming it. Hence her friendship with a "poor" girl from Tennessee.

Ugh is right. You can't imagine my school's awfulness, Lydia texted.

Feel for you. We have creeps at school too.

I bet Phillips Exeter has a different kind than Forrestville High. When does your school start?

Yeah, probably. September.

Hate you. (But in loving way)

LOL gotta run love. Hang in there at Hillbilly High.

Lydia set down her phone and began typing a post about the road trip to Nashville, shopping at Attic, and some thoughts on the first day of school. She got stuck and began looking for ways to procrastinate.

She downloaded her pictures from the Nashville trip to her new computer and sorted through them. Travis, leaning on his staff, doing his best to look grim. She opened a tab and pasted them into an email to him.

Can you believe it? We ran into Rainer Northbrooke (sp?) in Nashville. He said to say hi. Enjoy.

And then she started browsing through the pictures of Dill, looking distant. Lost. Haunted.

Lydia felt a familiar pang of guilt and sadness that she couldn't use the photos on her blog. When she'd gone to New York Fashion Week, there'd been a meet-up of teen fashion bloggers. A bunch of thirteen- to seventeen-year-olds talking about content and brand preservation.

"It *sucks* when your friends have a look that's off-brand and you can't talk about them or show them on the blog. It's so *awkward* to explain. What? Are you going to say 'Hey, sorry, but your style sucks so I can't tell people I hang out with you?' But that's the reality," a thirteen-year-old from Johannesburg said with a world-weary air, the others nodding sagely.

Lydia had just sat and listened. *Oh, I could tell you a thing or two about having friends who are off-brand.*

Travis was hopelessly off-brand, and he couldn't care less.

Dill? He was another story. He was tall and had these dark, brooding eyes with high, sharp cheekbones; thick, shaggy dark hair (that she cut for him); gaunt, angular features; and full, expressive lips—all of which placed him outside of the vanilla beauty standards of Forrestville but would make him a great Prada or Rick Owens model.

She did her best with him. And even though she dressed him as what he was—a musician from the rural South—his look wasn't what made him off-brand. In fact, he'd probably be a big hit with her audience, not that she needed to spend her time dealing with people crushing on Dill (not possessive, just busy).

His name was the problem. Her readers were inveterate Googlers. The last thing she needed was for them to see a picture of Dill, get curious, find out his name (They had ways. Oh how they had ways.), and Google it. Because guess what came up on a search for "Dillard Early." *Very* bad for the *Dollywould* brand.

People, Dahlia included, already treated Lydia with a sort of benevolent condescension *(You're so intelligent and open-minded for a Southerner! You have such sophisticated taste for living where you do!)*. They imagined her living in a house . . . well, like Dill's. *My house is probably nicer than yours,* she'd murmur to herself while reading their well-meaning comments. *My parents met at Rhodes College. There are two Priuses and a hybrid Lexus SUV in our driveway. I have a hundred gigs of music on my brand-new Mac laptop and Netflix and high-speed Internet. I'm not chasing raccoons around a trailer park barefoot, folks.*

She skipped through the pictures of Travis, Dill, and the

three of them; picked out the best pictures of herself and some of the pictures of her with April (who was on-brand); and dragged them to her computer desktop to use. She still didn't feel like working on her blog post, so she texted Dahlia. *Hey. **What are you doing right now? Can you talk?***

Sorry, darling, not at the moment. Just sitting down to dinner with Peter Diamond. Text me later.

Peter Diamond was the latest up-and-coming Brooklyn wunderkind literary sensation. He was two novels into a Proustian four-novel cycle that dealt, semiautobiographically, with the day-to-day (sometimes hour-by-hour and minute-by-minute) travails and ennui of being an early-twentysomething creative in Brooklyn. Captivating stuff, no doubt.

This is a good preview of what I have to look forward to in New York, Lydia thought. She loved Dahlia, but.

Maybe this is the universe telling me to stop putting this off. After a few false starts, she began her post about the first day of school.

Here's what I'm thinking about as I drive to Nashville today, my last day of summer before I begin my senior year: nothing makes you feel like you're trying to grab and hold on to a handful of sand like first days of school. And by "sand," I mean time.

The first day of senior year is when you realize that summer might never again mean what it used to. Before you even enter a classroom you learn that life is composed of a finite number of summers, passing us by in a haze of ice cream, fireflies, chlorine-scented hair, and skin that smells like coconut sunblock. We live in a series of moments and seasons and sense memories, strung end to end to form a sort of story. Maybe first days of school are to give us lines of demarcation, to make sense of these childhood moments and the life cycle of friendships and—

As she typed, a warm wave of excitement about her impending new life swept through her.

7

DILL

Dill surveyed the parking lot with glum resignation, watching his fellow students file in. *But this year, I don't even get to wish for the year to be over quicker, because that means no more Lydia.* Al Gore was parked in the rear of the lot, Lydia's preferred spot for quick after-school escapes. She even had a track of fast banjo music that she played on her iPod for these getaways. Somehow, they'd arrived with time to kill before class began. The hatchback was open and Lydia and Dill sat on the bumper.

Ms. Alexander, the cheerleading coach, walked past.

"I never thought she was as hot as everyone else does," Lydia said, after she'd gone.

"Me neither," Dill said.

Lydia looked satisfied, as though he had passed a test of

some kind. "I'd bet twenty bucks she ends up arrested for banging some thirteen-year-old student."

Lydia kicked her legs gently. She wore tights woven in an intentionally chaotic pattern with purposeful rips. They would have been a disaster on anyone else. Her calf tapped the A HEALTHY SMILE IS A HAPPY SMILE bumper sticker. Her dad had offered to remove it. *"Why didn't you let him?"* Dill had asked once. *"Because it's still as true as when he drove it,"* Lydia had told him. *"Plus, it's both creepy and hilarious."* "What hotness discount do you give her?"

Dill thought for a moment. "Seventy-five percent hotness discount."

"Oh damn. That's Dollar General pricing."

"People at this school confuse a tan and perfect teeth with hotness."

"But not you."

"Not me."

Lydia gave him the you-passed-the-test smile again. Her teeth were as chaotic and imperfect as her tights. And like the tights, Dill thought she pulled them off in style. She refused to let her dad fix them, just like with the bumper sticker. She explained to Dill once that it was similar to the way makers of Persian rugs would intentionally leave a flaw in their work, as a reminder that only God is perfect.

They kept up their red-carpet commentary until it was almost time to head inside.

As Dill was about to ask Lydia what she had first period, he heard laughter off to the left. He saw Tyson Reed and his girlfriend, Madison Lucas, approaching. His heart sank. *Here we go.*

"What up, Dildo? Senior year!" Tyson said with mock excitement, raising his hand for a high five. "Come on, player, don't leave me hanging!"

Dill went into defensive mode. He shut off and turned away, ignoring Tyson. He prayed in his heart. *Bless them that curse you, bless them that curse you, bless them that curse you.* And another thought ran parallel: *God is punishing me for dishonoring my mother and going to school. He won't allow me even an hour's peace.*

Lydia laughed a braying, sarcastic laugh. "Wait a minute, hang on . . . I see what you did there! You said 'dildo'? Like his name! But you add '-do' to the end! This is fun with these good jokes." She applauded.

"Glad you appreciate my joke, Lydia Chlamydia," Tyson said. Madison snickered from behind him.

Lydia's mouth dropped open. "Wha—Lydia Chl—*You did it again!* You made an extremely hilarious joke by rhyming my name with a funny sex disease! Tremendous!"

"You're tremendous," Tyson said. Another snicker from Madison. This one was louder and more pointed, as though he was finally treading the territory she hoped he would.

Something surged through Dill. Not courage exactly. More the realization that he had nothing to lose by getting kicked out of school. Maybe that was what God wanted for him anyway. He might be able to land a punch on Tyson before Tyson could react. He wouldn't be expecting Dill to do anything. Even Christ had chased the moneylenders from the temple, and Lydia's friendship was a temple to him.

Dill rose. He felt Lydia's hand, warm on his arm. He sat, his head spinning with adrenaline, trying not to visibly shake.

"Yeah, Dildo. Do it. Bring it," Tyson said.

Lydia crossed her legs, holding her knee and rocking back casually. "Tremendous, huh? Let's go with that and say I could lose, oh, twenty pounds. I can easily do that by not eating chess pie or bacon or any of the other things that make life worth living. But you"—she pointed at Tyson with an elaborate flourish—"are dumb. And there's nothing you can simply *not eat* that will make you any smarter. You'll die an idiot."

"You'll die from too many french fries, fatass Lydia Chlamydia."

"Do you really want to do this?" She wagged her finger between them. "A battle of wits? It's not even fun to destroy you because you're too dim to understand you're getting destroyed."

Madison lunged forward, her face resembling a spray-tanned fist. "You're an ugly person. Inside and out. You think you're better than everyone here because you've been interviewed in the *New York Times* and you're famous on the Internet."

Lydia studied Madison with the look she'd give a clogged toilet. "Since I know that you don't equate 'smarter' with 'better,' I'm going to say that that's not true."

"This is why no one can stand you," Madison said.

"Fabulous. I'd hate for it to be because of halitosis or something."

"Nice witch tights, by the way," Madison said, her voice dripping with scorn. "They come from the trash?"

"No, they were a gift from the Rodarte sisters. They're last season, but I hoped no one at Forrestville High would notice."

"All your fancy friends," Tyson said. "You gonna go cry about us on your blog now?"

Lydia gave Tyson a condescending smile, furrowing her brow. "Oh. Bless your heart. You think you're important enough to talk about on my blog. You are *still very important, though, you special widdle guy.*"

Travis walked up, looking exhausted. "Hey."

"Tyson, do one of your name jokes for Travis," Lydia said with a wicked grin. Travis's fight with Alex may not have raised his social status, but people still feared him. Travis had at least eight inches and almost a hundred pounds on Tyson.

Tyson grabbed Madison's hand. "Y'all can blow me. We've wasted enough time with your queer asses." They stalked off. Madison flipped Lydia the bird over her shoulder. Lydia, Dill, and Travis flipped them the bird to their backs. Dill's heart still thumped from the encounter, but he breathed again. Maybe God had a different message for him.

"They're really not over that interview, are they?" Lydia said.

"You did call Forrestville High a 'fashion wasteland,'" Travis said.

"Full of outlet mall–clad drones who smell like survivors of an Axe body spray tanker truck crash with a school bus," Dill said.

"Aw, you guys read it!"

"Why don't you unleash all your blog fans on the people who give you trouble?" Travis asked.

"Well, first off, the people who like my blog aren't very good at cyberbullying, which is fine. I would hate to be liked by people who are good at it."

They got up and walked to the school, a large, non-descript, 1970s-era building. It had all the charm of a state-run asylum.

"I gotta head this way, y'all," Travis said.

"Hey, why do you look like you got fifteen minutes of sleep last night? You okay?" Lydia asked.

"I was up late talking with friends from the Bloodfall forums. No big deal. Meet y'all after I get off work?"

"Yep," Dill said. He and Lydia kept walking. Lydia said nothing. She had the air of a boxer who'd won a bout: triumphant but bruised. That's how Dill felt.

"You're not fat or ugly," Dill said.

She laughed. "You're sweet, but I'm completely fine. I love myself and nothing Tyson can say will ever change that. One more year with these bipedal turds. Then I'll never see any of them again. I mean, unless one of them serves me french fries in ten years. Apparently I'm a big fan."

Dill thought that he'd managed to hide it, but he must have appeared bruised himself.

"You're not a dildo, you know," Lydia said. "I don't get why they haven't figured out "Dullard" as a nickname. It's funnier and more creative. But it also requires a larger vocabulary."

"Nothing *they* said bothered me."

"*They?* Did *I* say something?"

They got to the front doors and stopped as people hurried past them.

"It's fine; I'm fine." He started to walk inside. Lydia stopped him.

"Nuh nuh nuh, hold up. What?"

"When you talk about people still being here in ten years—"

Lydia rolled her eyes. "Oh man. Can we stipulate right now that I'm not referring to you when I say something like that?"

"It's just—What if I'm the one serving you fries in ten years? Does that mean you think I'm dumb like Tyson?"

"Really, Dill?"

"You asked."

"Fine, you're right. I asked. No, I don't think I'm better than you. No, I don't think you'll be serving me fries in ten years. Jeez, could you please not with the drama? After I stick up for you?"

"What if? What if I end up no better than Tyson?"

"I won't let that happen, okay? I'll hire you as my butler first."

"That's not funny."

"No, it's not, because you'd be the worst butler. You'd always be spacing out and playing the guitar while people knocked at the door, and then when you answered the door you'd be like 'Hey, isn't it weird how the Earth is flying through space all the time, and yet we can't fly,'" Lydia said, imitating Dill's voice, "and you'd get your butler panties in a twist every time a guest hurt your feelings a little bit."

"What about the thing you said to Tyson about how he's not important enough to talk about on your blog? You've never talked about me on your blog."

They stood and stared at each other.

"Do I honestly need to stand here in the entryway of Forrestville High School and tell you how important you are to me? What's really going on here, Dill? Something else is bothering you."

The five-minute bell rang.

Dill broke eye contact and turned. "We better get to class."

Lydia grabbed his arm. "What?"

Dill looked from side to side. "Last night, my mom tried to get me to drop out of school and go to work full time."

Lydia's mouth fell open, as it had with Tyson and Madison, but this time her astonishment and outrage were genuine. "*What?* That's so gross. Who does that?"

"My mom, apparently."

Vice Principal Blackburn strolled up the hall. "Mr. Early,

Ms. Blankenship, five-minute bell's rung. You may be seniors, but you don't get to be tardy. Move it."

"Yessir," Dill said, and watched until he rounded the corner. "My mom said something else."

"What?"

"She said someday I'd learn that I'm no better than my name."

"Well, she's wrong. And we'll talk about that and some other stuff when we get a chance."

They went their separate ways. As Dill hurried to class, he caught a whiff of some astringent industrial cleaning chemical.

• • •

Suddenly he's twelve years old, helping his father clean their church on Saturday morning so that it sparkles before Saturday evening worship. He's finished feeding the snakes in their wooden crates, and now he's scrubbing one of the pews when his father looks at him and smiles and tells him that God is happy with him and that by the sweat of his face shall he eat his bread. And Dill's heart sings because he feels that he's pleased his father and God.

• • •

Times are simpler when no one hates you because of your name and it doesn't occur to you to be ashamed of it.

8

TRAVIS

Raynar Northbrook's day's labors were almost at an end. As Lord of Northhome, he didn't need to soil his hands with work. He did it because he loved the sweet, spicy smell of cut wood and the rich, earthy smell of damp soil. A man's work kept the back and arm strong for war. And he would need every ounce of strength in the coming days . . .

"Travis!" his father shouted over the din of the saw. Travis glanced up. His father tapped his watch and made a circular motion with his finger pointed in the air. "Quitting time! Wrap it up."

Travis finished his task and switched off the saw. He'd only been working a few hours. He was on work release from school, so he got to leave early. He checked his phone. Two messages from Amelia. He felt a pulse of excitement.

How was your first day of school?

Oops forgot you're at work now huh.

Travis hurried to text her back.

Yeah, at work. First day wasn't bad. I was a little tired from how late we talked LOL. How was your day?

Hehe, tired too. Ugh every day of school sucks. I'd rather spend a month at the Siege of King's Port than one day at my stupid school.

But remember at the Siege of King's Port they had to eat rats and boiled leather until King Targhaer's brother broke the siege. I love food, Travis replied.

Hehe, true, me too. Maybe too much, which is one of the things I get crap for at school.

Don't listen to those people. I bet you look great. Travis blushed as he typed. He almost didn't hit "send." But he did.

He stood there for a couple of minutes waiting for a response. His heart sank deeper with every moment that none came. He knew he shouldn't have hit "send." He put his phone in his pocket and started to walk toward the office. His phone buzzed. He almost dropped it removing it from his pocket. Amelia had sent a picture of herself, taken at a sharp angle and heavily filtered. She had dyed bright-red hair, large gray eyes with dramatic eye makeup, and a soulful pout on her round face. She held a piece of paper that said "Hi, Travis."

I was right, Travis typed, his pulse pounding. He went through his photos and found the best one that Lydia had taken of him with his staff. He texted it to Amelia with the message **Here's me. Sorry, didn't have anything to write on.**

What a great picture. Nice staff! If we ever hang out, you have to bring it.

LOL, my friends hate it when I bring my staff places. Ok! Gotta go, my dad's waiting for me.

See you on the forums tonight?

Yep.

Bye bye!

Bye!

Travis pumped his fist, mopped the sweat from his forehead, and walked to the office, where his father and Lamar were sitting in the cool of the air conditioning, shooting the breeze, dipping snuff, and spitting in empty Diet Coke cans.

Lamar tossed Travis a cold Coke. "Got yourself a hot date tonight, boy?"

"No sir. Hanging out with my friends tonight and doing some homework," Travis said, enjoying the feeling that he may have been lying a bit. Or at least only telling half the truth.

"You realize you said 'Travis' and 'date' in the same sentence, Lamar? Don't you know him at all?" Travis's father said.

As if you know me at all.

"All right, all right. Tall young man, hardworking. There should be a girl or two out there," Lamar said.

"Maybe there is," Travis said, popping open his can.

"If there is, he don't care about it," his father said, as if Travis weren't sitting right there. "Too busy with them friends of his. Hey, guess who he runs around with?"

Lamar shook his head.

"Grandson of the Serpent King," Travis's father said.

Lamar looked from Travis to Travis's father and back. "Well. How about that. Dillard Early's grandson?"

"No," Travis said. "You're thinking of Dill's dad, not his papaw. Dill's dad is named Dillard Early too. He's the snakehandler."

Travis's father eyed him in wonderment. "No, I ain't talking about the Pervert Preacher. I mean Dill's papaw. You telling me Dill ain't told you about his papaw, the Serpent King?"

Travis shook his head, bewildered. "No. I didn't even know Dill had the same name as his papaw. He don't care to talk about his family."

Travis's father snorted. "You reckon?" He slapped Lamar on the shoulder. "Tell Travis the story of the Serpent King, old man. You remember it better than me. He ought to hear."

Lamar grunted and reclined in his chair, folding his arms across his beer gut. "Lord above. I ain't thought about the Serpent King in a long time. Long time." He rubbed his white beard and adjusted his Carhartt ball cap. "Well, first off—there's three Dillard Earlys. There's Dillard Serpent King. There's Dillard Preacherman, son of the Serpent King. And there's the one who you're friends with, son of the Preacherman. Now, he'd be Dillard III, but after his papaw died, his father became Dillard Sr. and he became Dillard Jr. Only reason I know how that works is that I'm the third Lamar Burns. But I became Lamar Jr. after my papaw died."

Travis pulled up a metal folding chair and sat down. "Okay."

"So Dillard Serpent King used to have a home place up Cove Road. They had a little spread of land and Dillard worked in town as an auto mechanic. Dillard Serpent King had two kids. Dillard Preacherman and a little girl named . . . I forget now. Ruth. Rebecca. Something of that nature."

"Ruth," Travis's father said. "I believe it was Ruth Early."

Lamar spit in his can. "Anyway, Dillard Serpent King loved that little girl. I'd see them every Saturday come into town; she'd be dressed in a pretty white dress and they'd go for ice cream. Now, story goes that one day, Dillard Serpent King is sitting on his porch, whittling or doing something, and he hears a scream. *'Daddy, come quick.'* So he runs toward the screaming and there's Ruth lying on the ground. A big old copperhead's bit her right in the neck."

Lamar formed a V with his two fingers and made a stabbing motion at his neck. "So Dillard Sr. shouts for Dillard Preacherman to go call an ambulance while he stays with Ruth. And Dillard Preacherman does, but it's too late. The poison from the snakebite goes right to her brain and *ffffffft*. Dead." Lamar drew a finger across his throat.

Travis felt cold in the air conditioning in his sweat-sodden T-shirt. Between the quick-decaying rush of excitement from seeing Amelia for the first time and the caffeine making his head spin, he was glad to be sitting.

Lamar continued. "So he buries his little girl on their land and then he goes funny in the head. Now, folks guessed at this part, but he started killing snakes out of revenge. Must have thought he'd better kill them all, since he couldn't say which one killed his baby girl. He keeps showing up for work, but after a while, he starts coming in with snakeskins pinned to his clothes, and snake heads worn on a string around his neck. Well, it's awful strange, but don't nobody want to say anything to the man because he lost his baby. He gets worse. He wears more and more skins the more snakes he kills. He quits bathing and shaving and cutting his hair and he stinks like something dead. He gets skinnier and skinnier. Looks like a snake himself. Finally, his job has to cut him loose. He's scaring the customers. He gets this weird look in his eye. I remember seeing him after things had really gotten bad for him. Shuffling down the street, snakeskins hanging from his clothes. That scraggly long hair and beard."

Lamar stared off, eyes unfocused, shaking his head. His voice became quiet. "Tell you what—you looked into his eyes? You saw a walking dead man. Gives me chills to think about it. I've seen things in my life. I been to Vietnam. I ain't never seen anything like the way grief rotted that man from the inside out. Chewed him up. That's when folks started calling him the Serpent King. They wasn't trying to be ugly or funny. They was just trying to make some sense of it, I guess. Folks do that when they scared. Look out, they'd say. Here come the Serpent King. Folks is afraid of grief. Think it's catching, like a disease."

Travis waited for Lamar to finish the story. "So what happened to him?"

Lamar shifted uncomfortably in his seat. "All I know's what I heard. That one morning, Serpent King went up to his little girl's grave and laid on top of it with a Coke bottle of rat poison and drank it down and died there. Say Dillard Preacherman found him lying there. Can you imagine that? Seeing that happen? I don't wonder why Dillard Preacherman got funny in the head himself. That ain't to excuse him. But."

No one spoke. Lamar gazed out the window, a troubled look on his face. "I don't like to tell that part of the story. Ain't fond of any of the story, t' be honest. But since your dad asked and he signs my checks."

"Don't be an old pussy, Lamar." Travis's father spit in his can with a little clink. "So them Dillard Early boys are all a little touched in the head, seems. Sooner or later. About the time they decide to mess with serpents."

Travis's stomach had started to feel like it had a snake or two writhing around in it. He shuddered. He tried to wrap his mind around Dill having this much darkness in his bloodline. Obviously, he knew about Dill's dad. But this was different.

"Such a damn shame. Think on that," Lamar said, holding up a finger. "One snake did all this to one family."

"Don't cry about it too much, Lamar," Travis's father said. "Ain't you heard the story of Adam and Eve? One snake already did us all in. Whole damn human family."

"Seem like at least the two older Dillard Earlys both tried to be the Serpent King in their own way. The first by killing them. The second by handling them," Lamar said, spitting in his can.

Travis's father spit in his can again, got up, and slapped Travis on the back. "You like kings and princes and shit? You still might not want to be around when your buddy snaps and tries to take his papaw's and daddy's throne. That ain't no lucky name he's got. That's for damn sure."

9

DILL

Dill preferred studying at the library to studying at Good News Coffee. For one thing, he hated feeling pressure to buy something. For another thing, Good News, a Christian-themed coffee shop, provided him with too many reminders of a world he didn't like thinking about, especially when he was with Lydia. But she insisted.

"I'll have the Luke Latte in the Good News Grande. Wait . . . Matthew Mocha . . . no, Luke Latte after all. Dill? I'm buying."

"I'm okay."

"Come on."

"Fine. Plain coffee in the Victory Venti size."

The girl behind the counter handed them their drinks with a cheery grin and wished them both a blessed evening. Dill and Lydia found their seats.

"How do we not have a Starbucks here yet?" Lydia asked. "I've literally seen a Starbucks that had another tiny Starbucks in the bathroom. And anyway, how is a coffee shop Christian?"

"It implies that normal coffee shops are satanic."

"Which they totally are. It's like, can I please just get a cup of coffee without having to kneel before Lucifer and pledge my eternal soul?"

"Here's your latte. Will that be cash, credit, or the blood of a virgin?"

They laughed, content to procrastinate doing their homework.

"We learned in church that the Starbucks logo is satanic," Dill said.

"Of course you did, and of course it is. What's the reasoning?" She made air quotes around "reasoning."

"Mermaid demon."

"Ah, yes. But your new church is slightly less nutty, right? No snakes?"

"No snakes."

"So while we're here in the temple of Christian coffee, do you still have the snake verse memorized?"

This was exactly what Dill hated talking about, but he humored her. "Mark sixteen eighteen. *They shall take up serpents; and if they drink any deadly thing, it shall not hurt them; they shall lay hands on the sick, and they shall recover.*"

"Bravo."

"You don't know if I got it right."

"Eh. It felt right. It felt Bible-y. I have such cred coming here with you."

"I'm not that faithful. I volunteered for the praise band because I was scared of the snakes."

Lydia sipped her latte. "Well, I assume you could also play and sing reasonably well, not that I've ever heard you do both at the same time."

Dill shrugged. "I guess."

Lydia appeared to be pondering. "Back to the snakes. Do you think that's what Jesus really meant? Maybe he was like, *'And theoretically, you could probably pick up snakes,'* and Mark's over there writing and he's like, *'You should literally pick up snakes. Cool, Jesus, got it!'* And Jesus is going, *'Well, calm down with the snake business. Don't be weird; just be a decent person. It's really more of a metaphor.'* And Mark is writing, *'Definitely pick up actual literal snakes and drink actual real poison like rotten grape juice or other Bible-y poison.'*"

"Who knows exactly what he meant?" Dill tried not to sound impatient with the conversation. He really did enjoy Lydia's showing interest in his life.

"I'm sorry, do you hate talking about this?"

"No, it's fine." *Let me just turn the temple of Christian coffee into a black pit of lies.*

"Am I going to hell for joking about it?"

"Not if we find some snakes for you to handle. And I slipped some arsenic in your latte when you weren't looking." They laughed.

Dill sighed, the way he did when he knew he'd procrastinated doing something for as long as he could. He fished around in his bag for his schoolbooks. "Homework on the first day of school," he muttered under his breath.

"Hey, Dill? Hang on a sec." Lydia spoke quietly, the snark gone from her voice. "There's something I want to talk to you about."

Dill's heart began to race. Over the past few years, when people had prefaced something they were about to say with "there's something I want to talk to you about," it proved to be nothing he wanted to talk about.

"There's something I want to talk to you about. Your father is in trouble."

"There's something I want to talk to you about. We need you to testify."

"There's something I want to talk to you about. Your mother was in a very serious accident coming back from visiting your father in Nashville, and she might not pull through."

"There's something I want to talk to you about. With the house, the church, your father's legal fees, and my bills from the accident, we're about two hundred seventy thousand dollars in debt."

"There's something I want to talk to you about. I'm leaving you behind to go on to a bigger and better life, and I'll never think about or speak with you ever again." Probably.

"Okay," Dill said.

"I want to do some school shopping with you. The kind where you actually shop for schools."

Dill eyed her blankly, not quite processing what she was saying.

"Colleges. I want you to go to college."

"Why?" Dill's heart continued to race. What Lydia said wasn't bad in the way he feared, but it still wasn't what he wanted to hear.

"*Why?*" Lydia appeared flustered, a rare condition for her. As though it hadn't occurred to her that she'd have to explain why. "Because. First of all, college is good. You learn how to function in the very big world outside Forrestville and you set yourself up better for life. College grads make way more money. Millions more over their lifetime."

"So I'll stay in Forrestville and I'll be fine. And I don't need millions of dollars. Only enough to live." Dill wouldn't make eye contact.

"Dill, who are you kidding? You're miserable here. All the whispers and stares. Come on. Plus, I would love it if you had some direction so that you weren't getting mad at *me* every five minutes for having some."

Dill folded his arms. "I wondered when we'd get to the part where this is about you."

Lydia took a loud, deep breath through her nose. "*Ergh.* This is not about me. It's about you improving your life and I happen to get something out of it—namely you not being so defensive about my refusal to spend my life stuck here. I'm trying to pull you up."

A sunshiny church youth group a few grades below Dill and Lydia came in and ordered cupcakes and smoothies. *That used to be me.* Dill waited for them to pass their table before responding.

"You're turning me into a project," he said, his voice lowered. "It's not enough to dress me anymore. Now you need to chart out my life for me."

"Are you kidding me? You think I see you as a project?"

"That's how you're making me feel. Like a craft project. Like a photo series for your blog. Except not for your blog because obviously I'd never actually be on your blog."

"Yeah. Okay. Fine. I'm making it a project to make your life better." Her voice crescendoed. Lydia had no discernible Southern accent until she got mad. "I'm so sorry for caring and trying to help you make your life better."

"Is it that or is it your fear of the stain of my sad life getting on you? So you have to polish me up and make me worthy."

"No, dude. You're way off here, and you're being gross about it. You're scared of the thought of leaving and you're projecting that fear onto me. *You're* the one trying to make this about me. You think if you can convince yourself that I have totally impure motives for wanting you to go, you won't have to face the possibility that you're just afraid."

A couple of the youth group kids peeked over. Lydia gave them a firm mind-your-own-business stare. They pouted. One whispered something to the other, as if to prove Lydia's earlier point about whispers and stares. Dill could make out "pastor" and "jail." He gave serious consideration to the possibility that Lydia had hired them as plants. Wouldn't surprise him.

"Look," he said, almost whispering. "I would love to go to college too. But I can't."

"Why not?"

"My grades."

"They're fine. Not spectacular, but there are colleges who'll take you just for having a pulse. But more importantly, you're extremely smart. I wouldn't hang out with you if you weren't. Next."

"I can't afford it. Even if my grades are good enough to get in, I can't get a scholarship."

"Financial aid and get a part-time job. Next."

"I still can't afford it because I need to start working full time to help my family get out of debt. I need to work more than full time, in fact."

"You'll be of more financial help to your family farther down the road with a college degree. Next."

"I never planned on it. Going to college isn't something Earlys are supposed to do. None of us have ever been."

Lydia rocked back in her chair with a smug bearing. "Finally, the real reason, and it's the dumbest one of all."

"Thanks, but they're all the real reasons. Especially the part about needing to help my mom. I'm all she has. My grandparents died. We don't have any other living family nearby who still associate with us."

"I'm not trying to convince you to go to the Sorbonne or Harvard, Dill. Go to UT. Go to MTSU. Go to ETSU. Go to TSU. You'll be close to home."

The youth group held hands in a circle, praying over their cupcakes and smoothies. Dill waited for them to finish.

"Why aren't you up Travis's ass about this too?"

"First of all, don't assume that I'm incapable of being

up more than one ass at a time. I can be up—" The youth group table cast dirty looks in her direction. She lowered her voice to a hoarse whisper. "I can be up many asses at the same time. Multiple asses. I cause rips in the space-time continuum with how many asses I'm capable of being up simultaneously. Stephen Hawking had to come up with a parallel universe theory to explain my up-asses omni-presence."

"So you're up Travis's ass?"

"No."

Dill did a double facepalm.

"Listen," Lydia said. "I'm not bugging Travis because he's fine here. And that's because he doesn't actually live in Forrestville, Tennessee. He lives in Bloodfall land. Trav will be happy stacking lumber during the day and reading books at night until he dies. That's who he is. But you? I can tell you don't want that life. Everything about you screams that you want a different life. This is how you do it."

"What if I moved to a different town and got a full-time job?"

"Don't do this halfway. Either go to college, learn something, and change your life, or stay here and be miserable. Don't move to the next county over to be miserable. You'll waste your time."

"This is all super easy for you to say. You have loving parents who support you and want you to succeed at stuff. You can afford college."

"So what if it's easy for me to say? Am I not supposed

to say important stuff because it's easy to say? Counter-intuitive much?"

"I can't. I just can't. And all you're doing is making me feel worse about my life. You're telling someone in a wheelchair *'Walking is awesome. You should get up and walk.'* It's not that easy."

"I'm telling someone in a wheelchair to walk who's in the wheelchair because his dad and mom were in wheelchairs and he thinks he doesn't deserve to walk, or he's not walking so he won't hurt their feelings."

"What gives you such access to my deepest thoughts and feelings? I never told you I wanted to leave Forrestville."

Lydia's voice began to rise again. "Oh, give me a break. Ask any gay person in the world"—more reproachful looks from the youth group table—"if not voicing a desire makes it any less real. How can I tell you want out? Because you've laughed your head off during every Wes Anderson movie we've ever watched together. Because you've loved every music mix I've ever made for you. You've read every book I've ever recommended to you. And because I am your best friend and *I want out of here.* You are curious and hungry for experience, and it couldn't be more obvious." Her eyes blazed.

"I have to work on my homework."

They sat and eyed each other.

Lydia's face softened. "Please think about it."

Dill took a sip of his coffee. "This has been the worst first day of school I've ever had. And that's saying something."

The nagging dread that had accompanied Dill to Nashville rematerialized. Now not only would he lose Lydia at the end of this year, but he would also disappoint her. And worse, somewhere, circling and flitting around that dread, was another awful feeling: nothing makes you feel more naked than someone identifying a desire you never knew you possessed.

10

lydia

She's in ninth grade, sitting up a row and a few seats over from Dillard Early in English class. He rarely talks. He's frequently absent. She's heard her dad mention that Dillard's dad got himself into trouble for having some pretty creepy porno on his computer and maybe that wasn't all. This confluence of perverse sexuality and strange religion is titillating stuff in a small town. Well, it is anywhere, really. It's made national news. It's the hot topic for hacky late-night comedians who can't resist the low-hanging fruit of snakehandling jokes. There are rumors that the porn was Dillard's, which would be somewhat less creepy, since at least Dillard is a minor himself. Still, people steer clear of him—even the couple of friends he had from church.

But it's not as if she's burning down the house in any

popularity contests herself. For the most part, she'd always preferred books to people her own age. Her one close friend, Heidi, moved to Memphis the year before.

They're reading *Lord of the Flies* and the teacher is asking the students about their understanding of the book, and generally teachers don't call on Dillard because either they figure he won't have an answer or they don't want to put him on the spot. But Ms. Lambert, bless her heart, she goes for it.

"Dillard, what do you think this book is trying to say?" she asks.

He raises his head from his desk. He falls asleep in class a lot. He fixes the teacher with those intense, unnerving, Pentecostal eyes, which so often have dark circles under them lately. He waits several seconds to speak. Not like he's gathering his thoughts, but instead considering whether the teacher is prepared to hear what he thinks.

"I think it's saying that we're all born with seeds in us. And if we let them see sunlight and air, they'll grow through us and break us. Like a tree growing up through a sidewalk."

Tittering from the class, but mostly awkward silence.

Ms. Lambert speaks quietly. "Yes, Dillard. I think that's very much what this book is about."

Logan Walker raises his hand and doesn't wait to be called on. "My mom told me that if you eat watermelon seeds, a watermelon will grow in your stomach." The class snickers. Dillard puts his head down on his desk again.

"That's enough," Ms. Lambert snaps.

But Lydia isn't paying attention to this exchange because Dillard has earned himself an instacrush. Not that kind. Within Lydia's taxonomy of crushes are innumerable subspecies, most of which contain no romantic element whatsoever. She once listed as many of them as she could in a post on her new blog. West-Coast-clean-hippie-girl-wearing-headband crush. Witchy-goth-British-female-singer-wearing-torn-dresses-and-going-barefoot crush. Sardonic-young-male-Jewish-comedian-who-is-only-handsome-from-one-angle-and-with-whom-she-wants-to-have-brunch-but-not-kiss crush. Et cetera and so forth.

And who'd have guessed that she had a slot for weird-outcast-rural-snakehandler-boy-given-to-apocalyptic-existential-pronouncements-in-class crush. But she did. She suspects there's a fair chance she'll end up regretting it and instead of being full of beautiful sorrow and loneliness and brilliance as she imagines, Dillard really is a complete Jesus/porn freak weirdo. But if that turns out to be the case, she can always drop him with no social repercussions.

She finds him in the cafeteria later, where he eats his free lunches alone, or sometimes with Travis Bohannon, another thoroughly odd duck with a sad story of his own. Today Dillard's alone, writing in a notebook. She asks if she can sit down across from him. He eyes her with suspicion, as if he's wondering how she intends to hurt him.

"Go 'head," he says.

She sits down with her baby carrots, pita chips, and hummus, all bought on a recent supply run to Trader Joe's in Nashville. Her mother's Lexus SUV groaned under the weight of all their groceries. They'd bought a "Trader Joe's fridge" to put in the garage, just for these runs.

"What are you writing?" she asks.

"Nothing."

Cut-to-the-chase time. "I'm not here to make fun of you, by the way. Maybe you haven't noticed that the people who do that to you don't care for me much either. I liked what you said in class about the book."

He continues to regard her warily. "Songs. I get ideas in my head and I write them down. Words, or melodies."

"You're a musician?"

"Yeah, I learned how to play the guitar and sing when I was really young so I could play in my dad's church."

"So are those, like, Jesus songs you're writing?"

"No."

"Do you like movies?"

"Yeah. I mean, I haven't seen very many."

"Every Friday night is movie night at my house. Wanna come this Friday?"

"My mom's pretty strict."

Lydia shrugs. "Okay. Maybe some other time."

Dillard hesitates. "But she's working on Friday night. She works pretty much all day every day and every night. So as long as I'm home before ten . . ."

"I'm no snitch. Snitches get stitches."

And for the first time she can recall, she sees Dillard Early smile.

• • •

Lydia pulled herself from her reverie just as Travis bumbled into Good News, his hair still wet from the shower.

"Sorry, I got held up at work. Telling stories."

He sat down next to Dill and pulled out his tattered copy of *Bloodfall*.

Lydia looked up from the blank page she was staring at on her screen while reminiscing. "You cannot possibly have read that book fewer than seven times."

"Eight times."

"So why—"

"Because *Deathstorm*, the final book in the series, comes out in March. And I'm rereading the whole series before then so I don't miss any details when I talk about it on the forums. They're brutal there. I don't want to look like a noob. I'm reading it with one of my friends from the forums. They're good books. You should read them."

Lydia rolled her eyes. "Yeah, no. I wouldn't read five thousand pages of something if it contained precise instructions on how to lose twenty pounds by eating Krispy Kremes and orgasming. Do you not have homework?"

"Damn, Lydia, you're everyone's mom tonight," Dill said. Travis gave him an inquisitive eyebrow raise.

Lydia raised her hands in surrender, still gazing at her screen. "Nope. Nope. I'm done. Y'all do your thing. This is what I get for trying to help." *This is what I get for trying to keep from having to watch your life wither and die on the vine in this stupid little town.*

Her phone buzzed.

OMG just got sneak peek at Vivienne Westwood pre-Fall. Mind-blowing, Dahlia texted.

JEALZ.

Cool things going on with subverting trad. ideas of femininity etc.

I ALREADY SAID JEALZ.

Soon, love. BTW spoke with Chloe this morning. Expressed interest in rooming with us in NYC.

Chloe Savignon was a young actress and fashion designer. Lydia had never met her in person, but had corresponded with her online and seen her movies. She was a fan of *Dollywould*.

I'm down, she texted.

She could barely process how different her life would be in a year. A change she had wrought through her own force of will and ambition. From a nobody in a nothing town at the edge of the Cumberland Plateau to rooming with actresses and fashion industry scions in the most glamorous city in the world, attending one of the finest universities in the world. The possibilities were so endless. Her new friends would dress and talk differently. They'd be from big cities and elite prep schools. They'd have beach houses where they'd spend weekends. They'd have late-night conversations about Chomsky and Sartre and Kraftwerk and

Kurosawa and the Givenchy spring line. Friends who would introduce her to new things instead of it always being the other way around. That's what would replace this. Not that this wasn't fun. Not that Dill and Travis weren't good friends to her. Not that she wouldn't miss them. Not that she wouldn't feel guilty leaving them behind. But.

A year from now, she wouldn't be sitting in a Christian coffee shop across from friends who resented her ambition, that was for sure.

This was a good mind place for her to start drafting her college admission essay. She began typing.

I was born and raised in Forrestville, Tennessee, population 4,237, according to the last census. Not surprisingly, technology startups, software companies, media conglomerates, and so forth are reluctant to set up shop in a town named for Nathan Bedford Forrest, Confederate general and founder of the Ku Klux Klan. Opportunity and possibility don't knock at your door in Forrestville. You have to create them for yourself.

The coffee shop faced out onto the town square. Her classmates congregated at the gazebo at its center and used the square as a turnabout when they cruised the main drag, ending up at the Walmart parking lot. She could see them beginning to gather.

Another text from Dahlia. *Meeting mum for dinner in hour. Wish me luck.*

Speaking of, any chance your mom would be into writing me a rec letter for college? I'll need a few, Lydia texted.

What am I doing? Lydia thought. *I just casually sort of asked for a letter of recommendation from one of the most powerful women in the media.* Lydia had met Vivian Winter all of one time, at Fashion Week (Dahlia's stockbroker father had chaperoned them in Nantucket). Fortunately, Dahlia loved opportunities to show off her influence.

Oh mum adores you. We'll make it happen.

With that small victory, Lydia resumed work on her admission essay.

When I was thirteen, I decided that there was no reason why only adults from big cities should have a voice in the national conversation on fashion, pop culture, and the arts—the three things I love most. So I started a blog called *Dollywould*. I drew my inspiration from a quote by one of my idols, a fellow Tennessean and strong woman: Dolly Parton. She said, "If you don't like the road you're walking, start paving another one." So that's what I did. I paved a new road. I wrote from my heart about the things I loved and people began paying attention.

I got tens, sometimes hundreds of thousands of unique visitors a month. I have over 100,000 followers on both Twitter and Instagram. *Dollywould* has been featured in *Teen Chic, Cosmopolitan, Elle, Seventeen,* and *Garden & Gun*. I've been invited to New York Fashion Week for the last two years and I've given an interview to the *New York Times*. I've been a guest judge on *Project Design* on the Bravo Network. I get packages weekly from designers giving me their pieces to feature on the blog.

My goal with *Dollywould* was to create a space that was empowering to young people—especially young women—who had tastes outside of the mainstream and felt lonely, like no one understood them. I can empathize. I have exactly two friends at my high school. One is the son of a defrocked snakehandling pastor who is currently serving a prison sentence. My other friend works at a lumberyard to make money to buy books.

A little Southern fetishism never killed anyone. Dill and Travis may have been off-brand for her blog, but they were resoundingly on-brand for her bootstrappy admission essay narrative.

11

DILL

Dill was in good spirits as he clocked out of work, took off his green apron, folded it, and put it in his backpack. Every year since he'd known Lydia, Dr. Blankenship had thrown them a back-to-school dinner on the first Friday after school started, before their Friday-night movie night. He always did it up right, with smoked pork shoulder, cornbread, collard greens, mac and cheese, sweet tea, and Mrs. Blankenship's chess pie for dessert. It was generally the best meal Dill ate all year. In the interest of enjoying it to the fullest, he even resolved to allow himself the luxury of forgetting that it would be the last such dinner he'd ever have.

He hummed a new song he was working on as he walked from Floyd's to Lydia's house. He could smell lighter fluid and a charcoal fire from one of the houses near downtown.

He passed in front of the appliance repair shop, which was about to close. The door opened and a woman dressed in a plain, homemade-looking dress and two children—a boy and a girl—stepped out.

Dill stopped in his tracks. "Sister McKinnon?" He didn't run into members of his old church very often. Most lived outside Forrestville. They weren't big town-goers.

The woman jumped at the sound of her name and stared at Dill for a moment before recognition flashed across her face. "Brother Early? My goodness, I almost didn't recognize you. You're about a foot taller now than last I saw you. When was that?"

"Must have been just after my dad—so, I guess three years or so."

"And how is your daddy doing?"

"He seems okay. I saw him about a week or so ago."

"What a godly man. I pray for his protection and health every day."

"Me too," Dill lied.

"I've always been a believer, but to see how the signs manifested in him . . . if ever I had any doubt, he cast it away."

"Come on, Mama," the boy said, tugging on his mom's arm.

"Jacob? Hush. Daddy's paying the man who fixed the washer and then we need to get it in the van."

Dill knelt down to give Jacob a high five. "This is Jacob? Whoa. The last time I saw him, he was half this size."

"They grow up too fast. So are you and your mom attending services somewhere now?"

"We both work a lot, but we go to services at the Original Church of God when we can."

Sister McKinnon nodded politely. "Oh, okay. Do they practice the signs gospel there?"

"No, not really. Just healing and speaking tongues."

She nodded politely again. "Oh, well, God's word is God's word, wherever you hear it."

"Mamaaaa." Jacob tugged at his mother's arm.

"Go inside and talk to Daddy. Go on. Take your sister." The two children ran inside. Sister McKinnon turned back to Dill. "We go to services now at a signs church in Flat Rock, Alabama."

"Wow, that must take—"

"It's two hours each way. About a hundred miles." She gestured at a battered white fifteen-passenger van. "We bought this and we give rides to the Harwells and the Breedings. They help pay for gas. Do you still run with Joshua Harwell?"

"No. We . . . grew apart, I guess." A thick silence. "Are you a youth group leader like you were at our church?" Dill asked. "You were my favorite youth group leader."

She gave a melancholy smile. "No. We don't get callings because we live so far. How about you? Do you play in the praise band at your new church?"

"No."

"That's a shame. You had a mighty spirit for music."

The shop door opened with a jingle, and Brother McKinnon and his son and daughter came bumping out with their washing machine on a dolly. Dill hurried and grabbed the door. Brother McKinnon thanked him without looking up, wheeled the washer to the back of the van, and stopped, panting and mopping his brow with a bandana. When he made eye contact with Dill, his expression soured.

"Hey, Brother McKinnon," Dill said, extending his hand, hoping to break the ice. To be honest, this was the reaction he expected from his former coparishioners.

Brother McKinnon was having none of it. "Well, how about this. I'd have thought you'd be too busy spending your thirty pieces of silver to be bumping into us."

Dill blushed and tried to form a response, but words didn't come.

Sister McKinnon touched her husband's arm. "Dan, please—"

He raised his hand. "No, no, I'm inclined to give Junior here a piece of my mind. I've wanted to for a long time."

Oh boy. This'll be fun. Dill started to turn away to leave. "Sister McKinnon, it was good to see you. I—"

Brother McKinnon grabbed Dill's arm and squeezed hard, his voice rising, spraying flecks of spit. "Don't you call her 'sister.' You know good and well what you done. And if you don't care to hear no more about it, well, maybe that's your conscience. But you made things hard on my family. I spend about every hour of daylight on Sundays just driving to church. Hundreds of dollars in gas. I hope you're happy."

Dill wrenched his arm away and stared at the ground. "I'm not happy. I'm sorry." Passersby on the other side of the street had stopped to gawk at the snakehandler-on-snakehandler violence that was unfolding.

Brother McKinnon gave a sarcastic chuckle. "Oh, you're *sorry*. Well, with your sorry and four hundred a month, I can buy gas so I can raise my kids in the true faith. You're sorry." He spat at Dill's feet.

Dill met Brother McKinnon's caustic gaze, his shame decaying into anger. "Yeah. I'm sorry things are bad for you. But what my dad did was not my fault. He got himself into trouble."

Brother McKinnon's voice took on a dangerous hush as he jabbed Dill in the chest with his index finger, punctuating his words. "You keep telling yourself that, Judas. But tell yourself that somewhere else, because the sight of you is making me want to do something I'll regret."

Dill said nothing in reply, but he turned and walked away fast, adrenaline coursing through him, making his legs rubbery, sickening him. He scurried up the street, feeling like a cockroach that someone had flushed out of hiding. As he walked, he decided without much consideration that he would renege on his commitment to let himself forget that this would be his last back-to-school dinner. *This is what I'll have left when she's gone. Spats in front of appliance repair shops with former members of my dad's church who think I sold my dad to the Romans.* He kept his head down and cast furtive glances from side to side, but by then the streets were mostly empty in the rust-colored light.

· · ·

Dinner was excellent as usual. Good food and friendship washed away the run-in with the McKinnons. But even after the sour of the encounter had faded, forlornness welled up around him. Of course, he always experienced a certain anguish when hanging around with Lydia's family at their home, by virtue of the contrast with his own family and home. Their light, airy, spacious house, filled with beautiful things and modern appliances, always perfumed with bright, clean white flowers and citrus . . . compared with his cramped, dark house, filled with decline, stinking of mold, old carpet, and the glue that held everything together. Lydia's close and loving family, engaged in warm conversation—Lydia an only child by choice . . . compared with his fractured family, his mother treating him like a child even though she was only eighteen years older than him—Dill an only child because God wouldn't give his parents any more (their words).

This time while he was there, it was like sitting on a beach enjoying the sun while the tide rose cold around his ankles. *This will be gone by this time next year.*

It also felt like sitting beside the hospital bed of someone who was having a good day, but who was expected to die. He knew because he had done that before.

12

TRAVIS

The harvest was good that year in Raynar Northbrook's lands, and they feasted often on the heavy oaken table that sat in his great hall. He called for bread and meat until he was sated and threw the unfinished scraps to the dogs who slept by the fire that roared in his hearth. He was in high spirits.

"I forgot to tell you, Dr. Blankenship, I love your table." Travis ran his hand over the reclaimed barnwood surface he was helping Dr. Blankenship clear.

"Thanks, Travis. You are a man of excellent taste."

Travis beamed. He didn't often get compliments on his taste—one of the inherent hazards of wearing a dragon necklace.

While Travis helped Dr. Blankenship tidy up, his phone buzzed. I'm bored. Sitting here playing with my dog. What are you doing? Amelia texted.

Travis put a plate in the dishwasher. **Just had dinner at a friend's house. Helping clean up. What's your dog's name?**

Sounds fun! His name is Pickles.

No way! My best friend's name is Dill!!!

LOL WHAT???? Someday we should get Dill and Pickles together.

Definitely.

"I've been on a Werner Herzog kick lately," Lydia announced. "And it's my turn to pick. So this week's Friday-night movie is *Cave of Forgotten Dreams*."

Lydia's parents retired to their front porch rockers with glasses of wine and books while Travis followed Lydia and Dill to the TV room.

As they watched the documentary about the 32,000-year-old cave paintings in France's Chauvet cave, interwoven with Herzog's heavily accented existential musings, Travis couldn't help but wonder what his father would say if he were there. *What's this fag talking about? Can't understand a thing that comes out of his mouth.* For his part, Travis enjoyed it, as he did anything that carried the whiff of the firelit, ancient, and mysterious.

"So, I've been thinking about permanence lately, and how we live our lives without the world ever noticing we've come and gone," Lydia said as the end credits rolled.

"Lots of Christians think the world is only six thousand years old," Dill said. "So think about that. Those paintings have been there for almost five times longer than that."

"Kinda makes you wonder what we'll leave behind," Travis said. "I want to leave something behind for people to remember me by. The way kings do. Or the cave painting people." He learned this about himself even as the words left his mouth.

They sat for a moment, contemplating.

"We should leave something behind," Travis said. "For people to remember us by. Our own version of cave paintings."

Lydia didn't have any joke at the ready, which meant she liked the idea. "But not a cave. I don't want to go crawling around in any caves."

"The Column," Travis said, after thinking for a bit. "None of us can draw, but we could write stuff on it that's important to us."

"This is good. I smell a blog post in this," Lydia said. "First things first. Everyone have something they can write? Dill?"

"I have some of my lyrics I can write."

"Trav?"

"I've memorized what Raynar Northbrook had engraved on the marker to his best friend's tomb. It's my favorite."

"Okay. So I'm the only one who needs something. Let me think while I change." Lydia ran upstairs and returned a few minutes later, having donned a more appropriate outfit for tromping through the woods.

"Okay," she said. "Permanent markers. Big ones."

"Walmart," Travis said. He was rarely the catalyst for their activities, and he was proud.

"Walmart on a Friday night? We'll get to see all our friends from school!" Dill said.

"Ohhhhh, yes," Lydia said. "We *have* been missing out on the Friday-night Walmart hijinks while watching Herzog documentaries. Let's reassert our social position."

Starlight filtered through the green canopy of towering oaks and magnolias on Lydia's street. Sweat trickled down Travis's back the minute he hit the muggy air. But he didn't mind. This was as good as Friday nights got.

• • •

They pulled into the Walmart parking lot as the moon was rising bright and silver in the sapphire sky. Whooping, giggling, and music came from a clump of parked cars in a corner of the lot as they parked and walked in. Travis left his staff in the car.

"Dilllllllllllldoooooooooooo. Chlamydiaaaaaa," someone shouted.

Lydia shook her head. "This is my life. Getting yelled at in a Walmart parking lot on a Friday night by somebody doing a bad impression of a PG-13 fart-joke-movie comedian."

"We were just watching a smart documentary, so it's not really your life," Travis said.

"I'm starting to think we haven't been missing out on much with the Walmart parking lot scene," Dill said.

"Got any cookies, Girl Scout?" someone else shouted.

Lydia never went anywhere without the perfect outfit. She wore a vintage summer camp T-shirt and a pair of khaki hiking shorts and boots from the 1970s.

"I guess I deserved that," Lydia said.

Do all the losers from your school hang out at Walmart on Friday night? Travis texted Amelia.

Definitely, she texted. It's like we live in the same town.

I wish. I love my friends but it would be so cool to be able to talk about Bloodfall with you in person.

They bought their markers and drove to the unnamed gravel road that ended in a stand of trees beside the Steerkiller River, which bisected Forrestville. The air smelled like kudzu, mud, cool gravel, and dead fish.

• • •

That smell. Suddenly Travis is fourteen. He's with his mother at Saturday-night worship at the Forrestville Original Church of God. A new family has been attending their small congregation. Crystal and Dillard Early Jr., the wife and son of Dillard Early Sr., the snakehandling Pervert Preacher. The Earlys' meager congregation has collapsed in their pastor's absence, and the Original Church is the best they can find in Forrestville to replace it. They'll get their speaking in tongues and Holy Spirit and laying on of hands to heal the sick. They'll have to handle their snakes and drink their poison at home if they're so inclined.

They sit in the back beside Travis and his mom. Neither looks like they've slept in months, and they probably haven't. Dillard doesn't make eye contact with anyone. He seems to be drawing little comfort from being in God's house. He looks friendless and forsaken. Travis has had a taste of that. He gets a lot of suspicious looks himself because of his clothes and proven penchant for reading un-christian books.

He also knows something about loss and sleepless nights. His big brother Matt had died in a roadside bomb blast in Afghanistan the year before. Their father had never been especially nice, but he was at his worst when he drank. He started drinking more when Matt died. A lot more. And Travis has changed too. He used to love books and video games about modern soldiers, but now they only remind him of Matt. They remind him of how Matt would email him pictures of him and his buddies sitting on their Hum-vee, cradling their weapons. Which means his old books and video games remind him of grief and loss and of not living up to Matt's legacy. So he gets his fix of heroism and combat from fantasy books. He thus manages to es-cape a world in which big brothers die in faraway places. As soon as his mother figures out how he's finding solace, she brings him home the first book in the Bloodfall series from a shopping trip to Nashville, a recommendation from a bookstore employee.

Travis catches Dillard's eye and smiles and waves. Dil-lard, expressionless, returns the wave. Something tells Tra-vis to speak with him. Travis has always been taught that the feeling to do good is the Holy Spirit speaking, and when you feel that call, you'd better answer. Plus, he's been feeling a bit lonely himself. One of the consequences of his decampment into the world of fantasy was leaving his mea-ger group of friends—mostly from church—behind.

He slides over to Dillard and offers his hand. Dillard shakes it.

The next time they're both at youth group, Travis asks Dillard if he wants to go see this cool place his brother showed him before he left for Marine Corps boot camp. It's a good place to sit and be alone with your thoughts. And Travis doesn't mention this, but it's a good place to escape your father when he drinks and watches football, and reminisces about what a great football player your dead brother was, and asks you how you'd like the job of coaching a bunch of African American (but he uses a different word) millionaires and won't let it go until—to appease him because his belt has been known to come off—you lie and tell him you guess you wouldn't want that job. And then you hate yourself for being a coward and not saying what you really think. You hate yourself for not being good at sports like your dead brother. You hate yourself for not being as brave as the people you love to read about. And you just want to be somewhere where no one makes you feel that way.

• • •

"Travis, you can bring the staff this time," Lydia said, yanking him back to the present. "This place always creeps me out a little at night."

"What if a possum or a raccoon sees you with me? Wouldn't that be embarrassing?"

"Bring the staff before I change my mind."

13

DILL

"I have my Taser and pepper spray too," Lydia said. "My mom's armed me well."

"What's your deal?" Dill asked. "You planning on running into like twenty murderers?"

"I'm a vocal woman in the public eye. I take precautions."

"Maybe Trav and I should start wearing suits and sunglasses when we hang out with you."

"Are you done?"

"Yeah."

They picked through the brush at the base of the railroad bridge. By the river, a chorus of whistling frogs joined the clamor of insects. Dill led the way with a flashlight from Lydia's car.

Lydia swept the ground using the LED from her cell phone. "I'm scared of snakes."

"If we have a problem with snakes, Dill can handle it," Travis said. "Get it?"

Dill slapped at a mosquito. "Yeah. I got it."

The turf grew marshy beneath their feet. Lydia tried taking a couple of pictures with her flash.

"Kinda cool," she said. "Getting a sort of Ryan McGinley vibe. Either of you want to strip down and run around naked in the dark while I take your picture?"

Dill stepped behind Lydia and peered at the photos. "Not especially."

"I'd crack your camera lens," Travis said.

"Oh come on, Travis. You have a beautiful body. Dill, tell Travis he has a beautiful body."

That line from *Freaks and Geeks*, one of Lydia's obsessions, had been a running joke with them ever since Lydia had made Travis and Dill watch every episode in a single day. The joke never failed to slay them.

They reached the large concrete bridge support column that rose out of the ground before the river. They made their way to the side, the mud sucking at their boots, where a small metal ladder covered in chipped green paint hung. To get to the Column—situated in the middle of the river—they had to climb up the ladder on the riverbank column, walk out over the river on the catwalk under the bridge, and climb down another ladder to the Column.

"I'm wondering if I should invoke the ladies-first privilege to avoid having to climb up after you on muddy, gross rungs, or if I want one of you to go first to make sure a giant spider hasn't made a nest up there."

"A giant spider like Sha'alar, the Spider Queen," Travis murmured, loud enough for anyone interested to ask who Sha'alar was. Nobody asked.

"Here." Dill gripped the ladder, raised a foot, and scraped his boot on the column before stepping on the bottom rung. He did the same with his other boot. "Best of both worlds. Now you won't get your muddy hands all over what's left of my body when Shalimar or whatever kills me."

They climbed up the ladder and squeezed through the tight hole at the top to a catwalk. Travis had to hold his breath.

"We need to remember to bring some butter next time so we can grease up Travis," Dill said.

Travis laughed, trying to suck in his gut. "Come on guys, give me a yank."

"Not before you buy a gal dinner," Lydia said in her best 1940s sexpot voice, flicking ash from an imaginary cigarette.

"If only you walked through holes as easily as you walked into that," Dill said.

They finally dislodged Travis and continued on the narrow catwalk out to the Column. Travis had to walk hunched over to keep from hitting his head. They got to another hole with a ladder and slipped down it.

"I have an easier time going down the holes than up them," Travis said.

"Not even touching that one," Lydia said in the 1940s voice.

"We are thoroughly violating this poor bridge," Dill said.

"I didn't mean it that way. God dang, you guys."

They finally reached the Column, where there was space to spread out. Dill discreetly kicked a condom wrapper into the water below.

"Every time we come here, I try to figure out why this ladder exists," Dill said.

Lydia rummaged through her bag for her book and their markers. "Right? It's like 'Hey, Butch, whyncha climb down and see if the Column is still there.' 'Okay, boss. Thumbs-up! The Column is still here!'"

"No, but you have to come down to clean and paint the metal parts and make sure the rivets and welds and stuff are sound," Travis said, slapping the Column. It made a hollow, metallic ring.

Lydia examined a wide, flat spot and brushed the dirt away. "How is it every time we're talking about the real world, you manage to bring up fantasy, and every time we're talking about fantasy, you manage to bring up the real world?"

Travis shrugged. "My fantasies are more interesting than the real world and machines and tools are more interesting than you guys' fantasies."

Lydia took a picture of a blank spot. "Sure. We'll go with that. Hand me a marker."

Lydia went to work on her spot, using her cell phone light. Dill and Travis went around to the other side with the flashlight and took turns.

Travis's marker squeaked. "Be really, really careful not to fall, guys. Safety first."

"There are probably worse ways to die than falling into a river, having a great time with your friends right up until the end," Dill said.

"What would be you guys' ideal way to die? If you could choose?" Travis asked.

"Jeez, Trav, way to go dark on us," Lydia said. "But hey, I smell more blog post fodder. Dill? You seem like you've thought about it. Kick us off. The conversation, I mean. Don't literally kick us off the Column."

Dill thought for a second. He looked out at the river, at its eddies and swirls, the patterns forming on its surface and disappearing. He listened to the ordered chaos of its sounds. The moon ascended, Venus beside it. On the horizon below, a radio tower rose into the indigo sky, its red lights blinking lazily. A warm evening wind carried a breath of honeysuckle and linden from the banks. A train whistled in the distance; it would soon rumble over them with a sound like waking up to a thunderstorm. He was a tuning fork, made to resonate at the frequency of this place, at this time.

"Here," Dill said. "This would be fine. Lydia?"

"Surrounded by servants tearing their clothing and wailing, begging to join me in the afterlife so that they can continue to serve me."

"I don't even know if you're joking right now," Dill said.

"Okay, fine." She thought for a few moments. "I'm fascinated with Martha Gellhorn's life and death. She was a journalist and hero of mine. She did all sorts of amazing stuff. She said she wanted to die when she got too old to think well or be interesting. So she popped a cyanide capsule when she was ninety or something. If there was a way I could explode with beautiful heat and light, like a firecracker, that's what I'd want. I want people to talk about me and remember me when I'm gone. I want to carve my name into the world."

They heard the train approaching. "I'll go after the train," Travis yelled as it thundered overhead.

When it passed, he spoke quietly, looking at the river. "I'd want to die with glory. On a green battlefield as an old warrior, with my friends around me." He paused, gathering his thoughts. "I could join the Marine Corps like Matt if I just wanted to die in war like he did. But that's not what I want. I don't want to die in Afghanistan or some foreign country. I want to die fighting for my home. For a cause that means something to me. That's why I wrote the thing I did."

Dill handed him the flashlight. "Let's see it."

Travis shined the flashlight on what he wrote.

Rest, O Knight, proud in victory, proud in death.
Let your name evermore be a light to those who
loved you. Let white flowers grow upon this place

*that you rest. Yours was a life well lived, and now
you dine in the halls of the Elders at their eternal
feast.*

"I had no idea those books meant *that* much to you, Travis," Lydia murmured. "Now I feel bad about making all those Bloodfall jokes."

"Does that mean you'll read them?"

"No."

"They're amazing. I forget about everything I'm not good at and everyone I'm not when I read them. They make me feel brave."

"Do we know how to party on a Friday night or what?" Lydia said.

"Hey, Lydia, maybe after you move away, when you come back to visit, we can all come here and add stuff to the Column," Dill said. "If that wouldn't be too boring."

"Totally. That doesn't sound at all boring." Lydia took a picture of what Travis wrote. "Okay, Dill. Show us yours."

They stepped around to the side of the Column.

Dill shined the flashlight on his writing. "I said I'd write some of my song lyrics, but I changed my mind and wrote some of my favorite stuff."

*Moonlight. Calm after thunderstorm.
Scarecrows. Dusty bibles. Abandoned houses.
Fireflies. Sunlight through dust. Fallen leaves.
Churchyard cemetery. Gray autumn sky.*

River levee. Gravel road. Wind chimes.
Wood smoke. Train whistle on winter night.
Kudzu on telephone pole. Hymnal falling
apart. White crosses by highway. Cicada hum.
Shadows. Sparrows. Rust. Railroad crossing
lights through fog. Crickets. Dance of leaves
in wind. Decaying barn. Field after harvest.
Clouds covering moon. Quiet dusk. Lightning.
Heartbeats.

Lydia took a picture. "I love these things too, and I had no idea until I saw this."

"I don't think these'll last thirty-two thousand years," Travis said, "but maybe they'll outlive us, right?"

Lydia showed them the Dolly Parton quotes she'd written on the Column.

Find out who you are and do it on purpose.

We cannot direct the wind, but we can adjust the sails.

If you don't like the road you're walking, start paving another one.

"Future generations need the counsel of this prophetess," she explained.

Then they lay for a while on their backs, gazing into the starry expanse through the railroad tracks, listening to the dark river below. *This might be it,* Dill thought. *This might be the best your life ever is. This moment. Right now.*

"I read somewhere that a lot of the stars we see don't exist anymore. They've already died and it's taken millions of years for their light to reach Earth," Dill said.

"That wouldn't be a bad way to die," Lydia said. "Giving off light for millions of years after you're gone."

14

lydia

Her mom had gone to bed when she got home. Her dad was wearing his bathrobe, sitting on the couch, eating a big bowl of popcorn and watching TV.

"Hello, princess," he said, as she entered the living room after washing her hands in the hall bathroom. "Have fun tonight?"

"Friday-night Forrestville fun. It's an alliterative party." She pulled off her hiking boots, sat on the couch, and snuggled up to her dad, putting her head on his shoulder.

He rested his head on top of hers. "You smell like summer night."

She pulled a piece of her hair to her nose. "The scented candles that are supposed to smell like summer night never smell this way. They always smell like scary-guy cologne." She reached into his popcorn bowl and grabbed a handful.

"I like your friends. They're good guys. You've made smart choices."

"They are. And don't sound so surprised about me making smart choices."

"You're lucky to have them. Good friends in high school aren't a given."

"Yeah, especially around here."

"Around anywhere. This hasn't been such a bad place to grow up, has it?"

Lydia raised her head off her dad's shoulder and gave him a solemn stare. "You did not just seriously ask me that in good faith."

"What? Sure I did. This is a nice place. It's quiet, safe. The area is beautiful. I grew up here and your mother grew up a couple of counties from here. Taking over Grandpa's practice reduced the stress our family would've experienced if I'd had to start my own from scratch."

"It sucks here. People are dumb and racist and homophobic. I don't have a single female friend at school since Heidi left."

Her dad picked up the remote control and muted the TV. "Hang on. You'd never have made friends with Dill and Travis if we didn't live here. Let me ask you this: do you like who you are?"

"Yes."

"Do you really think living here hasn't had a big hand in

who you've turned out to be? Do you think you'd have had the same drive to create *Dollywould* if we'd laid the world out for you at your doorstep?"

"Are you seriously saying that living in this shitty town was part of some grand strategy to make me a go-getter?"

"That was part of it. Yes."

Lydia reached out and smacked her dad on the fore-head, as if swatting a mosquito.

He winced and pulled away. "Look, do you think there's anywhere—any city, any high school—where someone as smart and talented as you can waltz in and do your thing and nobody will try to tear you down because they feel inferior to you?"

"I don't know." She rested her head back on her dad's shoulder.

"I went through what you did in high school."

"Oh please. Mom told me you were class president of Forrestville High."

"That doesn't mean I had a lot of close friends or that I fit in. It means that I was nice to everyone and they rewarded me for it. I still felt lonely."

"Then why did you come back here to raise your daughter? Look me in the eye and tell me that it wasn't because you were afraid of living in a bigger city."

"I don't think it was fear so much as the inertia of living in a familiar place that we feel connected to. Nowhere is perfect."

"And here I've been thinking that Forrestville couldn't be improved."

Her dad grabbed a handful of the dwindling popcorn. "Hey, I think it's fine, and when I was in high school I didn't even have two friends as close and loyal as Dill and Travis. I can see it on those guys' faces. They'd stand between you and a pack of lions."

"*Pride* of lions." She grabbed a handful of popcorn.

"Whatever. They wouldn't let lions eat you. Don't think you won't miss them when you've gone off to bigger and better things. Part of you will miss this life."

"I'll be too busy to miss stuff."

"No you won't. Listen, sweetie, these are real friends you have. *Genuine* friends. Two of them. That's two more than a lot of people who live in bigger cities and do fancier things have."

Her voice became faint, like it became when she knew she had to concede something but thought she could keep the universe from hearing. "I know."

"So stop hating your parents for making the choice we made about where to raise you. If we'd raised you in the big city, you might've gotten hit by a stray bullet in a drive-by shooting or something."

She lifted her head from her dad's shoulder and rolled her eyes after making sure he was watching. "I am *so* regretting that I made you watch *The Wire*. I should've guessed you'd be a total doofus about it."

"What are Dill's and Travis's plans after they graduate?"

She sighed. "I mean, I guess Dill's going to go full time at Floyd's and Travis'll work full time at the lumberyard. And they'll live their lives and go to Waffle House or whatever and get old and die."

"Hey," her dad said, more sharply than usual. "Don't."

Lydia gave him a reproachful, wounded glance, frowning. "Sorry. Jeez, don't be a creep."

"No, sweetie. I'm not being a creep. You're being very haughty and unkind about their lives. People live quiet lives and that's okay. There's dignity in that, no matter what you may think."

"I wish they wanted more out of life because I care about them. I hate thinking about Dill and Travis stuck here, living pathetic lives. It bums me out. I want Dill especially to go to college and do something with his life."

"I don't think they're trying to inconvenience you personally. Their circumstances are really different from yours."

"Duh, I know."

"Do you? Can you keep a secret?"

She gave him an of-course-I-can-how-dare-you-question-me look.

"You really can't tell because I could get in trouble for revealing patient information. But I think you should know. A couple of years ago, I replaced Travis's two front teeth. They said it was an accident at the lumberyard— that he was stacking some wood and a forklift hit the stack and drove a piece of wood into his face. So here's the funny thing about that. They called me the morning after. The lumberyard closes at five, like my office. So why not call me sooner? Did this accident happen at 4:59? I doubt it. Wouldn't you call the dentist immediately?"

"Oh my God," Lydia murmured. "It must have happened that night—"

"At home. And of course I have zero proof of anything and Travis insisted that it happened at the lumberyard. But first he said that he was pulling some lumber off a rack and it fell and hit him; then he said a forklift hit it."

"Trav's dad totally seems the type."

"Oh, Clint Bohannon *is* the type. He was two years ahead of me in high school. Meanest son of a bitch you ever met. Bully. Strutted around high school like nobody could touch him. Star quarterback. Did you really not know what Travis goes through at home?"

Lydia felt wounded and oblivious—neither was a feeling she enjoyed. "No. He—he doesn't talk about what goes on at home. I knew his dad was an asshole but I didn't know how big of one. How did Travis come from that? He's the sweetest."

"Anne Marie, his mom, was in my grade. Sweet, pretty. Cheerleader. Nice to everyone. We all thought she'd turn Clint a little nicer when they got married. Guess that didn't happen."

Lydia absorbed it all silently.

Her dad hugged her closer. "And I don't need to tell you

about Dill's issues. Point is, you've had a very different life and it's important for you to be understanding."

"Okay," Lydia said, shaken. *How did I not know that about Travis? How was I so blind? I'm a horrible friend. I should have seen. I should have made Travis feel like he could tell me.*

"You're destined for great things, Lydia. That comes at a price. Everybody wants to be close to greatness and get a piece for themselves. The day may come when it takes some discernment to tell when someone loves you for you and when someone wants to stand near your fire. You have two friends right now who may not be glamorous, but they love you for you."

"You're right," she murmured.

Her dad sat up in mock astonishment, fumbling for his phone. "Hold on, hold on! Can you repeat that so I can get it on film?"

"You're such a dork, I can't even deal. I have to go work on my blog." She got up.

"Don't stay up too late."

"I love you, Daddy." She kissed him on the cheek.

"Oh, by the way, a few things came for you today. On the kitchen counter."

Lydia went into the kitchen. A package from Owl, an up-and-coming online budget fashion retailer. A sundress and some wedges. Not bad. They'd make the blog. A small package from Miu Miu. A back-to-school gift—a necklace. Definitely blog-worthy.

And an envelope. She opened it. A letter, on the most

expensive-feeling stationery she'd ever held. It smelled as though scent scientists had engineered it to give off the whiff of walking past a high-end rare book dealer's shop in Paris or London. Written in powerful, sweeping, feminine handwriting:

Love the blog. Of course I'll give you a letter of recommendation. Write a letter for my signature and have Dahlia give it to my assistant. See that your grammar and spelling are impeccable. Above all, be generous with yourself; make signing this worth my while.
Cheers,
Vivian Winter

Excitement dissipated some of the melancholy of the conversation about Dill and Travis.

Just got letter from your mom, said she'd write rec letter for me!!! THANK YOU, Lydia texted Dahlia.

Her phone buzzed. *I told you she would*, Dahlia texted back. *Repay me by featuring me on Dollywould.*

You got it. We'll do profile and interview. Seriously thanks.

It's nothing. Chloe is in, btw. Three fab fashionistas in NYC. We better find a place with loads of closet space.

Now I need to get into NYU, Lydia texted.

You'll have no trouble thanks to mum and your brilliance.

Lydia began composing her blog post while she looked at the pictures of the things she and her two friends wanted as their messages to the world after they'd been dead for thousands of years and tried to think about what she could say that would do them justice.

15

DILL

Mr. Burson, the owner and proprietor of Riverbank Books, had always reminded Dill of a shambling, humanoid badger. He wore small, wire-rimmed glasses on the end of his nose, and for all but the hottest months of summer, cardigans covered in cat hair, buttoned across his rotund belly, usually over a Merle Haggard or Waylon Jennings concert T-shirt. Dill always liked Mr. Burson. As a lifelong bachelor who loved cats and books, he was the subject of plenty of whispering and judgment himself, so he wasn't about to visit it on Dill.

Dill, Lydia, and Travis walked in about a half hour before closing time (or the closest approximation thereto—Mr. Burson stayed open as much or as little as he saw fit), scattering three or four of the shop cats before them. Mr. Burson glanced up from his stool behind the counter, where he was reading some pulp sci-fi novel from the 1960s, absent-mindedly petting yet another cat. Several guitars hung on the wall behind the counter. A forest composed of stacks of used books loomed around him, the usual spicy-vanilla scent of pipe tobacco and old paperbacks wafting in the air. Mr. Burson's jowly face lit up when he saw Travis, one of his most loyal customers.

"Young master Bohannon!" he said in his wheezy voice, adjusting his glasses. "To what mysterious and fantastical lands may I offer you passage today?"

Travis leaned on the glass counter that housed Mr. Burson's tiny museum of early editions of Faulkner, O'Connor, Welty, and McCarthy. "Actually, we're here to find a present for Dill's mom for her birthday, but while I'm here, could I place a preorder for *Deathstorm*?"

Riverbank Books's stock was largely used. Mr. Burson traveled around in his battered and rusty 1980s Toyota pickup covered with nerd-joke (MY OTHER CAR IS THE MIL-LENNIUM FALCON), pro-reading (I'D RATHER BE READING), and vaguely political (COEXIST) bumper stickers, snapping up boxes of books at thrift shops and estate and library sales. But he carried a small stock of new books and took special orders for people who didn't use Amazon and/or preferred to support their local bookstore.

"Ah, yes, *Deathstorm*. The new opus from Mr. G. M. Pennington. Aren't you lucky I don't sell books by weight?" He chuckled, got out a tattered ledger volume, and scribbled a note to himself. "So, Travis, what do we think will become of House Northbrook in the final battle against the dark forces of House Allastair and their Accursed? Will the Queen of the Autumnlands intervene with her Raven Host? Will Rand Allastair's bastard throw a wrench in the Allastairs' plans by leading the Horsemen of the East in a gambit to capture the Gold Throne?"

Travis's eyes glistened. He didn't often get to talk about Bloodfall with real-life, flesh-and-blood human beings. He opened his mouth to answer.

Lydia interrupted them by making a time-out sign. "Hey-o, whoa, hang on, fair knights of the realm. Before thou dorkest out, we humble serfs beg thy assistance in finding a book for the woman who doesn't like anything."

"I mean, it's not that she doesn't like *anything*. It just has to be Christian. Really Christian," Dill said.

"Like the Bible barely makes the cut because Christ is only in the second half," Lydia said.

Mr. Burson snapped his fingers and dismounted from his stool with an involuntary grunt, letting his cat leap to the ground. He waddled from behind the counter, waving for them to follow. "This way, young friends." He led them past floor-to-ceiling bookshelves, haphazardly organized with piles of books on the floor in front of them.

They reached the section labeled CHRISTIAN/INSPIRATIONAL. He got down on one knee with much effort, grunting and puffing, the seams of his pants creaking like ship riggings. He pulled out a book called *The Templar Device*—a new book he'd shelved with the used books, his customary practice.

He adjusted his glasses and handed it to Dill. "This is a Christian adventure novel that was quite popular a few years ago. It's about an archeologist who unearths the tomb of one of the Knights Templar, to find part of a prophecy about the Antichrist inscribed on his shield. He's launched into a world of international intrigue and deceit as he tries to put together the other pieces of the prophecy. But"—he cupped his hand to his mouth and whispered—"spoiler alert: the Antichrist is in all of us if we don't accept Jesus."

Lydia made a zipping motion over her mouth, then locked it with a pretend key.

"I'm not sure the idea of adventure is even Christian," Dill said as he thumbed through the book. "The true believer has faith that everything will be fine and they'll be saved and go to heaven, which kind of makes adventure less of an adventure. But I'll risk it."

They stayed and browsed for a bit. Travis and Mr. Burson swapped theories about *Deathstorm*. Dill watched Lydia as she moved along the shelves, gently dragging her hand behind her along the books, touching each one, as if she were reading the titles with her fingers.

Lydia found a used copy of Patti Smith's *Just Kids,* her favorite book. "I pretend I'm buying it and getting to read it for the first time. Besides, I try to support Riverbank. It's basically the only semisophis . . ." She trailed off as Travis and Mr. Burson began acting out a pretend sword fight. She sighed. "Anyway, I try to support Riverbank."

They bought their books and stepped out into the late-August dusk. September was around the corner, but summer lingered in full force.

"Let's go watch some trains," Dill said.

Travis shrugged. "I'm in."

"Lydia?"

"I need to fill out some scholarship applications and get ready for my interview with Laydee."

"You're interviewing Laydee, the singer?" Dill asked.

"Yep."

"Wow. That's awesome. She's pretty much our age and her songs are all over the radio."

"Yeah. Anyway. Trains." Lydia checked the time on her phone. "I can go for a little bit. If we don't see a train soon, I gotta run."

"High five."

"When is the last time you and I shared a high five that wasn't completely awkward?"

• • •

There were several spots in Forrestville that were prime for train watching, but Dill favored Bertram Park. It was a little ways up from the bridge with the Column. The railroad tracks bisected the park, perhaps not the optimal design. Fortunately, the neglected park wasn't much of an attraction to kids. It had a forlorn baseball diamond and some oxidized playground equipment. A few spring-mounted teeter-totter animals that resembled sun-faded dollar-store rip-offs of Disney characters sprouted up through the sand.

They sat on a picnic table near enough to the train tracks that when they heard a train coming, they could get close.

Lydia checked her phone. "Watching trains. Dill's version of YouTube. You know this is a very weird thing to do, yes?"

"Said the girl currently wearing clothing from five different decades."

"Touché."

"Should we ask the guy wearing a dragon necklace if he thinks it's weird?" Dill asked.

"I don't think it's weird," Travis said. "Trains and big machines are cool."

"Why *are* you so into this?" Lydia asked.

Dill pondered. "I'm trying to think of the least weird way to put it."

"Uh-oh," Lydia said.

"Okay. So, when I watch trains, it makes me think about how much movement there is in the world. How every train has dozens of cars and every car has hundreds of parts, and all those parts and cars work day after day. And then there are all these other motions. People are born and die. Seasons change. Rivers flow to the sea. Earth circles the sun and the moon circles Earth. Everything whirring and spinning toward something. And I get to be part of it for a little while, the way I get to watch a train for a minute or two, and then it's gone." *The way I get to be part of your life before you're gone, and I'm left here, watching trains pass me by too.*

His cheeks flushed and he looked at the ground, preparing himself for whatever clever thing Lydia had to say. "Anyway. Sorry. Weird." He glanced over at her. She stared at the tracks.

"No," Lydia said, all teasing gone from her voice. "Not weird. I mean, obviously you're still generally weird—let's not get carried away—but that's not weird."

Almost on cue, a train whistle sounded in the distance.

As the train approached, they got up off the picnic table and stood near the tracks, close enough to feel the wind from the train. Dill experienced the familiar rapturous rush of excitement and adrenaline as it neared and began laying on the whistle. That orgasmic rise as the clamor and energy of it built, threatening to overwhelm his senses, until it was right upon him. He closed his eyes and listened to its various parts. Wheels squealing on the rails. The *chug-chug-chug* of one of the cars. He absorbed its violence and brawn as it slithered past, a massive steel serpent. That pounding, pulsing din stirred something in him.

• • •

He's thirteen and standing at the front of his father's church with the rest of the praise band. He's wearing his too-large electric guitar, playing as loud and fast as he can while the drums and bass jar the flimsy walls and low particleboard ceiling of the tiny church. He makes mistakes left and right, but nobody notices because they're caught up in the Holy Spirit, and the walls also vibrate with the exalted and chaotic glossolalia of tongue speaking. Shoes and boots muddy from the unpaved parking lot stomp and make the floor quake. Several congregants, including Dill's mother, pound tambourines.

Dill's father stands at the front of the congregation and raises a mason jar half-filled with strychnine before taking a long swig, his eyes rolling back. He shakes his head, wipes his mouth, and shouts, "Hallelujah!" He hands it off to Dill's mother, who sips it like it's lemonade, passes it on, and goes back to beating her tambourine.

Dill's father strips off his white dress shirt, down to his undershirt. He stands with his arms outstretched. Supplicants approach him and put their hands on his veiny arms and bony shoulders, seeking healing from maladies real or imagined.

A call goes up through the congregation and two of the brothers do a shuffling dance down the center aisle, a wooden box containing a snake in each of their hands. They stop and set them on the ground and Dill's father dances up to them, clapping his hands. They pull back the chicken-wire lids on their hinges and reach into the boxes with hooked poles, pulling out two rattlesnakes and two copperheads. The brothers begin distributing them among the congregants like so many neckties. Brother McKinnon holds a rattler inches from his face, spraying it with spittle as he prays, daring the serpent to strike and test his faith.

Dill plays faster, his heart thumping, sweating in the suffocating humidity of so many animated bodies pressed into one place. His father starts in his direction, carrying a copperhead draped around his neck. He stands in front of Dill and lifts the copperhead off himself. Dill's heart thrums in his ears. He stops playing. The bass player and drummer keep on without him, playing ever more furiously. He's always been afraid of the snakes. He's never taken them up before and he prays to God to cleanse his soul and to give him the faith, if this is to be the hour. *And these signs shall follow them that believe. And these signs shall follow them that believe. They shall take up serpents. And these signs shall follow them that believe. They shall take up serpents.* His breath leaves him.

His father reaches out to him with the thick, sinewy copperhead and Dill extends his hands. He imagines how the snake will feel when he holds it. Cool. Dry. Sleek. Pulsing with malevolent vitality. He meets his father's eyes. His father gives him a slight, sad smile and turns away, holding the snake above his head, triumphant, before handing it off to an elderly sister. Dill breathes again. He tries to pick up the rhythm but he's shaking too badly. He's relieved but disappointed that his lack of faith shines through his skin.

A week later, officers arrest his father.

16

TRAVIS

"Hey, Travis," Dill said as they left Bertram Park. "Any chance your mom might be able to help me by making a birthday cake for my mom for tomorrow? I . . . don't have a lot of the stuff you need to make a cake."

"Yeah, no problem. Especially for someone from church."

"I can come help after work."

"Naw. Sometimes my dad's weird about people coming over. You know."

Dill handed over a battered package of off-brand yellow cake mix that he appeared to have snagged from work for free. "Thanks. Sorry for the late notice."

Travis's mom was happy to do it. He didn't want to dump the project on her, though, so they made a little mother-son evening of it, with him pitching in to help. It was the perfect night, because his father was playing cards at a friend's house.

"Really now, this kitchen is an absolute pigsty . . . ," Travis said in a horrible British accent, imitating his mom's favorite cooking reality show host from the Food Network.

She giggled. "Oh Trav. You're too funny."

His mom's laughter was one of his favorite sounds. He didn't hear it nearly enough. Not since Matt died. He kept clowning. He dusted his face with flour and put on one of his mom's flowered aprons. He was trying to juggle some wooden spoons when they heard Travis's father stumble in the front door.

They immediately fell silent, hoping he might go right to bed or at least flip on the TV and pass out in front of it. Anything but coming in the kitchen and ruining their night. They stood a fair chance—Travis's father considered the kitchen to be his mother's exclusive domain.

No such luck. He staggered in, stinking of bourbon. The minute he saw Travis in the apron with flour on his face, he sniggered.

"Well, ithn't thith prethiouth!" he said, slurring and lisping, gesturing with a limp wrist. "Look at my two little girlth having the betht old time!" He affected a mincing gait.

Travis smiled uneasily, hoping this was his father's attempt at humor. The only problem was that his father never quite knew when a joke stopped being funny (or started being funny, for that matter) when he was drunk.

Travis's mom swept a stray bit of flour into her hand and

threw it in the garbage. "Did you have fun at your game, sweetie?"

"Oh heaventh yeth! But not ath much fun ath baking a little cake in my little apron." He staggered over to Travis and jerked hard on his apron strings, untying them. Travis turned away, avoiding eye contact. He removed the apron and quietly folded it.

"Clint," Travis's mother said softly. He ignored her and got in Travis's face.

"Talked with Kenny Parham tonight. He mentioned homecoming. Since I guess you ain't playing in the game, you at least taking a girl to the dance?" All hint of playfulness was gone from his voice.

Travis stared at the ground. "I don't know."

"You don't know. You don't know what? That you're going to the dance or that you like girls? You taking your boyfriend, Dillard Early the Serpent Prince, to the dance?"

"No sir. I like girls fine. Just not dances."

"You a fag?"

His father's breath made his eyes water. "No sir." He had a sudden impulse to show his father the picture of Amelia on his phone. But he knew his father would make him regret that too. Say something about Amelia's body or face. And Travis knew that would make him do something he'd regret.

"You just get your kicks from powdering your nose and putting on aprons and baking cakes with Mama, and not going to dances?"

"No sir." *Please leave. Please leave.*

His father got up even closer and spoke with menace. "If you're a fag, I'll teach you not to be, by God. You better man up." He gave Travis a push. Not an especially hard push, but it caught Travis by surprise and he stumbled backward a couple of steps. He almost looked his father in the eye, but thought better of it. He stared at the ground. *Just shrink away and he'll get bored and leave. Make yourself small. That's what he wants—for you to be small.*

"Clint, honey," Travis's mother said gently, as if she were talking to a dangerous animal or a recalcitrant child (or some combination of the two). "Travis is a Christian. Don't worry. Now can I fix you something to eat?"

Travis's father belched and sauntered over to the mixing bowl. "Nope, I'm fine." He dipped three fingers in the cake mix, and while staring Travis's mother dead in the eye, sucked them clean and then stuck his fingers back in the bowl for a second helping.

"Oh Clint. I wish you hadn't done that. That cake wasn't for us."

Travis's father walked over to his mother. "I. Don't. Care," he said, poking her in the upper chest, punctuating each word. She looked away. He stood over her for a second. Travis's fear began to turn to rage. He felt what he had felt with Alex Jimenez. *Please leave. And don't touch my mom again.*

"Can't wait to try the cake," his father said with a smirk. He pointed at Travis. "Better not be a queer." He stalked into the living room, where he flopped on the couch and clicked on the TV.

Travis breathed again. *Thank you, Jesus. Thank you.* So did his mother. They made eye contact. Travis started to speak. His mother put a finger to his lips as if to say *Don't. Be careful.*

"I'll go ahead and bake this one and your dad can have it. And I'll do another for Crystal. I have another yellow cake mix in the pantry. In fact, it's better than the mix Dillard gave you."

"You want help?"

She gave him a sad half-smile. "No, sweetie pie. I'll take it from here," she whispered.

"Dad didn't always used to be this bad," Travis whispered.

"I know." She picked up a damp cloth and gently wiped the flour from Travis's face. From the living room, they heard Travis's father cackle at something.

Travis's mom dumped the batter from the mixing bowl into a cake pan, bent down, and got another cake pan from under the stove. She put the mixing bowl in the sink and started to wash it with quaking hands.

Travis walked up to her and put his arms around her neck, hugging her from behind. She put her hand on his arms. "I love you, Mama," he whispered.

He managed greater stealth than usual and sneaked past his father, who was absorbed in some sitcom rerun. Safely in his room, he turned on his decrepit laptop. It whined to life. While he waited for it to boot up, he ran hypothetical scenarios in his head—ones where he stood up to his father. Where he didn't slink around and shrink from him. Where he didn't let his father make him feel small and worthless. His loathing of his father kept circling back to self-loathing. *Why aren't you braver? At least for your mom's sake? You're nothing like Raynar Northbrook. He would stand up to a bully. Of course, even if you stood up to him, you'd probably just screw it up and feel even worse, like what happened with Alex.*

He wanted to text Amelia. But also he didn't. He didn't want to look weak in front of her. But he also didn't feel like being alone right at that moment. He didn't think Lydia would understand because her family was so awesome. And he didn't think Dill would understand because his family was so awful.

Travis went around in circles until finally he just did it.

Hey, he texted.

Hey yourself mister, Amelia texted back, almost immediately. How are you?

Rough. I got into it with my dad.

OMG. You ok?

Yeah. I guess I just needed cheering up.

If I were there I'd give you a huge hug and remind you that Deathstorm comes out soon.

That's working!

His phone buzzed again. It was a photo of a baby elephant playing with a beach ball.

Yes!

A funny Bloodfall meme. And then another. And another. Travis almost laughed out loud but caught himself.

Thank you!

When we meet in person, I'm going to give you a million hugs and tell you it's not your fault your dad is an asshole.

As Amelia's disembodied words of encouragement continued to stream in, the warm sugar-buttery smell of baking cake filled the house.

17

DILL

He lit the candles the moment he heard her pull up. There were only five of them.

"Dillard, you home?" she called out when she entered the dark house.

"In here, Mom."

She walked into the kitchen, where Dill stood behind the cake, candlelight illuminating his face. "Happy birthday!"

She shook her head and set down her things. "Dillard Wayne Early, what have you done?"

Dill grinned. "I made you this cake. Sort of. I got the stuff and Travis's mom made it. It turned out a lot better than if I'd done it, I promise."

She smiled. "I don't even—"

"Well. What are you waiting for? Blow out the candles. Let's have a piece or two."

She sat down and blew out the candles. They sat in the dark for a second while Dill fumbled for the light switch.

"Did you make a wish?"

"I sure did. I wished for—"

"No, no, you can't tell me. Then the wish won't come true. Besides, I can probably guess."

"Wishes don't matter anyway. Prayer does."

Dill got up and grabbed a knife, two forks, and two plates. He pulled out the candles and cut two large pieces of the vanilla-frosted yellow cake.

"Did your work do anything special for your birthday?"

"The gals on the cleaning staff put their money together and got me a twenty-dollar gift card to Walgreens. I think I'll buy a little something and see if they'll cash out the rest. We need stamps to write your father."

"I think you should spend it on yourself," Dill said.

"There isn't anything I want."

"Get some of your favorite candy or lotion or something."

She thought for a second. "Maybe we'll go for an ice cream."

"I really wish you'd spend it on yourself. It's your present."

"We'll see." They sat silently and ate their cake. Dill finished his first. It was delicious. And as they sat there, something came over him. It seemed as good a time as any to bring it up.

"While we're talking about money, what if there were a

way for me to make us a lot more money than I'd make at Floyd's, even as a manager? What would you think about that?"

She gave a rueful laugh through a bite. "Oh, that'd be great. As long as you aren't proposing to sell drugs."

"No. But what I'm talking about would mean that we still have to spend a few more years with me not making as much as I'd make full time at Floyd's."

She took another bite of cake. "I'm not following," she said, but her eyes said *I hope I'm not following.*

"I'm talking about what if I were maybe to go to college. People who—"

She shook her head and put up her hand. "No."

"But Mom, listen to me. You didn't let me finish."

"No. No need. I know what you're going to say and what my answer will be."

"Mom, I talked with Lydia, and she told me about how much more money college graduates make over non–college graduates and—"

"Oh Lydia, of course. She sure does say the things that are easy for her to say, doesn't she?"

"But she has a point. If we sacrificed a few years so that I could go to college, I could get a better job and help you more. It'd be like"—Dill racked his brain for some Bible analogy that would encompass the idea of short-term loss in favor of long-term gain—"how we sacrifice the opportunity to do certain sinful things, so that we can live in heaven with Jesus."

"Sin is not an opportunity. Following Jesus isn't a sacrifice. He did all the sacrificing."

"I was trying to come up with something to compare it to."

"Come up with something else."

"Think of all I'd learn in college."

"You'd learn that you're too good for God. That we came from monkeys. You'd learn a lot."

"College would give me more options in life."

"You don't need options in life. You need Jesus. Options are fine if you've got them, but we don't. We don't have the money."

"I can get financial aid."

"Oh great, more debt. That's what we need. I could use another few holes in my head while you're offering."

"You always say 'our debt.' I didn't rack up this debt. You guys did. Why should it fall on me?"

"Because we're a family. And families go through hard times together, that's why. They don't run off by themselves and leave the others alone to fend for themselves. I dropped out of high school to marry your father and have you. I bathed and fed you. I've worked six days a week cleaning motel rooms by the highway and six nights a week at a gas station to give you the best life I could. And it's not much. But we have each other and we have Jesus."

"I want more."

"That's greed and pride talking."

"I'm tired of this town. Do you know what it's like? To

have his name? To wear that millstone around your neck? The stares and whispers? The weight of this blood?"

Her eyes blazed. She stabbed the last pieces of her cake with her fork. "Do *I* know what it's like? Of course I do. You think people don't whisper about me? They whisper about me most of all—wonder where I went wrong. Why I didn't know. Why I wasn't good enough. What more I should have done. God gives us trials. This is our place to experience them. You think I'll let gossipers drive us from our home and fail God's test? Think again."

Guilt seized Dill. He felt that he was once again failing a test of faith. Like he was afraid to pick up yet another serpent. He hadn't intended to bring up college. Certainly not on his mother's birthday. In fact, he hadn't even realized he'd been thinking about it.

"Mom, I'm—"

She didn't look up. "This is the last I want to hear of this. I've not said much as you've gone running around with Lydia and Travis all the time. But now? I want you to honor me."

Dill hung his head. "Okay. Fine. Sorry." He wanted to tell her how much he'd miss Lydia when she left; that that was part of the reason he wanted to go. So that his life wouldn't end right as Lydia's began. But his mother surely would have been even less sympathetic about that.

A long silence between them. They listened to the clatter of their decrepit refrigerator and the ticking clock on the wall.

"Did I ruin your birthday?" Dill asked.

"Never cared much about birthdays," his mom said, getting up to take the plates to the sink. "You're a year older. That's all." *But she didn't say no.*

The book. Perhaps his redemption. "Hey, I almost forgot. Hang on. I got you something." Dill jumped up and ran to his bedroom. He hadn't bothered to wrap *The Templar Device.* They didn't have any wrapping paper, and he sucked at wrapping presents anyway.

He returned to the kitchen, the book behind his back.

"Dillard. You shouldn't have," his mother said. Of course, she didn't say it in the sense of *you shouldn't have . . . kept me waiting so long,* the way most people did. She meant it.

He handed her the book. "Mr. Burson down at Riverbank Books thought you might enjoy this. Happy birthday."

She looked up at him. "Is it—"

"Of course it's Christian."

She leafed through it. Sure enough. Jesus. She leaned forward and kissed him on the forehead. "Thank you, Dillard. You're a sweet boy. Between this and the call I got from your father earlier, I feel very blessed."

"I'll clean up in here, Mom. You can go read your book or take a hot bath or something. That'd make your back feel better."

Dill went to the sink and washed the dishes. Soon, his guilt for bringing up college and excitement over getting his mom a gift she didn't immediately hate had both worn off. A sort of dull ache mixed with anger replaced it. Anger at Lydia of all people. It was unfair to direct his frustration at her, even inwardly. It was unfair to blame her for the fictional zero-sum game of her successes equaling his failures. And yet he indulged the feeling. It wouldn't be fair to be angry with his mother on her birthday.

18

lydia

First things first. I need to thank all of you who read and shared and said nice things about my interview with Laydee. That's already become the most-viewed article here (thanks to all of you who retweeted it). I was so, so nervous, but she was so, so awesome and lovely and everyone buy her music, please and thanks.

Here's a picture of me looking very happy indeed thinking about the whole affair. I'm wearing a Missoni top over a dress I snagged at Attic in East Nashville. My bag is from Goodwill. The wedges are from Owl and the necklace is Miu Miu.

It's the end of September. So what, you ask? So if we consider autumn to be the Saturday of the year—and we should, because autumn is the most awesome part of the year, just as Saturday is the most awesome part of the week—then that makes September the Friday of months. Which means it is also awesome. Which means I'm officially on the lookout for good autumnal movies. Autumn porn, if you will. Leave me suggestions in the comments. I love wearing autumn colors. I love it when it gets cool enough for me to start doing interesting things with layering. I'm addicted to jackets (big surprise there, Dear Reader). Autumn basically turns me into a fifty-year-old woman. I go to Cracker Barrel and buy my Autumn Harvest Yankee Candle (the only thing with "Yankee" on it that makes it past the front door of most Southern households). This is only one component of my insatiable hunger for coziness. Pumpkin spice everything is another component. I would eat pumpkin spice scrambled eggs in the middle of October. I would eat a pumpkin spice steak. I would eat [insert personal choice of food that would be disgusting in pumpkin spice form].

I love a witchy, dark, gloomy autumn day, when it rains from the time you wake up until the time you go to bed. And you can listen to Leonard Cohen and wrap yourself up in a warm blanket of exquisite melancholy.

I will say this for Tennessee: it does autumn well. We break out the wreaths, the cornstalks, the hay bales, the wood smoke, and the scarecrows. The leaves are amazing. I can't believe this is probably my last autumn in Tennessee for a while. I'll miss it. I hope wherever I end up rocks autumn at least half as well.

I'm in one of those periods where every ounce of my

mental energy is being diverted elsewhere (college-y stuff, etc. and so forth), to the point that I don't feel like I have anything particularly important or insightful to say. That's when I'll sometimes answer frequently asked questions because HEY, FREE INTERNET CONTENT. Anyway, let us begin.

Q. Why do you always spell "Forrestville" as "Forestville"?

A. Because Forrestville is named after Nathan Bedford Forrest, the founder of the Ku Klux Klan, which makes my town's name roughly as awesome as if it were "Hitlerville." Oh! And bonus! It's in White County (not named after white people, as far as I know). Point being: it's the worst. And as I always say, forests are way better than racists. So I always write "Forestville" because YOU MUST BE THE CHANGE YOU WANT TO SEE IN THE WORLD. Anyway, the dropped "r" from Forrestville stands for "racist."

Q. What year are you in school and where are you going to college? What do you want to study?

A. Senior and that remains to be seen. Here's my list, starting with my first pick and then in no particular order: NYU, Oberlin, Smith, Brown, Sarah Lawrence, Princeton, Harvard, Yale, Columbia, Cornell, Vanderbilt, Vassar, Wellesley. I want to study journalism.

Q. Who are your style icons/role models?

A. Both real and fictional (please feel free to Google copiously): DOLLY PARTON (obvs), Margot

Tenenbaum, Zadie Smith, Debbie Harry, Natasha Khan, Angela Chase, Veronica Mars, Jenny Lewis, Patti Smith, Dee Dee Penny, KatieJane Garside, Meg White, Donna Tartt, Florence Welch, PJ Harvey, Beyoncé, Stevie Nicks, Joan Didion, Frida Kahlo, Martha Gellhorn, Anaïs Nin, Flannery O'Connor.

Q. Who are your favorite designers/houses?

A. Rodarte, Rick Owens, Vivienne Westwood, Prada, Billy Reid (I'm still a Southerner).

Q. Are you a lesbian?

A. The answer to this very much depends on who's asking. If it's any of the above-mentioned ladies, the answer is an emphatic yes. The Birthday Party–era Nick Cave? No. Young Willem de Kooning? No. *Labyrinth*-era David Bowie? No. *Bottle Rocket*–era Luke Wilson? No. *The Royal Tenenbaums*–era Luke Wilson? Also no.

　　If the asker is yet another random Internet troll who literally believes, in this day and age, that it's an insult to call someone gay—in a passive-aggressive manner no less—then the answer is whatever makes you the most uncomfortable, threatens your sense of self, and throws your tiny brain into a tizzy. So the answer is probably yes, I am a raging lesbian. All other askers I take on a case-by-case basis.

Okay, that's enough for now. More later. In the meantime, enjoy these pictures of my haul this last Saturday from the antique store up the street from my house. That's the other thing the South rocks, by the way. Antique stores.

• • •

As she uploaded her post, she looked across the library table at Travis. He was texting vigorously with a faraway expression on his face. He didn't look carefree, per se. But as close to it as she'd ever seen him. Travis read a text and started giggling silently. He put his forehead on the table and shook with muted laughter.

His laughter was so infectious and jubilant, she couldn't help but be taken in. "Okay, dude. What? Who are you texting?"

He wiped his eyes. "No one. Nothing."

She regarded him with good-natured suspicion. "You are the world's worst liar."

19

DILL

Dill finished loading Ms. Relliford's groceries in her car.

She reached out a shaky hand with a dollar. "Here you are, young man. Thank you so much for your help. Have a blessed day."

Dill accepted the dollar and tucked it in his shirt pocket. "Yes ma'am, thank you. Have a blessed day."

He took his sweet time walking the cart back into the store, relishing the brief moment spent outside before returning to the air-conditioned cold and slight smell of rotting meat and spoiled vegetables of Floyd's.

Dill loved being on bagging duty on these early evenings in late September. The sun was still strong, but it lacked the vitality of the summer sun. It felt faded. He caught a subdued hint of cut grass wafting from somewhere. *How was it possible for love of a place and hatred of it to exist so comfortably side by side?*

As he approached the store, wrestling the cart *(how did shopping carts always have at least one bum wheel?),* a little girl rode the chipped, plastic coin-operated pony ride out front.

Dill smiled at her.

She giggled. "I'm riding the pony!"

"Yeah, you are! Good job, lil' cowgirl!"

The ride stopped and the little girl swung her leg over the pony to dismount. In her rush she caught her sandal on a curl on the pony's mane, and tumbled face-first to the hard concrete. She scraped her chin. She looked at Dill for a second with huge, blue eyes filling with tears.

Uh-oh.

She began to wail. Like a tornado siren.

Dill ran over and knelt beside her, rubbing her back. "Oh no! Sweetie! Hey, hey, don't cry. It's okay. It's okay. Shhhhh. Where's your mama?"

She was inconsolable.

Dill picked her up gently, murmuring in her ear. "Hey now, hey, let's go find Mama, okay? We're gonna find Mama."

Then, from the end of the parking lot, frantic shouting. *"Hey! Hey! What are doing?! Put her down!"*

Dill looked up to see a wild-eyed woman sprinting toward him. He set down the little girl, who was still howling. "Ma'am, is this your—"

"What did you do to her? Why is she crying?" the woman shrieked. She knelt and shook her daughter by the shoulders. "Daisy. Daisy, honey, what's wrong?"

A crowd had begun to gather. "Go get the store manager," someone said. "Allison, is everything okay?" someone else called.

Dill's face burned. "Ma'am, I was just walking by and she was riding the pony and she f—"

The woman stood and got in Dill's face, radiating wild fury. "You stay away from her. Stay away. I know who you are. You're Dillard Early's son. You don't touch my child. Got it?"

"Allison, I think Daisy—" someone called.

"I don't care! I don't care! He does not touch or get near my daughter."

Mr. McGowan, the store manager, pushed through the crowd. "Okay, okay, everything all right here? Ma'am?"

Her voice still had its brittle razor's edge. "I go to put the groceries in the car. I leave Daisy on the ride. I turn around and he"—she pointed at Dill, a contemptuous curl in her lip—"is right there and Daisy's crying." Daisy continued to wail, as if there were some doubt that her mother was telling the truth.

"She fell," Dill said. "I was trying—"

Mr. McGowan raised his hand, cutting Dill off. "Dill, why don't you go back inside. Ma'am, I'm very sorry this happened. I'm sure Dill meant no harm."

That's enough. That's enough of this. Dill's voice rose with his temperature. "Hang on. I didn't do *anything* wrong. I think she just feels guilty because she ran off and let her kid get hurt."

"*How dare you?* You can't talk that way to me. You've no right. I'm a good mother."

"Dill?" Mr. McGowan said sharply. "I will handle this. Please go inside."

Dill and the woman exchanged final mutually reproachful glares, and he turned and walked inside. He went straight to the dimly lit employee break room, where a sit-com rerun played on the decrepit TV. He slumped at the table and ran his hands through his hair.

After a few minutes, Mr. McGowan came in. Dill started to speak. Mr. McGowan cut him off. "My Lord, Dill! What's gotten into you, son? You can't talk to customers that way."

Way to stand behind your employees, Floyd's. "Mr. McGowan, I did not do anything wrong. I was helping that little girl. What was I supposed to do? Just let her cry?"

"Well, you could come get me—"

"You know why that woman acted that way."

"Yeah," he said softly. "I do. Allison's husband, Chip, is a Church of Christ pastor. So she probably wasn't keen on your dad even before all that mess. People don't like when other people say they ought to be twirling snakes around to be right with God."

"Yeah." Dill didn't say anything. He just stared straight ahead. "Well, I better get back to work."

"You got . . . what . . . fifteen minutes left on your shift?

You can go ahead and go. I'll clock you out regular." Mr. McGowan sounded apologetic.

"Okay." Dill rose from the table without meeting Mr. McGowan's eyes, removed his green apron, and walked slowly to the library, where he was meeting Lydia and Travis. He felt thoroughly battered.

• • •

When Dill got to the library, he saw Lydia and Travis sitting at the table farthest from the ever-vigilant eye of the librarian, Ms. White, who was quick to shush.

Lydia made a grab for Travis's phone. He giggled and held it out of reach. She stood and leaned over the table, making another grab, almost tipping onto the table as Travis leaned back in his chair, holding the phone still farther from reach. She came around the table, sat next to Travis, and started tickling him. He squinched up, giggling, as she pawed at his phone. Ms. White cast a withering glare in their direction and shushed them.

"Dill, help me," Lydia said in a loud whisper as Dill walked up and set his backpack on the table.

"No, Dill, help *me*," Travis whispered. "We've been friends for longer."

"Yeah, but I keep Dill from looking like a dingus. Come on, Dill. I suspect Travis is texting a secret girlfriend. We need to know about this."

Dill tried to look happy and play along, but he wasn't succeeding. And seeing Lydia and Travis, apparently without a care in the world between them, horsing around while he basically got accused of being a child molester, was more than he could handle. "No, I'm good. I need to use the Internet while I have the chance."

He gave his library card to Ms. White and took a computer. He didn't actually *need* to use the Internet so much as he needed to not be near happy people.

He told himself that he wasn't consciously looking for an excuse to ruin Lydia's mood. He told himself that it was a bad idea for him to read Lydia's blog at that moment. So that's exactly what he did.

Resentment grew in him as he read post after post.

I'm so excited for college. I'm so excited to leave all this behind. I have no friends so I spend all my time alone writing cool blog posts and vintage shopping and taking pretty pictures. Nope, I don't have a single friend. At least no one worth mentioning. No one I'm not embarrassed to mention.

By the time he logged off and got back to where Lydia and Travis were sitting, Lydia was back working on her computer, and Travis was back texting.

"Dill! I got his phone. He's been texting someone named Amelia. Travis has a girlfriend, dude."

Travis blushed and he scowl-smiled. "No I don't. She's just a friend from the Bloodfall forums."

Lydia turned to Dill. "I think Travis has Bloodfallen for this girl. See what I did there?"

Travis began to protest. Dill tried to laugh, but the rising black dome of rage pushing up through his chest and lungs cut him off. "Yeah."

Lydia sat for a second, her mouth agape, her hands outstretched in front of her. "*Dude.* Come *on.* We have the chance to tease Travis about a girl and you're just letting it fly free like a dove."

And then the black dome of rage burst and hot lava flowed through him. "Let me ask you a question."

"Okay."

"Just curious. How come you have never *once* mentioned either Travis or me on your blog? Are we that embarrassing to you?"

Lydia's good cheer crumbled away in an instant. She stared at Dill with an acid expression. "I'm sorry, do I owe you an explanation for what I say or don't say on *my* blog?"

Dill tried to affect a casual, who-cares tone, with little success. "No. I just think it's sad you have friends you're embarrassed by. That's all."

Travis, who had clearly been pretending to be absorbed in his texting, shifted uncomfortably in his seat. "Dill, come on. Leave me out of this. I don't care."

Dill glared at Travis. "Sure, dude. Take her side like thirty seconds after she was trying to embarrass you."

"I just think you're being rude. I—"

Lydia cut off Travis's response. "What's this about, Dill? Why have you chosen this exact moment to bring this up? After years of being friends."

"Oh, we're friends? Sorry, I only read your blog so I didn't know you had any. I told you. Just curious."

"Horseshit." She was no longer whispering.

"All right you three," Ms. White called over. "I warned y'all once. Y'all need to take your discussion outside."

Lydia rolled her eyes, slammed her laptop shut, yanked the plug from the wall, and started shoving things in her bag. "Thanks, Dill."

"You're welcome."

They left, hanging their heads, avoiding eye contact with anyone. They got to the parking lot and formed a circle behind Lydia's car.

"You still haven't answered my question," Dill said. "How come you've never once mentioned us?"

"I answered your question with a question. What makes you think you're entitled to be mentioned?"

"I don't think I'm entitled to be mentioned. I just think I'm entitled to be treated like a real friend you're not embarrassed to know."

She popped open the hatchback and put her bag inside. She stood there with her hand on her hip and gestured for Dill to throw his in too. "Get in so I can finish tearing you a new asshole."

"I'm parked over here. Y'all, please stop fighting," Travis said. "It's not worth it."

Dill and Lydia both glared at Travis.

Travis's voice took on an angrier tone than Dill had ever heard before. "Y'all are ruining my good day. I already have enough people to ruin my good days; I don't need you two doing it. Just *stop*."

Lydia squared off her five feet, two inches against Travis's six feet, six inches. "Look, Travis, we're going to work this out. Until then, please butt out, okay?"

Travis threw his hands in the air. "Okay. Whatever." He walked away.

Dill and Lydia got in her car. They sat there for a moment, not moving. Not saying anything.

"I mean, what do you even want?" Lydia asked finally. "I know you don't care that much about fashion. You want a bunch of pictures of yourself on there or something?"

"No."

Lydia pulled on her hair with both hands. "*Errrrgh.* So what *do* you want?"

"I want you to understand that you wear the fact that we live in a small town and don't have many friends like it's some fashion accessory. You can put it on and take it off at will. But it's my shitty reality."

Lydia's voice rose. "A fashion accessory? Oh boy. Here we go." She started the car, put it in gear, and pulled out of the library parking lot.

"Yeah. I read your blog. You love casting yourself as the misunderstood misfit with no friends in some dead-end Southern town. Very romantic. But you've got a ticket out of here. You're actually totally fine. But your friends—who you do have, but never mention, by the way—are stuck."

"Okay, wow, I guess we're just gonna shift topics. But I'll

go with it. You are not stuck. You're making a choice to stay. I've tried to convince you to get out. I've addressed all your arguments. But you think you have to stay. Whatever. It's your life and I can do without your lame jealousy stemming from hating your choices."

Dill's voice rose to meet hers. "My choices? It was not my choice to have my dad go to prison and leave my family with a mountain of debt. You love talking about choices, don't you? Pretty easy when they're served up on a platter."

"First of all, don't pretend like you know everything about my life or that my life is roses. *Now* look who's casting himself in the role of 'boy from the wrong side of the tracks who's misunderstood by blithe rich girl.' "

"I don't care that your family has more money than mine. I'm trying to make you understand that it really hurts my feelings that you not only pretend I don't exist, you can't wait to get away from me. It makes me feel worthless. I get that from enough people. I don't need it from you."

"What is your deal with viewing everything I do in the most unfair light possible? As if I'm out to intentionally hurt you in some way? As if I run my blog to hurt you? As if I'm leaving for college to hurt you?"

"That's not what I'm doing."

"It is."

"It isn't."

"Maybe instead of dwelling on everything I *don't* do for you, you should think about what I *do* do for you. If it weren't for me, you'd have sat on your ass at home a whole lot of nights, playing your guitar."

Dill made a mock worshiping motion. "Oh, thank you, savior. Thank you for saving me. Sitting on my ass and playing my guitar is better than hanging out with someone who's embarrassed by me and looking through me to the next thing."

They pulled up in front of Dill's house.

"We can certainly arrange for you to do that more often," Lydia said, a frigid edge to her voice.

Dill suddenly felt as though he'd tried to swallow a huge ice cube, and it had gotten stuck in his throat. He knew the smell of impending loss, how it felt to have parts of his life erode from under him and be swept away. Panic seized him. Like he should take a mental photograph of Lydia and everything surrounding her, in case he never saw her again.

The way she sat too close to the steering wheel, staring straight ahead, one arm on the windowsill, her head propped on that hand. The other hand—chipped blue nail polish, the color of a vintage car—resting on the wheel. The line of her neck as it met her shoulder. The piece of black tape that covered her perpetually illuminated "check engine" light starting to peel off. The five or six spent vanilla air fresheners hanging from the rearview mirror. The ornaments adorning her wrists and fingers.

Please God. Quicken my tongue. Make me mighty of speech. Please let me not be prideful in this hour. Let me say exactly the right thing I need to say to keep from losing one more part of me.

"Fine," Dill said. *Not what I had in mind, God. Guess you've gone to bed and left one of your lesser angels at the duty station.*

Then he remembered the church sign. One last chance for God to speak to him. He looked up the street. IF GOD SEEMS FAR AWAY, GUESS WHO MOVED.

Good one, God. A message about moving apart. That's helpful right at this moment. He got out. Not a sideways glance from Lydia. Not a goodbye. He barely managed to close his door before she sped off with a squeal of her tires.

Her taillights faded into the darkness and disappeared.

20

TRAVIS

*R*aynar Northbrook *sat at his table, holding the latest missive from Lady Amelia of the Southern Lands in his eager hands. He pored over her flowery script as she recounted the happenings of her life. His heart sang every time he heard news of her.*

So what are you up to today? Travis texted.

I'm going to take Pickles and visit my grandma and grandpa. You hanging out with your friends today? Amelia replied.

I don't know. Lydia's in New York visiting colleges. I haven't heard from Dill. They're being kind of weird.

Aw.

Yeah. I love my friends and I don't want to say bad things about them, but I feel like they don't get me sometimes.

I get you.

I know. That's why I like you.

You're lucky to have even two good friends at school. I don't really have anyone.

Oh yeah, I know, I just wish

Travis's phone rang in the middle of composing his reply to Amelia.

Speak of the devil. "Hey, Dill, what's up?"

"Hey, Travis, do you have to work today?"

"Nope, yard's closed on Sundays. Why?"

"I could use your help. My mom's car won't start, and we need to get it fixed before Monday so she can get to her jobs. But I don't know anything about cars and we can't afford the mechanic. Do you think you could help me try to figure it out?"

"Oh yeah, no problem. Let me eat some quick breakfast and wet down my hair and I'll be over."

"Hey, Travis? I'm sorry about the other day. Being a jerk."

Travis laughed. "Don't worry about it, man. I'll be right over."

Most people wouldn't be excited to get a call on a quiet Sunday morning, asking them to help fix a car. But Travis loved helping people do things; being with his friends; being away from his father; and pulling a diseased part out of a car, holding it in his hands, and then replacing it with a shiny new one that resurrected the car. Dill offered him the chance to do all four things. Plus, he was in the mood to talk to Dill. He felt like it was time to tell him about Amelia. Dill wasn't as good with the jokes as Lydia, so Travis felt safer telling him.

Travis went into the kitchen, where his mom had some warm biscuits and gravy, bacon, and eggs ready. He hugged her and told her where he was going, then texted Amelia goodbye. He wolfed some food, grabbed his toolbox—he suspected Dill wouldn't have much more than a screwdriver and a pair of needle-nose pliers—and headed over to Dill's. As a bonus, he didn't even see his father, who had gone bowhunting.

Travis parked his red Ford pickup behind Dill's mom's Chevy Cavalier. Dill had the hood open and was studying the engine.

"You looking for the on/off switch?" Travis said, grinning, as he got out of his truck.

Dill smiled, stepped aside, and ran his hand through his hair. "I really hope you can help me figure this out."

"Let's see what it's doing." Travis took the keys, got in, and tried to start it. "Lights work fine, so it's not the battery," he mumbled. He turned the key. Nothing. No click, no sound whatsoever. He turned the key again. Nothing.

He thought for a second, running through some scenarios in his head. If it were the alternator, the battery would be dead and the lights wouldn't come on. If it were the fuel system, the engine would turn and chug, but not start.

He got out of the car and closed the hood. "I think you've got a bad starter motor."

"You sure?" Dill asked.

Travis readjusted his baseball cap. "Nope. But it's the best guess I've got."

"Are starter motors hard to replace?"

"Nope."

"Are they expensive?"

"Probably fifty, sixty bucks for this car."

The look on Dill's face said that even that was expensive, but they'd have to manage.

They got in Travis's pickup and rumbled off to the auto parts store. Travis had another reason he was glad to be helping Dill. Something else had been weighing on him. "So, I know she's been gone most of this week looking at colleges with her mom, but have you talked to Lydia since last Friday?"

Dill took a deep breath and exhaled through his nose. "No."

"Not a word?"

"Not a word."

"Don't you think you should say something?"

"What would I say?"

Travis fiddled with the heater and craned to see any oncoming traffic before turning left. "I dunno. Sorry?"

"I'm not."

"You should be."

Dill snorted. "How you figure?"

"You sorta freaked out on her."

"Yeah, so? I was having a bad day."

"Even if I were having a bad day, I wouldn't take it out on you or Lydia."

"Don't you think Lydia's been acting different this year?"

Dill asked. "Ever since she realized that she's getting out of here? Snobbier or something?"

"No, not really. Maybe it's your imagination."

"I swear it's not, dude. I swear she's being different."

"Man, I think you're being hard on her. I mean, it's good she's getting out of here to go to a bigger city with lots of fashions, right? Be happy for her."

Dill frowned. "Speaking of, do you ever read her blog?"

"Yeah, sometimes. Not religiously."

"Doesn't it bother you that for all the pictures she takes of us, and all the stuff we do together, neither of us has ever once been mentioned on there? Like she even put up pictures of the lady who owns that store in Nashville. They were friends for fifteen minutes. Doesn't it seem like she's embarrassed by us?"

Travis shrugged. "That lady was really pretty, though, and she wore nice clothes. You and I aren't big fashion guys. Why would we be on there?"

"I guess. Still bugs me. Makes me feel like she thinks we're less than her or something."

They pulled up to the auto parts store and went in. An older man and a younger man, both wearing green vests and baseball caps, stood behind the counter, chitchatting.

"What can I get for you, bud?" the younger man asked.

"Need a starter motor for a '92 Chevy Cavalier. Four cylinder," Travis said.

"See what my computer tells me." He squinted at the screen. "Says we got one in stock. Wait here a sec, let me put my hands on it." The man wrote something on a slip of paper and headed for the back.

The older man nodded at Dill. "'Scuse me, young man, you don't mind my asking, you ain't Dillard Early's grandson, are you?"

Apprehension flashed across Dill's face. "Yessir, I am," he said quietly. He seemed to be hoping the old man would be careful with what he said. Travis had never mentioned to Dill that he knew anything about the Serpent King. Dill surely preferred it that way.

"My goodness," the man said. "I used to work with your papaw. At the old Gulf station on North Church. It's a Conoco now."

"Yessir," Dill said, looking at his feet.

"He was a hell of a mechanic, by God," the man said with a nostalgic chuckle. "Fix anything. Could sense what ailed a car. Good with his hands. And he could sing. Sang the old-timey songs while he worked. Lord, he could sing. You take after him that way, son?"

"Which way?"

"Any way you please."

"I sing all right."

"Bet you can fix a car up too, if you care to. Things like that run in the blood."

"Yessir. Lots of things do."

"You look like him."

"People tell me that. I've just seen pictures. He died before I was born."

"Yeah," the old man said softly, nodding, looking off. Then he gazed straight at Dill. "Son? He was a *good* man. I want you to know that."

Travis knew the look in the old man's eyes. It was the same look in Lamar's eyes when he told the story of the Serpent King. It was the look of a man who had lived long enough to understand grief's consuming fire. The look of an old man who feared a bad death.

The younger man came out with a dirty cardboard box and set it on the counter. "All right, boys. That'll be seventy seventy-five with tax and a fourteen-dollar core charge."

Dill handed over some wadded bills. As they left, Travis stole a backward glance. He saw the old man move toward the younger man and point outside. The younger man was about to hear the story of the Serpent King. Travis would've wagered a lot of money on it.

• • •

"So it doesn't bother you that Lydia's leaving?" Dill asked.

"It does—I'll miss her—but we always knew this day would come. She's been talking about getting out of here forever. Think how bummed she'd be if she stayed."

"You ever think about getting out of here?"

"Where would I go? This is my home."

"College?"

"Naw. Grades suck. Anyway, I only like to read the stuff I want to read. Not what a professor wants me to read."

"We still gonna hang out after Lydia's gone?" Dill asked.

Travis laughed. "Yeah. I mean, I can't promise we'll have such creative stuff to do. And you may get outvoted on me bringing my staff places. Especially since it looks like I'll be driving us anywhere we go."

"The staff never bugged me the way it does Lydia."

"You mean it's been two to one all this time in favor of the staff?"

"I didn't say *that*."

Travis saw his opportunity to confess. "So . . . remember how Lydia was trying to get my phone at the library?"

"Yeah."

"I've been texting with this girl named Amelia Cooper, who I met on the Bloodfall forums. She lives in Alabama. Things are going pretty good."

Dill stared at Travis for a few seconds, then grinned and punched him in the arm. "Man, look at you go. Working it with the ladies."

Travis giggled and adjusted his cap. "Anyway, I really like her. I think we might end up being more than just friends someday. I hope so. We're for sure gonna meet up at the Tennessee Renaissance Festival in May. Maybe even sooner. She thinks my staff is cool."

"She thinks your staff is cool, huh?" Dill said, with an impish lilt.

It took a couple of beats, but Travis got it. He giggled again and punched Dill in the arm. "No dude, not like that. That's not what I meant. God dang." He grinned slyly. "Anyway, you ought to be glad to hear that friends can maybe become more."

Dill's mouth dropped open. "Whoa, hold up."

Travis gave Dill an oh-come-on look.

Dill shook his head and looked away. "You're way off, man."

Travis gave Dill the same look. "Say it to my face."

"No. You're driving."

Travis laughed and punched Dill in the arm again. "I knew it! How come you never—"

"Because."

"Why?"

"I don't want to wreck things. And I would."

"Maybe not." *But actually, yeah, Dill, there's a good chance you would.*

Dill gave Travis an oh-come-on look. "I maybe already did wreck things. Besides, she's leaving. She wouldn't want to. I'd be too much of a complication for her plans."

"You don't know until you try. Thing about girls is—"

Dill chuckled and punched Travis in the arm again. "'*Thing about girls,*' huh? Now look who's an expert."

"I know a thing or two."

"Like hell you do. Maybe you know *a* thing. You don't know *two*."

• • •

They pulled up to Dill's house. The day begged for work outside—cloudy, crisp enough that you needed a long-sleeve shirt but not a jacket. The air smelled of brown grass and clothes drying somewhere.

Travis determined they'd need to get at the starter motor

from below. They jacked up the car and put supports under it. Travis wiggled underneath with a set of wrenches.

"Can you help me get the end of my wrench over that top bolt?" Travis asked.

"Sure." Dill helped him maneuver onto the bolt. "Where'd you learn how to work on cars?"

"My dad." Travis grunted and broke the bolt free. He ratcheted the wrench to loosen it.

"Was that fun? Working on cars with your dad?"

"Not really." Travis hoped Dill wouldn't ask why. He didn't.

Travis unhooked the electrical connection from the starter motor and clanked around with the wrench until he got onto the other bolt. He strained and loosened the bolt, supporting the old starter motor with his hand while he ratcheted the remaining bolt. The bolt came free and he lowered the starter motor. He wriggled out from under the car.

"You ever think about teaching your kids how to work on cars someday?" Dill asked.

Travis brushed dirt off his pants. "I haven't thought much about having kids. But if I did, I'd teach them all kinds of things. And I'd let them read whatever they wanted." Travis pulled the new starter motor out of the box and hefted it. He lowered himself to the ground and wriggled underneath the car.

He fitted the starter motor in place. He could see Dill's face above him, through the engine compartment. They made eye contact. And all at once, Travis felt an overwhelming urge to relieve himself of one more weight that day, while he was on a roll. "Can I ask you kind of a weird question?"

"Sure. As long as it's not about Bloodfall. Save that for Amelia."

Travis slid one of the starter bolts in and hand-tightened it. "Did your dad ever hit you? Before he went away?"

Dill hesitated before answering. "Yeah, I mean, he spanked me. Sure."

Travis finished tightening the bolt with the wrench. "That's not what I mean. I mean did he *hit* you hit you. Really hit you?"

He and Dill made eye contact again.

"No. Not like that." Dill didn't ask why he asked. Travis gave thanks for that. Asking the questions indeed made him feel lighter. Less alone, somehow.

"When I have kids, I won't lay a finger on them. I mean, except to hug them and stuff. But never to hurt them." Travis slipped the other bolt in and hand-tightened it, finishing it with the wrench. He hooked up the electrical connection and scooted out from under the car.

"Okay," Travis said. "Moment of truth. Say your prayers." He sat in the car and turned the key. The engine spun immediately to life. It didn't sound healthy, but it never did. At least it ran and would get Dill's mom from point A to point B for a little while longer.

Dill whooped and high-fived Travis. "Dude, you're awesome. You did it."

Travis slapped Dill on the arm. "*We* did it. Now let's go get your fourteen-dollar core charge."

"I owe you one," Dill said, as they got into Travis's pickup.

"Pay me back by making up with Lydia. It sucks for me when you guys are mad at each other."

21

DILL

Dill didn't mind walking the couple of miles to Lydia's house. It had just rained, and the streets were covered with wet leaves; their earthy tobacco scent hung in the air, mixing with the spice of wood smoke. A wispy veil of clouds covered the sky and the bright waxing gibbous moon. Dill pulled the denim jacket (that Lydia had picked out) tighter around himself and buttoned it. While he walked, he rehearsed what he'd say. *I'm sorry. I was wrong. I only want what will make you happy.* Even his church sign had been semihelpful (this once): GOD DOES NOT FORGET THE SINNER, HE FORGETS THE SIN.

I could use some forgetfulness. He knocked on Lydia's door, his heart racing. Her dad answered.

"Hello, Dill. How are you?"

"I'm good, thanks. Is Lydia home?"

"Yes. Come in, come in. Lydia?" he called upstairs. "You have company, sweetie."

Lydia appeared at the top of the stairs, wearing yoga pants and a hoodie, her hair in a messy ponytail. When she saw Dill, she folded her arms and glared at him for a moment. Dill gave her a kicked-puppy-dog look. She waved him upstairs and stalked back to her room. Dill started to head up.

"Hey, Dill, before you go, remind me to show you this new Strat of mine, okay?" Dr. Blankenship said.

"Will do." He went upstairs.

Lydia sat at her desk, composing a document on her new laptop. It appeared to be a college admission essay. She didn't turn around when Dill walked in.

Dill took in the ordered chaos of Lydia's room. The sheer amount of visual information always overwhelmed him. Records. Books. Magazines. Posters. Photos. Stuffed animals. Weird antiques, including a terrifying dental phantom from the 1930s that her dad had given her. Clothes and shoes, everywhere—all representing her ever-shifting obsessions. What was different this time were the piles of marked-up college admission essay drafts. Half-filled-out college and scholarship applications. The incidents of a life moving forward with great velocity and determination.

Her room always made him feel wistful and envious for the abundance in which she dwelled—a stark contrast with his even starker room. The piles of college materials didn't help. Her bed creaked as he sat on it behind her.

Lydia still didn't turn around. She highlighted a line and deleted it. She appeared determined to make this hurt. "So. Talk."

Dill faltered. His carefully planned apology speech—formulated on the walk over—evaporated. "I'm—I'm sorry. For the stuff I said."

Lydia continued typing.

"And I've missed you."

Typing.

"And I want us to stay friends."

Typing.

"And I'm starting to feel stupid now, so I'll leave." Dill rose from the bed with another creak.

Lydia turned her chair around and sat cross-legged on it.

"All right. I accept your apology. But seriously. I can't deal with the continued drama. I have too much to think about. So it has to stop, Dill. I mean it."

Dill sat back down on the bed. "I can't promise that I'll be all smiles every time something reminds me that you're leaving. That's a promise I can't keep."

Lydia got up and walked over to her candle shelf (yes, a whole shelf) and lit two of her autumn candles. "I'm doing a mélange of autumn leaves, combining top notes of cider and cinnamon with a firewood-scented candle, bringing in bottom notes of cedar, birch, and vanilla. I should become a candle sommelier. Is that a job?"

"Did you listen to me?"

"Yes, I did. And I don't expect you to be happy. I expect

you to not allow your unhappiness with the situation to manifest in the form of unhappiness with me personally."

"Okay."

"If the tables were turned, that's how I'd roll with you."

"Okay."

"I promise that not a teeny little thing I do regarding college is with the intention of hurting you. And I also promise that I have very good reasons for protecting your privacy by not talking about you on my blog. So promise me in return that you'll start doing an amazing job of not taking out your issues on me for committing the sin of trying to make my life better."

"Fine."

"Say it."

"I promise."

Lydia's face finally softened. "Look. I'm not happy we're getting separated either. I get that what I'll be doing might be more fun than what you'll be doing. But I'll miss you. I missed you this week."

"That's an understatement to say that what you'll be doing *might* be more fun than what I'll be doing. It *will* be more fun."

She sat next to Dill on her bed. "Come on," she gestured. "Hugs."

Dill gave her a long hug. Her hair smelled like oranges and magnolia blossoms. He hadn't realized how long his heart had ached with a low-frequency hum until the ache melted away at that moment. And then there was the thrill of hugging Lydia on her bed—which was its own thing. *If only.*

"So. Where're you at in the process?" Dill asked.

She flopped back on the bed and stared up at the ceiling. "My NYU early decision application is due in two weeks or so. That's the biggie. I'm polishing my essay now."

"Good luck," Dill murmured.

She sat up. They regarded each other for a moment.

"It's not too late," she said.

It was Dill's turn to flop backward onto the bed. He covered his face with one of Lydia's pillows. "I can't," he said through the pillow. "I even talked with my mom about it."

"And?"

"And how do you think? She went *'Sure, Dill, go off to college and have fun and learn about evolution and pay tuition and go to class instead of working, and I'll hold down the fort here and it'll be cool.'* No. She crapped herself, obviously."

"You knew she would. Why are you letting that weigh on your decision?"

"Um, because she's my mom."

"And the Bible says you're supposed to respect her."

Dill rolled his eyes. "Don't. Come on."

"*You* come on. Do you honestly believe that your mom's not wanting you to go to college is in your best interest as opposed to hers?"

Dill sat up again. "I don't know what I believe anymore. About anything. There's definitely part of me that thinks that whatever's in her best interest is in mine too."

"How do you figure?"

"Because she's my mom."

"*Fantastic answer.* Hang on." Lydia put an imaginary phone to her ear. "Hi, Debate Trophies 'R' Us? Yes, I'll need one of your premium models."

"You're hilarious. Look, it's just not happening."

Lydia flung her hands up. "Whatever."

"Now you have to promise me you'll stop bugging me about college."

"Nope, not gonna do that."

"Why do I have to make all the promises?"

"Because I'm asking you to promise to stop being lame, and you're asking me to promise to stop being awesome, which I cannot, in good conscience, do."

"Please don't make me feel shitty for making the choices I have to make."

Lydia got up from her bed, walked over to her desk, and opened a drawer. "Nope again. But I will allow you to change the subject temporarily." She pulled her old Mac laptop out of the drawer and wound up the power cord.

She returned to Dill and dropped the bundle in his lap. "Here. Merry early Christmas, happy late birthday, happy Halloween, happy whatever."

Dill's jaw dropped. "Wait. Hold on. You're giving me this? Are you serious?"

"Yep. I don't need two computers and I got a new one for college. That one's about four years old. It's what I started *Dollywould* on, so it's got a lot of sentimental value to me. So maybe don't break it. It still works pretty well. A little slow sometimes."

Dill hugged Lydia again, knocking her glasses crooked. "Thank you. Thank you thank you thank you."

"Okay, easy. Don't thank me by breaking my glasses. Oh, and the best part is that because I'm not an awful, gross dude, the keyboard is one hundred percent semen free."

Dill glowed, joyous. Not just because of the computer. Because he and Lydia had made up. The gift was evidence of that.

"Oh, here," Lydia said, taking the laptop and opening it. "Let me show you how to take video of yourself with it. Then you can start recording your songs."

"I've never recorded myself before," Dill said. "We haven't even owned a computer since the police seized ours."

"Seriously? You've never recorded yourself? Okay, well, it's time to start. That's your first assignment." She demonstrated how to shoot video and record using the laptop's built-in videocamera and microphone. "You got it?"

"I got it."

"Excellent." She got up and sat back down at her desk. "Now scoot, because I have a lot of work to do," she said, with a whisking hand motion.

"Lydia. Thanks."

"You're welcome." She scrolled through her document, not looking up. "Oh, by the way, I have to cancel this week's Friday movie night. Too busy with college and blog stuff."

Dill's face fell. Lydia gave him a cautioning glance and raised a finger, mouthing the words *you promised.*

Dill nodded, turned, and left.

• • •

When he got to the bottom of the stairs, Lydia called down, "Hey, Dad, I gave my old computer to Dill. He's not stealing it."

"Okay, honey. Hey, Dill, come in."

Dill stepped into his study. Antiques filled the room. Leather-bound books. A large Dolan Geiman collage made from found materials hanging on one wall. A couple of guitars hanging on another wall. A vintage Fender amplifier.

Dr. Blankenship rose from his desk and got down one of the guitars: a gorgeous 1960s Fender Stratocaster in a tobacco sunburst pattern. He handed it to Dill, who handled it like it was a museum piece. It must have cost a fair penny.

"This is beautiful, Dr. Blankenship."

"Put it on. Let's play a couple licks, huh?"

Dill set down his new computer on Dr. Blankenship's desk and slung the guitar over his neck. He played a quick run to limber up his fingers. Dr. Blankenship got out a cord and flipped on the amp. They waited for it to warm up.

Dill strummed a chord. "Where did you get this?"

Dr. Blankenship plugged in the guitar. "An estate sale in Nashville. Let 'er rip!"

Dill played, tentatively at first.

"Go on, go on! Screw the neighbors!"

Dill played harder and faster while Dr. Blankenship grinned and gave him the thumbs-up. It felt good. He played and played. And then a stab of nostalgia. The last time he had played the electric guitar in front of anyone was in front of his father, before his father decided not to hand him the snake. Before his father was arrested. He stopped playing and took off the guitar.

Dr. Blankenship took it from him and hung it back on the wall. "So? What do you think?"

Before Dill could answer, they heard Lydia calling down from upstairs. "Daddy, what's happening down there? Why does your guitar playing sound so much better than normal? I'm scared. What did you do with my daddy?"

"I love my smartass daughter," Dr. Blankenship muttered. "Anyway, you were interrupted."

"Yeah. It's beautiful. I'd say you scored on this one. I haven't played an electric guitar in a long time."

"Do you have one?"

"I used to. After . . . everything happened with my dad, we had to sell a bunch of stuff, so we sold it and my amp. It's okay. I don't have anywhere I can play it anymore."

"How often do you get to see your dad?"

"A few times a year. Next time I go, it'll be around Christmas. Assuming our junker car is still running by then."

"If you need a ride to Nashville around Christmas to see your dad, I'd be glad to take you. I get my Christmas treats at the Trader Joe's there. I could close the office for the day."

"Are you sure? I mean, that'd be really cool, but I wouldn't want to be any trouble."

"It wouldn't be any trouble. And to be perfectly honest"—he lowered his voice and looked both ways—"it'd be nice to hang out with another male every now and again. There's a lot of estrogen in this house."

"I totally heard that," Lydia called down. "Don't be sexist and gross."

"Yeah, I can see what you mean," Dill said, picking up his new computer. "You tell me when works for you."

"I will. Hey, did Lydia offer you a ride home?"

"No."

"Do you want one?"

Dill smiled. "No thanks. It's a beautiful night."

As Dill walked home, a brisk wind blew, drying the leaves, which skittered and danced in front of him in the moonlit shadows. Their scratching on the pavement was a song to him.

22

lydia

They sat at a cafeteria table, alone and apart as always. The cafeteria, reeking of fish sticks, buzzed around them. Dill had his unappetizing free lunch. Travis had a massive container of his mom's mac and cheese. Lydia had her baby carrots, pita chips, hummus, and Greek yogurt. Travis read his Bloodfall book and Dill had in his earbuds, working intently on something on his new laptop.

Lydia read *The Diary of Anaïs Nin.*

Dill popped out one of his earbuds. "Hey, Lydia, any chance you could upload some videos to YouTube for me tonight? I tried, but the school's got YouTube blocked."

"Sure. What?"

"Some videos I made of me playing my songs. Five of them."

"*Five?* I gave you that, what, two days ago?"

"I had a bunch saved up."

Hunter Henry, Matt Barnes, and DeJuan Washington, three football players, walked by their table.

"Hey, Dildo, the police know you've got a computer now?" Hunter asked. His friends snickered.

"I think the school blocks kiddie porn," Matt said. More snickers.

Dill popped his earbud back in and ignored them. Travis visibly tensed up, but he kept reading, also ignoring them. Dill and Travis knew the drill.

Lydia set down her book with a smile. "Yeah, we informed the police at the same time we put your names on the National Micropenis Registry. Don't be surprised if you have trouble at the airport. Among other places."

"I'll show you my dick," Hunter said.

"Remember, I wear glasses." Lydia picked up her book.

"Yeah, how could we forget because they make your face so butt-ass ugly," Matt sputtered.

"You *could* forget because you lack the ability to form semantic memories, which is why Tullahoma High humiliated you guys by running the same play twice in a row last time they beat you in the fourth quarter," Lydia said, without looking up from her book.

"What do you know about football, bitch?" Hunter said.

"Well, that you're supposed to score more points than the other team, and that's hard to do when you—and specifically you—fumble in your own end zone like you did against Manchester last year, allowing a game-losing safety."

Hunter turned red.

"Leave it, bro," DeJuan said. "She ain't worth it. She's trying to make you do something stupid."

"I never have to try very hard," Lydia said.

Hunter slapped Lydia's book out of her hands, onto the floor, before the three stomped away.

Dill popped out his earbuds, picked up Lydia's book, and handed it to her. "I didn't know you were a football fan."

Lydia leafed through her book to mark her place. "I'm not. I only keep track of our team's losses and individual humiliations and shortcomings. I put them in my mental file on every player who gives us shit. It's really more fun than actual football. Anyway, I gotta run to class. Give me your computer; I'll take it home tonight and upload your videos."

• • •

Chloe & I have been scoping apartments for fun. What's your budget? We found a cute place for 3K/month, Dahlia texted.

I can swing 1K/month, no prob, Lydia texted.

LOL I wish. 3K each.

Well, she thought, *looks like I'm about to become the Dill of my new group of friends—financially at least.* Forrestville dentist and real estate agent money wasn't much of a match for *Chic* editor-in-chief money and actress money. She'd have to start thinking of ways to make being the "poor girl" part of her charm and appeal. The way Dolly did, in fact.

Oof. Maybe out of my budget, Lydia texted. **Plus haven't gotten accepted to NYU yet, so.**

You'll get in.

As we say in TN, don't count chickens, etc.

Lydia felt anxious for no specific reason. Not just about the rent situation, although that contributed. Her head ached from filling out college and scholarship applications, revising her admission essay, and working on a lengthy blog post critiquing the designs shown at Paris Fashion Week. Time for something different.

She pulled out Dill's computer, went to YouTube, and set up an account for him. Password: LydiaisaBenevolentGoddess666. She found the folder with Dill's videos and opened one.

What she heard stopped her short. *Whoa. That's Dill?* He had so much confidence and poise. He was mesmerizing. Singing transformed him. She realized that she had never seen Dill play and sing one of his own songs. And it was an exquisite song. She started uploading the video and opened another. Again. Mesmerizing. Haunting. Soaring. And another. Until she'd watched all of them. Her anxiety melted away completely.

Whatever else he had inherited from his father, he had inherited a dark charisma. The sort that makes people want to follow and confess. The sort that makes people feel saved. The sort that makes people want to pick up venomous snakes and drink poison to be nearer to their God. He sang like a river of fire flowed in him, like music was the only beautiful thing he owned. His songs made her heart ache. Watching him, in fact, she felt a little . . . she took a deep breath and shook her head. *Okay, that's quite enough of that sort of thinking.*

While she was visiting colleges with her mom, during the time she and Dill weren't speaking, he'd weighed heavily on her mind. She imagined him stuck in Forrestville, unhappy, unfulfilled. *This changes things. I can use this. I can work with this.* She began to formulate a plan.

"Lydia?"

Lydia jumped and turned in her chair. Her mother stood in the doorway.

"Sorry to startle you. What were you listening to? It's beautiful."

"Oh . . . this guy I came across."

"It's nice." Lydia's mom began to go on her way.

Lydia was horrified to find herself calling after her, "Hey, Mom. I'm . . . working on a blog post. Did you ever have a friend who you were sure would always just be a friend, but then you started developing feelings for said friend?"

Her mom came back, set down the laundry basket she was carrying, leaned against the doorjamb, and folded her arms with a sly smile. "Yes, as a matter of fact. I have some experience with that."

"What happened?"

"One night, we were hanging out at this burger place near the college, and we were eating ice cream cones and sitting on one of the picnic tables outside, and the moonlight caught his face in just the right way and he was the most beautiful thing in the world. And I wasn't ever able to go back to seeing him as anything but."

"Who was he?"

"Denton Blankenship."

"Oh. Right. This would've been a pretty awkward moment otherwise, I guess."

"Yep." Her mom picked up her laundry basket and left.

Once her mom was out of earshot, Lydia watched Dill's videos again.

• • •

"No, I'm not playing the Forrestville High School talent competition. Are you high?"

"Hear me out," Lydia said.

"Talent competitions are dumb."

"Yes, they are. But listen."

"Class is about to start." Dill stood up from where he sat on Lydia's bumper. He blew on his hands and rubbed them together. "Plus, it's freezing out here."

"Stop. Hear me out. What would be the sweetest feeling in the world? What would be the biggest middle finger in the faces of people who have done their best to make your life miserable? To stand in front of them and sing. That would be so badass, because you're so good. And what if you won? Fifty bucks. That's like a million dollars in adjusted Dill dollars."

"Why should I do it?" Dill sat back down.

"Besides every reason I just gave? Because we should do things we're afraid of. It makes it easier every time we do it." *And if I can get you to do this, maybe I'll be able to get you to do other stuff you're afraid to do, like leave this town and go to college. Maybe we just need to break through your comfort zone this once.*

"I don't want to get laughed at."

Trump card time. "Even if you get laughed at, I happen to know for a fact that you aren't laughable in general. And I have proof." Lydia opened her laptop. She pulled up one of Dill's videos. It had 9,227 views and forty-nine comments. All positive.

Chills.

This song is amazing.

OMG loved this, thank you. And so on.

Dill looked stunned. "How—Didn't you barely post this? Maybe last night?"

Lydia closed her laptop and gave him a smug pat on the head. "I tweeted it out last night. I didn't say you were my friend. If I had, it would have looked nepotistic. So I didn't use your name. I called you *Dearly.* Get it? D. Early?"

"People really liked it."

"Do this for me," Lydia said. "For all the times I've stuck up for you."

They heard the bell ring. They were late.

"I've never performed one of my nonhymn songs in

public before. Much less at the high school Christmas talent competition in front of six hundred people, most of whom hate me."

"You've performed plenty of times in front of venomous creatures. You'll be right at home."

23

DILL

Practicing for the talent show gave him focus. It took his mind off Lydia leaving. It took his mind off his upcoming visit with his father. Still, in the intervening month or so between promising Lydia he'd do it and the show's date, he'd had plenty of time to lose his nerve. Every time he waffled, though, Lydia would whip out her phone or her laptop and show him the steadily increasing number of views, comments, and likes "Dearly" had. She bought him a new set of guitar strings. She called it an early Christmas present.

But then, in the final days before the competition, Dill stopped being afraid and started being excited. He kept thinking about the fifty dollars and how much he wanted it. He was going to spend it on Lydia. Take her to dinner.

Buy her something. Anything but throw it down the black hole of the Early family debt.

The day came slowly, but it came.

Dill was nauseated that morning. He couldn't eat breakfast. He and Lydia didn't speak at all on the way to school. He couldn't pay attention in class. The talent show assembly was after lunch. He trembled as he filed into the auditorium, guitar case in hand, Lydia and Travis flanking him—a gladiator heading to a fight for his life.

"Hey," Lydia said. "Breathe. You'll do great. Remember: you have fans and you have friends. Nobody here can do anything to you or take anything from you."

"Why did I let you talk me into this?"

"Because I'm awesome and you're awesome and you're going to do something brave."

"It's cool you're doing this," Travis said. "I watched your videos again the other night, and they really are amazing."

Dill said nothing but nodded and gripped his armrest. Every nerve in his body hummed as he sat through the introduction of the three judges (all teachers—not fellow students, fortunately), interminable lip-syncing and dance routines, corny comedy sketches, duck and turkey calls, and awful karaoke. Until finally his turn came.

"All right," Principal Lawrence said, stepping to the microphone, paper in hand. "Next up we have"—he squinted at the list—"Dillard Early."

A mumble swept through the crowd. Hushed giggling. Whispers. Shifting of feet. Cell phones surreptitiously removed from pockets to film the spectacle.

Dill drew a deep, shaky breath. "Here goes." He stood on unsteady legs.

Lydia grabbed his arm and pulled him close to her. She put her lips to his ear. "Dill, keep your eyes on us. Don't look anywhere else. We're standing with you."

She had never whispered to him so intimately before. Her breath on his cheek felt like the caress of a lover. A different electricity coursed through his body. And for a moment, he forgot his fear.

It rushed back, though, as he made his way to the front, head down. He hit his guitar case on one of the seats. *Bwongggg.* The crowd tittered. "Sorry," he mumbled to nobody in particular.

Please God. Attend me this hour. Do not forsake me. He carefully ascended the steps to the stage and walked the seeming half mile to the middle, where two microphones stood.

He pulled his battered and scarred acoustic guitar from its case. He slung it around his neck and walked the last few feet to where Principal Lawrence stood. He kept his head down. The lights on the stage blinded him.

Principal Lawrence gestured for Dill to take his place and stepped aside. Dill stepped up to the microphones. He adjusted the vocal mic for his height and then the guitar mic. A screech of feedback. Laughter. "Ow," someone said loudly. Dill's head pounded. Black-red began to creep into the margins of his field of vision. He held his breath and felt his heart palpitating. *Can they hear it? Is the microphone picking it up? Please God. Stand with me now.* He closed his eyes. His heartbeat drummed in his ears.

Someone faked a cough. "Dildo!" Giggling. Someone else faked a cough. "Dildo!" More giggling. Angry shushes from teachers scattered through the crowd and from Lydia and Travis. Dill's heart sank.

Principal Lawrence nudged Dill aside and spoke into the microphone. "Okay, I hear another outburst, we cancel the rest of the assembly, and everyone writes a ten-page paper about manners, understood? Okay, Mr. Early."

Dill took his place again at the microphones. "Here's a song I wrote." His voice echoed in the auditorium. He didn't recognize it. It was too loud. He waited for the laughter. For someone to yell out "Dildo" again. But there was quiet, which was almost worse.

He couldn't remember how to play the guitar. He couldn't remember where to put his hands on the strings. He couldn't remember the words to his song.

He looked up, straight into Lydia's eyes. Her eyes were filled with . . . what? A new something he had never seen before in her. He couldn't name it, but it made him strong. It swept the black-red from the margins of his eyes and turned the contemptuous crowd beneath him into a faceless blob. It made his heart beat a different rhythm.

· · ·

For a fleeting moment, he's standing once more at the front of the praise band. He's wearing his guitar and they're playing, playing. And the congregation begins to pass around the deadly serpents. His father approaches him with a copperhead. He stops playing. His father smiles and gently hands it to him. He reaches out and accepts his father's offering. It is cool and dry and sleek. It pulses in his hands. His faith is strong. It binds the serpent's jaws. It cannot hurt him. He stares into its face.

· · ·

Dill took a breath and began to play and sing. He sang like the Holy Spirit had descended on him with a cleansing fire. He heard his voice and guitar echoing through the auditorium. He opened his eyes only once during the performance—to make sure Lydia was still watching him. She was, with even more of the something. The room melted away below him.

He finished, and his last notes decayed into silence. He got a smattering of polite applause, but a standing ovation from Lydia and Travis. *Probably not the reaction the winner would get, but at least no one is yelling insults at me. And it's over.* He put his guitar back in its case and left the stage, barely hearing Principal Lawrence taking the microphone and saying, "All right, that was a very nice song from Dillard. Thank you, Dillard. Next up we have . . ."

Dill collapsed into his seat. Travis glowed and was nearly bouncing. "That was so cool! You're like a professional singer!" he whispered, grabbing Dill's hand in a vigorous handshake.

Lydia clutched his arm and pulled him close again. Probably closer than she needed to. "That was amazing," she whispered, letting her lips brush his ear. "I knew you could do this. Remember how you feel."

Dill basked in his relief, like he was swimming in a warm, starlit lake. He listened with his eyes closed as five of the football players lip-synced to a rap song, to thunderous applause that dwarfed his own. *Thank you, God. You have not always given me the things I wanted or needed, but you gave me this, and I'm grateful.*

The competition ended, and Principal Lawrence took the stage again, holding three envelopes. "All right folks, the results are in from the judges. In third place, for her karaoke version of a Taylor Swift song, we have Lauren Ramsey. Congratulations, Lauren. You win a coupon for twenty-five percent off a tanning session at Tropical Glo tanning salon." Lauren, a cheerleader, accepted her prize, beaming, to riotous applause and whistling.

"Okay, in second place, for his fantastic duck and turkey calls, we have Austin Parham. Austin, you let me know if you're available come spring turkey season. Austin wins a ten-dollar Applebee's gift certificate." Austin, a baseball player, accepted his prize. Again, an enthusiastic response.

It's going to really suck losing to duck and turkey calls. Let's just get this over with.

"Now, for the grand prize winner of fifty dollars cash money. I want to remind y'all that our judges considered many factors in their decision, including originality and creativity. I also want to remind y'all to be respectful if the person you thought should win didn't win. And now, our grand prize winner is . . . drumroll please . . ."

Dill stomach flipped. It was then that he stopped being completely aware of what was happening. He knew that he heard his name called. He knew that he sat, paralyzed, while Lydia and Travis stood, whooped, and tugged him out of his chair, pushing him toward the stage. He was vaguely cognizant of the tepid applause and rush of grumbling that met the announcement. He was standing on stage again, accepting the envelope and a handshake from Principal Lawrence. And then he was sitting by Lydia and Travis again, clutching his envelope.

The assembly let out and the students streamed into the hall. Travis still buzzed with excitement. "Dude," he said, strutting alongside Dill. "I would totally buy all your albums if you made albums!"

Dill grinned. "You don't even like music."

"Yours is different."

"Hey, Dill." Alexis Robbins approached. She was pretty and popular. She never talked to him or his friends, but was never unkind to them either. They existed in separate worlds.

"Congratulations on winning," she said. "I didn't know you did music."

Dill blushed. "Oh . . . thanks. Yeah. I do. Thanks."

"Anyway, good job. Bye."

Lydia poked Dill in the ribs. "Look at *you* go. Girls *love* musicians." He laughed and squirmed away. "I'm serious, Dill," she said. "That was hot. Talent is hot. Bravery is hot."

Dill thought he could not be more filled with triumph.

But the moment Lydia said that, he realized that he contained yet undiscovered spaces being flooded with it.

He didn't get a chance to revel. "Dill!" Hippie Joe walked quickly toward them. Hippie Joe was a guidance counselor in his fifties. His name was Joseph Bryant, but everyone secretly called him Hippie Joe. He had a bushy mustache; shaggy gray hair; and wore round, wire-rimmed glasses. He favored joke ties and Converse with his khakis and button-down shirts. "That was fantastic! I've never seen a student perform like that! You had the ghosts of Bob Dylan and Neil Young in you! Well, they're both still alive, but you know what I mean. Great job! I think you've got a future in music!"

"Thank you, Mr. Bryant."

"Tell me when you have a gig somewhere. I'll come watch you."

"I will. Thank you."

Nobody else said anything. They got outside to the parking lot. "I propose we go get something to eat. Specifically, I propose that I buy Dill some late lunch/early dinner, since he hasn't eaten a thing today," Lydia said.

"I'm down," Travis said. "And I'm helping buy."

Lydia beamed as they drove, as though she knew some great secret. She appeared as joyous as Dill felt. He couldn't stop his legs from bouncing up and down. He kept peeking in his envelope, at the crisp fifty-dollar bill inside. He felt carved from something beautiful and indestructible. Light. Air. He wondered how long he could ride the wave of that feeling before it crashed again onshore.

• • •

Less than a week, as it turned out.

"I changed my mind," Dill said. "I'm calling Dr. Blankenship and telling him I'm not going."

His mother wore her cleaning uniform, ready to leave for work. They stood in their living room. "You will not. You'll go. It's almost Christmas and your father is expecting you. You haven't been to see him since the end of summer."

"I hate visiting there."

"He's your father. You go."

"Every time I go, he's weirder and weirder. I hate seeing him that way. I'm not going."

His mother's eyes narrowed and she drew near him. "You hate seeing him that way? Maybe you deserve to feel uncomfortable seeing as how *you* put him there."

His mother had implied this many times. But she had never outright said it until then.

Dill struggled for words. "What do you mean, *I put him there*? Huh? What are you saying?"

"I'm saying your father's lawyer gets up and makes every single police officer and TBI agent admit that this porn shows young girls. All of them admit that your father has a teenage son. All of them say that they don't know if you have access to the computer. All of them admit it's possible you did it. All of them admit they can't tell exactly who downloaded it. And you get up and testify against your father."

Dill paced. His voice rose. "The state called me to testify. What could I do? Refuse? The judge would've thrown me in jail."

His mother pointed in his face. "You could've testified it was yours. The DA wasn't about to prosecute a juvenile. Your father would be a free man right now if you hadn't done what you did."

Dill was aghast. His heart ached like it was trying to beat around a screwdriver. "So lie? I took *an oath* to tell the truth. I swore on *the Bible* to tell the truth. All I said was that it wasn't mine. I didn't say it was Dad's. I didn't testify *against* him. I testified *for myself.*"

"I didn't say to lie," his mother said quietly, looking away.

Dill grabbed her arm and turned her to face him. "What do you mean?" he whispered. "What did you mean by that? Do you think I could've testified truthfully that that sick shit was mine? Do you think—"

She slapped him. "Don't you curse in this house."

His face felt singed where her hand hit. *Don't let her see you cry. Don't let her see you cry.* "Is that what you've thought this whole time? That I downloaded that crap and got up and lied and let Dad take the blame? That's what you think of me?" *Don't cry.*

Her eyes seared, ferocious and condemning. "I think we're all sinners. We wouldn't need Jesus if we weren't. But the serpents never lied. If your father hadn't been pure of spirit, he wouldn't be in jail now—he'd be dead. The serpents would've taken him. Or the poison. But you never passed that test. You never took up the serpent. So you ask me, between you and your father, who I think Lucifer ensnared? God has given me that answer. I don't need to guess."

Dill couldn't get enough air. Nausea gripped his stomach. "So what about Kaylie Williams, huh?" he screamed. "What about her? When she testified that Dad got her alone after church one night and wanted to talk about sex with her? Was she lying too? She was *eleven years old*. Her family moved away because of it. Her brother was my friend."

"Teaching a member of your flock about sex before she gets herself into trouble is no crime, and that's why the state never charged your father with anything over it. You and I both know that Kaylie was a fast girl. She needed guidance or she'd have gotten pregnant in high school like—"

"Like who?"

His mother turned to leave. "You helped put your father in prison. If it weren't for that, he'd still be here. If it weren't for that, I'd never have had the accident coming home from visiting him there and my back and neck wouldn't hurt all the time. And then you have the gall to talk about prancing off to college and leaving me with the mess you made. I'm through discussing this with you. You will visit your father. You will give him comfort for what you've done. You owe him and you owe me. You've got your own debts."

"This has destroyed my life. Even having to deny that it was mine destroyed my life. It made me look guilty. I've lived with this. Nobody will let me forget it."

His mother glared at him. Grim, unblinking. "You keep forgetting that this life is nothing. The next is the only one that matters. I wish you'd remember that." And she left.

Dill collapsed onto the sofa, running his fingers through his hair. He wanted to vomit. The tears he had been restraining broke out and poured down his cheeks in a torrent. He screamed. It felt good. He did it again. He punched the sofa. Again. Again. Again. He grabbed the lamp off the table, and cocked his arm as if to throw it and smash it against the wall. Only the realization that he used that lamp for songwriting during long winter nights stopped him. He set it on the table, lay in the middle of the floor in the fetal position, and cried, with the reek of their musty carpet in his nostrils.

By God's own grace, Dr. Blankenship proved no more punctual than his daughter, which gave Dill a solid twenty minutes to compose himself and wash his face, and for the redness and puffiness to mostly subside from his eyes. He didn't look great, but he was more "didn't sleep much last night" than "had a screaming fight with my mother wherein she accused me of being a sexual deviant and putting my own father in prison."

Dr. Blankenship arrived in the Prius that had replaced the one he gave Lydia. Dill got in. Christmas music blared on the stereo.

"Thanks, Dr. Blankenship. If this is any inconvenience at all, it's totally okay if we don't go."

"Please, call me Denny. Even though I've told you that

lots of times and you never do. And it's no inconvenience whatsoever."

"Don't be afraid to say so. If it's even a little bit."

"No problem at all."

He didn't get it.

• • •

The leafless branches of the trees surrounding the prison were skeletal against the iron-hued December sky. They looked as barren and lifeless as Dill felt.

Dr. Blankenship dropped off Dill with instructions to call when he finished. Into the prison. Through security. Into the visiting room. Waiting.

Dill tried to smile as his father approached. "Hey, Dad. Merry Christmas."

"Merry Christmas to you." Dill's father had more new ink. Tattoos of snakes that spiraled around both of his forearms ended in snake heads in each palm. They covered and wove in and out of several sets of snakebite scars on his arms. The sign of faith wasn't that the snakes never bit you—it was that as sick as you became, you didn't die from it.

"You got some more new tattoos." *But at least we never want for an icebreaker as long as you keep getting them.*

Dill's father quickly opened and closed both hands, one finger at a time, making the serpents on his forearms ripple and writhe. "Ecclesiastes tells us there is nothing new under the sun."

"Yeah, but—anyway, Mom put some money on your books instead of buying you Christmas presents. She figured you could get what you wanted at the commissary."
Not my fifty dollars, though. My fifty dollars is safe and sound.

"Are you working hard and helping your mother pay off our debts?"

"Yep." *I'm doing great; thanks for asking. Love our visits.*

"Good."

His father seemed more alien every time he came here. But then again, maybe that foreignness had an upside. Maybe his father had changed, diverged from his mother. Maybe prison had given him some new perspective. Dill had a sudden inspiration. "Speaking of paying off debts. I had an idea. What if I were to go to college so that I could get a better job and help pay off your debts faster?"

Dill's father regarded him with cold skepticism. "College? Is that where you mean to learn true discipleship?"

"No sir, just learn what I need to get a good job."

He drew his face close to Dill's. "College will teach you that God is dead. But God is not dead. He is alive and he shows himself to those whose faith shows signs of life."

"I wouldn't believe that God is dead."

Dill's father laughed curtly. "Your faith was weak. Your faith failed you on the hour it was given you to take up the deadly serpent. You were as Peter, trying to walk on the waves of the Sea of Galilee, but sinking. You need instruction and learning, but not the sort college provides."

"I have faith."

"What sign proves it?"

"I played in the school talent competition. That took faith."

His father leaned back, the slightest glimmer of pleasure on his face. "Did you? Did you preach the gospel through song?"

"No."

The glimmer of pleasure faded. "What did you sing about?"

"Loving someone."

"Oh. *'Loving someone,'*" Dill's father repeated back, mockingly. "Did you risk death for Jesus's name at this talent show?"

"No."

"What did you risk?"

"Ridicule. Humiliation."

"The true Christian risks that every day. We are fools for Christ. You risked nothing but your pride. I have inmates in my ministry whose faith is stronger than my own son's. Thieves. Murderers. Rapists. You have my name. Not my faith."

Dill felt fury building in him. "If my faith is weak, maybe it's because of you. *You're* one to talk about faith. Where was your faith when it came time to resist temptation?"

His father bent in and spoke in a hiss. "Your faith was weak even before Satan's work destroyed our signs ministry."

"Satan's work? How come you didn't tell the jury that?

Why didn't you tell them that Satan came down our chimney and downloaded kiddie porn? How come you told them it was my fault?"

His father gave him a cautioning scowl. "Satan is no joking matter. Satan has no body. He works with weak flesh."

Dill stabbed his finger at him, his voice faltering. "*Your* weak flesh. *Yours.* Not mine. You and I both know it. And God does too."

His father exhaled slowly, as though waiting for a wave of rage to subside. He spoke in measured tones. "Do you not see God's hand in guiding me here to minister among the imprisoned?"

"No. I don't see that. I see a man who's let my mother think I got her husband locked up. I see a man who tried to save himself by destroying his own son's reputation. I see a man who seems to be doing fine in here while Mom and I work our asses off to repay *your* debts."

His father's eyes darkened. "Watch your tongue. *Our* debts. Did you not eat at our table? Did you not live under our roof?"

"*Your* debts. And now I'm paying for *your* sins by watching the world move on without me. I can't go to college like my friends because of you."

Dill's father pointed, his face a mask of contempt, and spoke with a perilous hush, his voice trembling with bile. "You are no savior of mine. Do not make yourself a Christ. Christ made me free. You made me a prisoner."

Dill jumped as his father slammed his hand on the table, a sharp crack in the still room, and stood. "Goodbye, Junior. Give your mother my love." He waved to the guards, who had tensed up at the noise. "I'm done here."

He left without a backward glance.

• • •

Dill thought—incorrectly, as it turned out—that his exchange with his mother that morning had somehow inoculated him against more pain. He sat in the parking lot, his head in his hands, feeling as gray as the sky. Dr. Blankenship pulled up. "Hey, Dill," he said with a cheery smile. "Candy cane truffle?"

Dill forced a smile in return. "No, thank you."

They drove for a while before saying any more.

"I'm sorry I'm not talking, Dr. Blankenship. I don't mean to be rude."

"I understand. Don't worry about it."

More miles passed. They listened to a Christmas mix on Dr. Blankenship's iPod.

Dill fought for composure. He assumed that he had a finite reserve of tears that he had already exhausted for the day. Wrong on that count too. He could feel a welling inside him that he couldn't contain much longer.

"So . . . um." He started to lose his grip. He choked back the tears until his throat ached the way it did right after he gulped a glass of ice water. "Things aren't so hot with me and my dad." And then he broke completely. He felt naked and ashamed. Adam in the Garden of Eden. But he couldn't control it anymore.

Dr. Blankenship glanced over at him, his brow furrowed. "Hey," he said gently. "Hey." He pulled the car over to the side of the road. Dill had his head against the passenger window, sobs racking his shaking body.

"Hey." Dr. Blankenship placed his hand on Dill's shoulder. "It's okay. It's okay."

And out of nowhere (at least as far as Dill was concerned), he fell onto Dr. Blankenship's shoulder. Dr. Blankenship hugged Dill while he cried. Dr. Blankenship smelled like warm cashmere, sage, and dryer sheets. Dill pulled himself together as quickly as he could, which took several minutes.

Dill drew a shuddering breath. He was a mess. "I'm sorry. I'm really sorry. I'm keeping you from getting home. This probably isn't what you expected when you offered to give me a ride."

Dr. Blankenship rummaged around for a travel pack of tissues. "Actually, it's sort of exactly what I expected, which is why I offered you the ride. You want to talk about it?"

Dill wiped his eyes with his palms and accepted a tissue. "Not really."

"Okay."

But then he did anyway. "My mom and dad both think I'm responsible for putting my dad in prison because I wouldn't lie for him. And because he's in prison, we have all these debts, and because of all these debts, I can't do a lot of stuff. And my dad thinks my faith is too weak to do anything anyway. I feel trapped. I think God is punishing me."

Dr. Blankenship sighed. "Let's take these one at a time. First off, I'm sorry, but your dad's predicament is not your fault in the slightest. I followed your dad's trial. I understand why you had to testify. The jury believed you and didn't believe him. End of story. That's not on you. That's on him. And if he tries to put it on you, screw him."

Dill rested his head in his hands.

Dr. Blankenship rubbed his thumb on the steering wheel, looking uncomfortable. "Sorry. I'm not meaning to be rough on your dad."

"It's okay."

"I get mad when people say that kind of stuff to kids who have their whole life in front of them. Make them doubt themselves. Your faith is plenty strong to do anything you want to do. You think God wants anything for you but your happiness? No way. And don't let anyone tell you otherwise. Your dad doesn't have license to crush your spirit just because he's your dad."

Dill sniffled and wiped his nose. Another shuddering breath. "Please don't tell Lydia about . . . this."

Dr. Blankenship patted his shoulder. "If I know my daughter, there's no way she'd tease you for this. She'd give you the hugs I'm here to give you."

"Yeah." Dill paused. "That's another thing. I'll really miss Lydia. Like a lot. So I guess that's another thing that sucks." His throat constricted.

Dr. Blankenship's eyes welled with tears. "Aw man, Dill. Look what you did. I'm right there with you, buddy." His voice quavered. "I'll miss her too. That sucks for both of us."

Dill handed him a tissue. "Don't worry, I won't tell Lydia about . . . this."

Dr. Blankenship dabbed his eyes. "Funny thing is, she wouldn't tease either of us for crying individually. But the two of us, sitting by the side of the road, both crying simultaneously? Over *her,* no less? We'd never hear the end of it."

"This can never leave this car," Dill said.

"Hell no."

They sat for a moment, composing themselves.

"I officially declare this meeting of the Lydia Fan Club adjourned," Dr. Blankenship said. "Let's hit the road. You better grab that whole bag of candy cane truffles from the backseat. I think we need them in our emotionally fragile state."

"You won't lose your dentist license for encouraging me to eat candy?"

"This'll be another of our secrets."

They drove in the winter gloaming. Here and there, a house off the side of the highway lit up in a glowing motley of Christmas lights. Dill withdrew into his thoughts. It felt like wrapping himself in a wet wool blanket. *Did you see your dad? Did you see what he's becoming? You better start performing your own mental and physical inventory of sanity more frequently and consciously. Madness seems to sneak right up on the Early men. You can never let down your guard. You can never stop being vigilant. You're never safe from yourself. Your own blood will poison you.*

Dill glimpsed a billboard with a father and son on it as it flashed past. He spoke before his preoccupied brain could stop his mouth. "I really wish you were my dad."

Dr. Blankenship was quiet for a moment and then glanced over at Dill. "I would be proud if you were my son."

24

TRAVIS

"When are you guys telling me where we're heading?" Travis asked.

"Nashville. The rest is a surprise," Lydia said, exchanging a knowing glance and smile with Dill.

"But my birthday was weeks ago. Christmas too."

"Irrelevant," Lydia said.

"What's in Nashville?"

"Non-Christmas, nonbirthday surprise."

"Give me a hint."

"Dill, help me here. What's something wizardy that will shut him up?"

"Oh man. Asking the wrong person. Uh . . . hey, Travis, if you keep asking questions . . . you'll break some sort of important spell. And you'll spend the rest of your life diarrheaing yourself."

"That works. Travis, you were born to a wizard family, and adopted by a normal family. But a very powerful sorcerer enchanted you so that if you ask more than . . . oh . . . say, three questions on your birthday, you'll have horrific diarrhea."

"It's not my birthday, remember?"

"There's a one-month window on the spell. And we're a half hour from the next rest stop."

They neared Nashville. Lydia's GPS squawked directions to the airport.

"The airport . . . ," Travis started to say, with a questioning lilt in his voice.

Lydia raised a finger in warning. "Diarrhea."

". . . is a very cool place for airplanes to take off and land," Travis finished.

They took the exit to the airport and approached the terminal.

"We're right on time," Lydia said, looking at her phone.

"*On time* on time or the Lydia version of on time?" Dill asked.

"No, genuinely on time." Lydia pulled into a parking lot where cars waited to pick up people at the terminal.

They waited several minutes. Travis started to say something.

"Dude, trust me. You will not want to have diarrheaed yourself for this surprise," Lydia said, cutting him off. "You'll want to be at your most diarrhea-free for this surprise."

Her phone rang. "Lydia Blankenship," she answered.

That was odd. That wasn't how she normally answered the phone.

"Okay . . . okay . . . so you've got your bags. Okay, great. We're in a light-blue Toyota Prius. Lots of stickers. Okay, great. Okay, see you in a minute. Bye." Lydia hung up.

"And so it begins." She started the car and drove to the terminal. They sat and waited. Travis stared ahead.

"Travis, look at that man over there in the coat and maroon sweater," Dill said.

"Where?"

Dill pointed. "Over there. The guy with the—"

"Fisherman's cap," Lydia said, pointing. "Bushy white beard, glasses, portly. Holding a Cinnabon box."

"Who does that look like?" Dill asked.

Travis laughed. "Oh wow, it totally looks like G. M. Pennington."

He studied the man for a second more. His heart rate doubled. "No way," he whispered. Lydia and Dill grinned. "It *is* G. M. Pennington! *And he's walking toward us!*" Travis squealed. He bounced up and down in his seat. He frantically reached for his phone to text Amelia, and realized that he'd left it at home again by accident. *She won't believe this. She's going to die.*

"Calm down," Lydia said. "Show a little dignity. You're about to meet your hero."

She got out and walked toward Mr. Pennington, extending her hand. "Mr. Pennington, Lydia Blankenship. Good to meet you. This way."

He gave her a jolly grunt and tipped his cap. "Mademoiselle. I'll follow where you lead."

She led Mr. Pennington to her car. "Sorry, we don't have something fancier."

He waved off her apology. "I would gladly ride in such an ecologically righteous conveyance over the finest limousine any day. Limousines are for sociopathic oligarchs."

"Mr. Pennington, I think we'll get along fine. Dill, get in the backseat," Lydia said. "Bestselling authors get automatic shotgun."

Dill got out and shook his hand. "Sir, Dillard Early. Pleased to meet you."

"The pleasure is mine," he said, sitting. "And please, all of you, call me Gary. My real name is Gary Mark Kozlowski, but who wants to read a fantasy novel by a Polish serial killer, right?" He chuckled. "But I'm told that one of you probably already knows my real name. You must be Travis."

Travis sat paralyzed, his mouth agape, looking like he'd seen an angel. Which was, frankly, how he felt. "Me, sir. Gary," he squeaked.

"Sir Gary? I accept my knighthood, Mister Travis. Pleasure to meet you." He offered his hand and Travis took it, trembling.

"Gary," Lydia said, "how long is your layover?"

"Three hours."

"What do you want to do or see?"

He stroked his beard. "I judge a city by its ice cream. And there's no conversation better than the kind you can have over ice cream. So lead on, friends. Transport me to your finest ice cream."

"Done," Lydia said. "I know a place." They sped away.

"How—" Travis started to ask before he cut himself off.

"It's okay, Travis. You can start asking questions now. The spell is lifted." Lydia looked over at Gary. "Don't ask."

"How?" Travis asked.

"I'll start," Lydia said. "I wanted to make this happen for you before I left for college, so I called my friend Dahlia, whose mom is the editor of *Chic*. She put me in touch with her mom's literary agent. Her mom's literary agent knew Mr. Pennington's agent. I got his schedule and found out he was stopping over in Nashville on his flight home to Santa Fe from meeting with his publisher about the upcoming *Deathstorm* release."

"But," Gary said, "that's not the whole story. Lydia clearly did her homework and discovered an obscure interview I did before any of you were born, in which I talked about what a special place I have in my heart for my rural fans who dream of a bigger world than the one they inhabit. And I know this because Miss Lydia had at the ready for my agent the population statistics for . . ." He snapped his fingers.

"Forrestville," Lydia said.

"Ah, yes. Forrestville. And my agent would be in big trouble if I weren't at least given the opportunity to spend some time with one of my small-town readers who made the trip all this way. So we changed my flight to the red-eye so I'd be able to spend some real time with you."

"I can't even tell you both what this means to me," Travis said. He wanted to cry. This was already the best night of his life.

"My pleasure," Lydia said. "I had to go big."

They arrived at Five Points Creamery and got in line.

"Mr.—Gary, please let me pay for you," Travis said.

Gary laughed. "My boy, it's no secret to you that I have sold many books. I am a millionaire many times over. *I* will be buying the ice cream this evening for all of you, thank you very much. Buy *Deathstorm* when it comes out if you must repay me."

"Oh, I will. You better believe I will."

Gary approached the young man behind the counter and pulled a fat, intricately tooled wallet from his pocket. "I'll be paying for my young friends here. And whatever they order"—he leaned in with a conspiratorial wink— "make it a triple. All around." He drew a circle in the air with his finger.

They all sat down with their ice cream.

"So, Travis, what house are you?" Gary asked, spooning ice cream into his mouth and grunting with delight.

"Oh, Northbrook. Definitely Northbrook," he said, without a moment's hesitation.

Gary pointed his spoon at Travis. "Indeed! I had you pegged as a Northbrook, but I was prepared to talk you out of whatever other ideas you may have had. House Tanaris? House Wolfric? Who knows how people think."

Travis beamed.

"All right, then," Gary said. "Let's put your friends in their rightful houses, shall we?"

"Yeah! Dill's a musician. So . . ."

"Minstrels' Brotherhood," Gary and Travis said simultaneously. They grinned.

"All right, Lydia . . . she's supersmart and she loves to read and write . . . so . . . House Letra?" Travis said.

"Yes, yes," Gary said, rubbing his chin. "Or . . . The Learned Order?"

Travis considered the proposition tentatively, not wanting to contradict his idol, but realizing he might have no choice. "Only thing is that there's a lifelong chastity vow."

"I forgot about that," Gary murmured.

"Nope," Lydia said. "My chastity vow extends only to high school. I'll take the other choice. Hey, I don't want to interrupt the Bloodfallery, but Gary, how did you become a writer?"

He finished a bite of ice cream. "I grew up on a farm in Kansas. Wheat. Corn. We had some animals. We worked from dawn until dusk. I loved the books of C. S. Lewis, J. R. R. Tolkien, and Robert E. Howard. As I worked, I would create worlds in my mind. Characters. People. Languages. Races. Battles. It was my escape. Pretty soon, I had too much for my head to hold and I needed to put some on paper."

"I do that!" Travis said. "I work at a lumberyard and I imagine stuff while I work. What did your parents think about you becoming a writer?"

A wistful smile. "My father . . . was not a kind man. He drove me hard and he thought writing was foolishness. And maybe he was right. But you couldn't have told me that then and you couldn't tell me that now."

A moment of quiet. Gary finished another bite of ice cream. "Are you a writer, Travis?"

"Oh no."

"Why not?"

"I mean . . . I can't write."

"Well, have you ever tried?"

"No."

"Then of course you can't! Writing is something you can learn only by doing. To become a writer, you need an imagination, which you clearly have. You need to read books, which you clearly do. And you need to write, which you don't yet do, but should."

"Don't you need to go to college to be a writer?"

"Not at all. Listen, we live in a remarkable time. There's free advice everywhere on the Internet. Have you ever read Bloodfall fanfic?"

"Yes," Travis said, hesitating. "But I'll stop if you want me to."

Gary laughed. "Nonsense. Start there. Write some Bloodfall fanfic. Borrow my characters. I give you permission. Get practice writing. And then begin to create your own. I sense something special in you. A great imagination. I sense that you have a story to tell."

Travis glowed. Something began to grow inside of him.

Something that might be able to grow through the rocks and dirt that his father had piled on him.

• • •

He and Gary spent an hour and a half discussing the Bloodfall series while Dill and Lydia sat outside and talked. Travis told Gary about Amelia. He borrowed Lydia's phone and they took many photos together. The time came to leave. They returned to the airport.

"Before you go, can I tell you one of my favorite parts of all of the Bloodfall books?" Travis asked.

"Please," Gary said.

"I don't know why I love this part so much. But I love the engraving Raynar Northbrook put on Baldric Tanaris's tomb after the Battle of the Weeping Vale."

Gary gave a melancholy smile. "I remember that part well. I wrote it right after my first wife passed away. I was deeply depressed, and I was thinking a great deal about what it meant to live a good life. And I decided that it was so your friends could write something of that nature about you when you were gone."

"I think that's why I like it," Travis said. "It makes me want to live a good life."

Gary beamed. "Good," he said softly.

As Gary was about to get out, Lydia gasped. "Wait! I almost forgot!" She pulled a hardcover edition of *Bloodfall* from her bag and handed it to Gary. "Please sign this for my friend Travis."

"Indeed, indeed!" Gary pulled a gold fountain pen from his jacket pocket and signed the frontispiece with a flourish. *To Travis of House Northbrook, my new friend, large in stature, strong of imagination. Become who you were meant to be.*

Lydia handed the book to Travis. "You need to lend me your old copy of *Bloodfall,* since I need to read it."

Travis got out to give Gary a last handshake. Gary chuckled. "We're friends now, Travis. I hug friends goodbye." He grabbed Travis in a huge bear hug and they took one last picture together.

• • •

"I can't believe this night happened. I can't believe this really happened. Lydia, you're so amazing." He repeated this mantra. His bouncing up and down in the backseat made the car rock.

"I'm pulling over if you don't stop." Lydia had a teasing lilt in her voice. "You're going to make us run off the road."

"Sorry. Y'all, I'm going to do what he said. I'll start writing. Maybe I can take some classes at the community college in Cookeville or something."

"Do it, Trav," Dill said. "You've got what it takes."

His mind buzzed the whole way home. It was rare for his real life to be so good that it would displacc his imaginary life. But this time it was.

He formulated his plan. He'd get some sleep *(yeah right, especially once I start texting Amelia)*, and the next day, when he was done at school and the lumberyard, he'd get on the Internet and start looking for writing advice. *Maybe I should get a notebook to keep it in. I should start saving up for a new laptop and writing classes. And I should get someone who knows writing to read it. Maybe Lydia will. But I better write fast before she leaves for college and gets too busy.* Exuberant purpose filled him.

They dropped him off after more fevered thank-yous. As he walked up to his house, he again lamented that he forgot to bring his cell phone. Yes, Lydia got plenty of pictures, as usual, but he wanted to send Amelia photos of himself and the master and upload them to the Bloodfall forums as soon as possible. *They'll never believe that G. M. Pennington—sorry, "Gary"—bought him ice cream and hung out with him for more than two hours. Oh, and the signed copy of* Bloodfall.

He entered the dark house. His father sprawled on the couch in the flickering glow of the TV. When he saw Travis, he picked up the remote and turned it off.

"Where were you?" he asked, slurring.

Travis knew his father's tone. His heart sank. *Please not tonight. Please not tonight of all nights. Let me just have this.* "With my friends, like I told you, remember?"

"No, I don't remember."

"Well, sorry. Anyway." He started for his room.

"Get your ass back here. We ain't done."

Travis turned, yanked thoroughly back to Earth. *And so it begins.*

"I got a call come in at four-thirty needing a load of pressure-treated for a deck. Five-hundred-dollar order. And guess what? I didn't have nobody to deliver it."

Travis began to sweat. He felt queasy. "I'm sorry. I told Lamar, and he said he'd cover deliveries."

"Lamar's oldass brain forgot. You left me high and dry. I tried calling you. Bunch of times."

"I forgot my cell phone."

"Yeah, no shit." Travis's father stood up. "I got it right here in my damn hand."

He hurled it at Travis. It hit him in the sternum with a meaty thud. He managed to grab it on the rebound before it hit the floor. He caught a glimpse of the screen. Fourteen missed calls. All from his father.

Travis's father walked unsteadily toward him. "Five hundred you cost me today. What you got to say about it? Huh? Think we can afford that?"

"I'm really sorry, Dad. Can't we deliver tomorrow? They probably didn't think if they called that late—"

"No. No. We can't deliver tomorrow."

"Why not?"

"What's that?" His father pointed at Travis's newly signed copy of *Bloodfall*. "Huh? What's that? More faggy wizard shit?"

"It's nothing."

"Huh? *That what you cost me five hundred dollars for?*" he shouted.

"I'll take the delivery tomorrow. Before school. I'll—"

Travis's father tore off his baseball cap and whipped Travis on the back and face with it.

"Huh?" *Whip.* "Huh?" *Whip.* "That what cost me five (*whip*) hundred (*whip*) dollars?"

Travis tried to shield his face but one of the whips caught him across the eyes. They watered profusely. He blinked and wiped at them. He began to churn and froth inside. "You're drunk, Dad. Please let me go to bed." *Please don't make this the night. Please don't make this the night you knew was coming. Please don't make this the night.*

His father grabbed for the book. "Gimme that."

Travis yanked it away. He heard his mother. "Clint, sweetie, you woke me up. What's going on?"

His father lunged at him again. Travis again yanked the book from his reach. His father pushed him into the hutch where Travis's mother kept the china and her doll collection. He shattered the glass doors. His mother screamed.

"Gimme that piece of shit," Travis's father seethed through gritted teeth. He managed to snatch the book. He turned away from Travis and started ripping pages out of it.

Something rent inside Travis, making a sound in his mind like a thousand tearing pages. He howled like a wounded animal and threw himself at his father's back. It was a solid hit. Had this been a football game and had he not been the target, it would have made Travis's father proud. Instead, it sent him careening into an end table, knocking a lamp onto the floor and shattering it. The book fell from his hands. Travis dove on top of the book and covered it with his body.

Travis's father got up and stood over him. "You think I'm some beaner wetback kid you can take? I'll whip your ass right now." He slapped at Travis's head, boxing his ears. He tried to get at the book, but Travis sheltered it completely. Travis's father unbuckled his belt and whipped it off with a swift motion, popping loose one of his belt loops. He raised his arm and scourged Travis's back with the belt. Again.

Again.

Again.

Again.

Again.

Again.

Again.

The belt whistled and cracked across Travis's skin. *Bear it in silence; it's the only way you can win,* Travis commanded himself, but he cried out each time it struck. It felt like someone was painting his back and ribs with stripes of gasoline and chili pepper and setting them ablaze. Travis's mom jumped at his father. "Clint! You're hurting him! Stop it!" She tried to catch the belt. Travis's father grabbed her by both arms and pushed her onto the ground. Hard. Her head hit the floor with a thud and she lay there, weeping softly and holding her head.

But she'd managed to distract Travis's father long enough for Travis to jump to his feet. His father turned, saw him standing, and swung the belt at him again. Travis snagged it with his free hand and tore it away. He stood there for a second—belt in one hand, book in the other—tears and sweat running down his cheeks, facing down his father, who glowered at him, ruddy and panting.

Travis tried to sound as brave as he could. He tried to speak with a clarion voice. The way Raynar Northbrook would speak to his men before a battle. But the pain was too searing. His heart pounded too ferociously. His voice hitched and caught as he spoke—gasping, faltering, and stuttering.

"I'm n-not . . . afraid of you . . . anymore. You'll n-never . . . make me . . . hate myself . . . like you hate me."

He helped his mother to her feet while his father watched, fists clenched, still ready to fight, breathing loudly through his nose as his jaw muscles tensed and relaxed.

Travis threw the belt into a corner, looked his father dead in the eye, and pointed, his hand shaking like his voice. "You lay a hand on me again, I'll break it off your arm. You lay a hand on my mom again, I will fucking kill you."

His father pointed at him with his own trembling hand. "Get the fuck out of my house," he said softly.

Travis kissed his sobbing mom, got his staff, and left.

25

DILL

Dill was in heaven. Lydia had left all of her music on her computer when she gave it to him. It was a sort of secret intimacy with her. Every night he'd lie on his bed, the laptop resting on his chest, earbuds in his ears, exploring and discovering, swimming in the Sea of Lydia.

Tap tap tap.

Dill paused the music and listened for a moment. Nothing. He hit "play."

Tap tap tap.

He paused the music again and got up.

Tap tap tap.

Dill looked out his window to see Travis's face. He jumped.

"Man, you about made me piss my pants," Dill whispered

as he jimmied open the window, letting in a blast of freezing air. Travis appeared to have been crying. "You all right?"

"I'm not doing so great. Can you sneak out and go for a ride?"

"Yeah. Hang on." Dill put on his boots and jacket. He started to climb out the window.

"Wait. Do you have any aspirin or anything?" Travis's face said that he would explain later.

"One sec." Dill tiptoed into the kitchen and retrieved their rapidly dwindling bottle of ibuprofen. He returned to his room and handed Travis three pills. Travis popped them in his mouth and swallowed.

Dill climbed out the window and shut it behind him, leaving himself enough space to get his fingers under it and open it again when he returned. He and Travis sneaked through the shadows to Travis's pickup, parked around the corner. They got in. It was still warm. Travis moved painfully. When his back hit his seat, he sucked in his breath. He took a second to gather himself before starting the engine. Dill decided he wouldn't ask any questions. He'd just let Travis talk.

"Let's go watch some trains," Travis said.

They drove to Bertram Park without speaking. When they arrived, Travis parked as close to the train tracks as he could, leaving his truck running and the heater on.

Travis pushed back his cap and rubbed his forehead. "So I told my dad tonight that I'd kill him. Maybe."

Dill looked wide-eyed at Travis. "You did what?"

"I got home. My dad was drunk. Talking about work.

Saying I cost him a job. He tried to rip up my book that G. M. Pennington signed. I mostly kept him from doing it but we got into it pretty good."

"Damn."

"Yeah. He took his belt to me when I wouldn't let him at my book. My mom intervened and he threw her down. I got the belt from him and told him I'd hurt him if he ever hit me again. Told him I'd kill him if he hurt my mom again."

"You mean it?"

"Yeah. Yeah, I sure did." Travis sounded grim. "Things ain't been great with me and my dad for a long time. You probably figured that out from when we were working on your car."

"You okay?"

"I hurt pretty bad, if that's what you mean."

"I mean in every way."

"My dad kicked me out. Told me to get out of his house. But I stood up to him. I looked him dead in the eye. Told him I was done being scared."

"What'll you do?"

"Haven't thought that far ahead yet. I guess I'll sleep in my truck and go into school early to shower."

They heard a train whistle in the distance.

"You gonna call the cops?" Dill asked.

Travis gave a quick, bitter laugh, then drew in his breath. "No. The lumberyard would shut down. I'd lose my job. My family would lose its income. My mom couldn't get by on the little sewing jobs she does."

"Yeah."

"Has it been a good thing for your family to have your dad locked up?"

"No."

"You can't tell Lydia about any of this. She wouldn't get it. She'd call the cops for sure."

"I won't."

The train took its time getting there. Train whistles always carried farther on winter nights. It came and passed. They didn't bother getting out of the truck.

They sat with the heater on, saying nothing.

"You know," Travis said, staring forward, "Gary made me believe in myself more tonight than my dad has in my whole life."

"Yeah. I know how that feels. Your dad not believing in you. That's a bad feeling right there."

"Things are going to change. I'll make them change. I won't live this way the rest of my life."

Dill sat silent and listened. Travis had a steadfastness and purpose in his voice that Dill had never heard before.

"I think when we graduate," Travis said, "we should get a house together and be roommates. Even if you can't pay much rent. That's all right. I'll pay most of it and you can play me songs to pay for the rest of your part of it. Cheer me up if I'm feeling sad."

"I like that idea. Even though my songs aren't cheerful."

"And we'll both work hard at our jobs, but when we're done, I'll write and you'll do your music. We can have a room with desks right next to each other. Maybe I'll build us desks using scraps from the lumberyard."

"Count me in."

"And we'll have a really fast Internet connection so you can put up your videos and I can post my stories. And we'll still do Friday-night movie night. Maybe we can even have Lydia do it with us, on video chat or something. And maybe Amelia because by then I'll have asked her to be my girl-friend. And no dads are allowed in."

Dill smiled. A genuine smile.

Travis looked him in the eye, that steely resolve in his voice. "I mean it, Dill. I really mean it. We need to take care of each other from now on. We need to be each other's family because ours are so messed up. We need to make better lives for ourselves. We gotta start doing stuff we're afraid to do. I think you should tell Lydia how you feel."

Travis meant it. Dill could see that. And despite feeling guilty for drawing hope for his own life from his friend's desperate circumstances, he felt hopeful all the same. *Maybe Travis is strong enough to keep me from falling when Lydia leaves.*

"I'll think about the Lydia thing. Until we get that house, though, you better park around the corner from my place and sleep in my room. My mom won't notice. She sleeps heavy from being so tired."

"You sure? I can sleep in my truck."

"Yeah. You need a warm, safe place to sleep. We'll get you a water bowl and a can to pee in."

Travis giggled. "Dude, don't make me laugh. It hurts to laugh."

"You positive you're okay? You need a doctor?"

"I've had worse. No broken bones. No teeth knocked out. Just welts and bruises. What would the doctor do?"

"You think you'll be okay sleeping on the floor? We'll make you a bed out of my clothes and blankets and stuff. I'd let you sleep in my bed and take the floor myself, but what if my mom peeks in?"

"I'll be okay."

They sat mute for several minutes.

"We'll get through this, Travis."

He choked up. "I wish he hadn't wrecked my amazing night."

They drove back to Dill's house.

"Hey, Dill, can I have a few minutes alone in here before we go in?"

"Yeah, take all the time you need."

As Dill opened his window to climb into his bedroom, he caught a glimpse of Travis. He had his head down on the steering wheel, his body shaking, as he sat solitary in the frozen January midnight darkness.

26

lydia

Lydia opened the front door. "Travis. What's up?" It was unusual for Travis to show up at her house unannounced.

Travis held a sheaf of notebook paper. He looked nervous. "Hey, Lydia. So. I wrote this story. And you know writing and stuff. I wonder if you could read it for me and tell me what to do better."

"Already? Wasn't it two weeks ago that G. M. Pennington told you to consider becoming a writer?"

"Three."

"Ah, right. It's almost as though that date sticks in your head more than it does mine."

Travis smiled.

"How familiar do I have to be with *Bloodfall* to understand it?" Lydia asked.

"You don't need to know anything. It's original."

"Because I started reading *Bloodfall* after we met Gary. He was so awesome. I owe it to him. And you. But I'm not even close to done."

Travis grinned. "Finally!"

She held out her hand. "Yeah, yeah, blah, blah, finally. Anyway, of course I'll read your story. But fair warning, I'm pretty no bullshit when it comes to writing. If something sucks, I'll tell you. And since this is your first try, there'll probably be stuff that sucks."

Travis handed her the papers. "I'm pretty used to criticism. I can take it."

Lydia remembered what her dad had told her about Travis and she felt a stab of guilt. *I can take it, he says. That and more.* She leafed through the papers. "Wow, handwritten? Who does that? Look at you go, Shakespeare."

"I haven't had much access to my laptop the last few weeks."

Another pang—this time of worry. "Is everything okay? Like at home?"

"Yeah, fine." Travis sounded nonchalant. But not too nonchalant.

If he was lying, he was doing a better job of it than when he lied about Amelia. "Gotcha. What are you and Dill up to tonight?"

"Dill's working; I'm out selling firewood," Travis said.

"Are you serious? You're handwriting stories and selling firewood? Could I maybe show you a flashlight and have you worship me as a god?"

"I finally inherited the firewood sales. Lamar, a guy I work with, did it for years. We get the scraps of lumber we can't sell and bundle them and sell them as firewood. But I guess he got tired of doing it. It makes me extra money to save for a new laptop and writing classes."

Lydia looked out the window and saw Travis's truck laden with firewood.

"Dad!" she called. "Come buy some of Travis's dumb firewood."

Dr. Blankenship came padding to the door in slippers, holding his wallet. "Travis! Hello."

"Hi, Dr. Blankenship."

"I take it you're still working at the lumberyard?"

"Yessir. Most likely'll keep doing that after I graduate. In the last few years, business has kind of slowed down, so I'm one of the only employees left."

"You enjoy it?"

"Yessir. I like the smell of cut wood and it gives me time to think."

"Do something you love and you'll never work a day in your life," Dr. Blankenship said.

"I didn't tell Lydia to tell you to come buy my wood, by the way," Travis said.

"Oh, I know that. If you'd told her to tell me, she'd have said no."

He bought half of Travis's supply.

As Travis left, it occurred to Lydia that there was something different of late in his smile, with its two fake front teeth. Triumphant. Like he had forded a raging river and come to the other side. Or survived some great battle. He shone bright, as if burned clean by fire.

• • •

A couple hours after Travis left, Lydia's phone buzzed.

Sitting here with fat envelope from NYU, Dahlia texted.

OMG open it.

A few minutes later, her phone buzzed again. A photo of an NYU acceptance letter.

CONGRATS!!!!!!!

I'm dying here. You have to tell me when you get yours.

"Hey, Mom?" Lydia called downstairs. "Did the mail come yet today?"

"The flag is down."

Lydia jumped down the stairs, four at a time. She ran outside barefoot, her feet freezing on the ice-cold pavement. She yanked open the mailbox door. Letters. She jammed her hand in so hard to get them that she got a paper cut. She couldn't breathe.

Junk mail. Junk mail. Something for her mom. Something for her mom. Something for her dad. Junk mail. Junk mail. NYU.

Literally the last item in the stack. She closed her eyes, held her breath, and tore. She almost couldn't bring herself to read it. But she did.

Dear Lydia,
Hello and greetings from NYU Undergraduate Admissions.
First and foremost—congratulations on your

acceptance to NYU. We are thrilled to congratulate
you on this achievement!

She stopped reading and screamed. And jumped. And
jumped and screamed. Her mom rushed out to see what
was wrong. Lydia showed her the letter. They jumped and
screamed together. Her dad rushed around from the backyard, where he was stacking his new firewood. They all
jumped and screamed together.

27

DILL

"Everything look okay, Mr. McGowan? I unloaded that pallet of pasta and got it on the shelves and I mopped produce."

Mr. McGowan ran down his clipboard with his pen, mumbling to himself. "Looks good to me, Dill. You got done early, but I'll clock you out normal. Great work."

"Thanks. See you tomorrow night."

"Hey, real quick, Dill. You still available full time come the end of school?"

"Yessir. As many hours as I can get."

"Great. I'll tell the big boss. He'll be glad to hear it."

Dill took off his green work apron, put on his coat, and walked outside. Not a bad night to walk home. It was one of those February nights with the smallest breath of warmth beneath the cold.

"Want a ride home, mister?" Lydia sat on the bumper of her Prius. Her voice startled him. Not only because he wasn't expecting to hear it, but because (and he could have been completely wrong about this) it had a flirtatious quality that had appeared with greater frequency after the talent competition. Dill attributed this to her being impressed with his bravery. Anything more would have been too much to hope for.

"What are you doing here? I thought you had blog stuff."

"Not tonight. That's actually why I'm here. Can we talk?" She must have noted the look of anxiety that passed over Dill's face. "It's good news. Kinda."

"Yeah, sure."

"Cool. Hop in. We're heading to Good News Coffee. I thought the name was appropriate. I'm buying."

They were mostly quiet on the drive.

"Can you give me a hint?" Dill asked.

"Let me have my big announcement."

"You got into college somewhere. NYU?"

"Please let me have my announcement."

They got to Good News, ordered their Christian-themed beverages, and sat.

"Okay," Dill said. "Let's have it."

"I got my acceptance letter from NYU today."

A sharp pain in his chest. A quick electric shock to his heart. The jolt spread lower and lower, into his stomach, like droplets of blood diffusing into water.

• • •

It's like when his name was called at the talent competition, the way his mind freezes and goes somewhere else. He's at some college campus. Maybe NYU. He can't say because he doesn't know what NYU looks like. And Lydia is sitting on a bench with some guy. He's handsome and well dressed (probably by her), with an insouciant, shaggy casualness that bespeaks money. They're talking and laughing. Autumn leaves fall around them.

And Lydia is sitting at a coffee shop with the guy. There are books stacked high around them—the way opportunity and possibility are stacked around them.

And then the guy is sitting in a car with Dr. Blankenship, and they're talking and laughing. And he's sitting at the Blankenships' table beside Lydia, across from Dr. and Mrs. Blankenship.

And Dill is wearing his green Floyd's apron. He's outside in the cold, watching them through the window. He can see his reflection in the glass, and he looks exhausted and used up. And it makes perfect but agonizing sense why the guy is sitting with Lydia and he's not.

• • •

Dill did his best to smile. "Congratulations," he said softly. "I—I knew you would get in. I never doubted it." *If only I could have doubted it. If only I could have pretended even for a second.*

"Thanks. For believing in me and being my friend."

"So. Are you going?"

"Yeah. I am." She said it gently. She must have heard the hopeful lilt in his voice.

She got up, walked around the table, and gave him a lingering hug, running her fingers through the back of his hair. She'd been finding more excuses to hug him lately.

"What was that for?" Dill asked.

"Because you looked like your heart stepped on a Lego."

Dill stared at his Hosanna Hot Chocolate. "I'm happy for you. You wouldn't be happy here and I wouldn't want you to be unhappy."

"I know."

"Please don't forget about me."

"I never will. You're my best friend."

"Have you told Travis?"

"Not yet. He's out selling firewood tonight. Did you know he was doing that?"

"Yeah, I did." *And that's not the only thing we've kept from you.*

They sat and nursed their drinks. They heard the wail of sirens. They turned and looked outside to see an ambulance speed past, followed by two police cars.

"So, I have some good news too, I guess. A little more of a plan for when I graduate," Dill said.

Lydia raised her eyebrows. "Oh yeah? Tell me."

"Trav and I are going to rent a place together and be

roommates. We're both superexcited. He'll write stories and I'll write songs. And our lame dads won't be allowed."

Lydia tilted her head and smiled. "That sounds awesome. A tiny bohemian artists' colony right here in Forrestville."

Dill grew more animated. As if trying to persuade Lydia that it really was awesome, which was what he was doing. As if trying to persuade himself, which was what he was doing. "We're planning on having Friday-night movie nights still. We thought maybe you could join us sometimes on video chat. Not every time, because obviously you'll be busy."

"I would sincerely be honored." After a while she said, "Is this what you want, Dill?"

"It's as close as I'm going to get," he said, after a moment's reflection.

"That's all I've ever wanted for you—that you be happy and live the life you want to live. I thought you'd need to leave here to do that, but maybe not."

"Maybe not."

And Dill realized that maybe he wasn't so easy to read. If he were, Lydia would have asked him why he looked as though he felt like his heart was being pulled from his chest, fiber by fiber, cell by cell, molecule by molecule. And instead of killing him, it only hollowed him out.

28

TRAVIS

Raynar Northbrook perched atop the isolated redoubt, keeping his lone vigil by the river. If any scouts of Rand Allastair's came this way, they would meet a fiercer foe than they had anticipated. There were others who could and gladly would sit at this lonesome post in his place, but he did not ask of his men that which he was unwilling to do himself. And they loved him for it.

Travis sat on top of the remnants of his firewood. It didn't seem like it would be a great spot—it was right by the river and not especially close to any houses or businesses. But Lamar recommended it, and he was right.

How's the firewood selling? Amelia texted.

Pretty good night, especially after Doc B bought so much. Few more nights like this and I can afford a new laptop, Travis replied.

When do I get to read the story you wrote?

LOL once Lydia tells me what I need to fix. I want you to see the best version.

I bet it's great already. You're so smart.

Aw thank you. Hey I just got an idea.

TELL ME.

When Deathstorm comes out, we should meet in between where we live and read it together!!

I LOVE THAT IDEA!!!!!

Ok we'll do it!! We can get blankets and lie in the back of my truck and read with flashlights.

PERFECT!! OMG CAN'T WAIT!!!

Travis shivered and thought about closing up shop, but he wasn't sleepy yet, and sleeping was about all he could do when he sneaked into Dill's house each night. Not a word had passed between him and his father at work. His father certainly hadn't invited him home—not that he would have accepted such an invitation. He talked with his mom regularly when he went by to pick up food while his father was out. He didn't tell her where he slept, but he assured her—on his honor—that it was in a safe, warm place.

The other reason Travis saw no reason to close up yet was that he was reading *Nightwinds,* the fifth book in the Bloodfall series, by flashlight. He'd managed to reread *Bloodfall, Raventhrone, Swordfall,* and *Wolfrun* in time to put away *Nightwinds* before *Deathstorm* came out in March. And that was even with starting his writing career.

His phone buzzed. A text from Lydia. *Have big news. Tell you when I see you.*

Hope it's that you gave my story to G. M. Pennington's agent and they want to publish it LOL, he texted back.

A set of headlights in the distance. An older model white Nissan Maxima slowed and pulled up behind Travis's pickup. He set down his book, clicked off his flashlight, and hopped down. Two men got out of the Maxima. Travis didn't recognize either of them; they were both wearing hoods that obscured their faces.

"Hey, gentlemen," Travis said. "Get you some firewood on this chilly night?"

One of the men hung behind a little bit. The other stepped forward. "Yeah, man. How much?"

"Small bundle's five dollars, big bundle's ten. Cut you a deal on the whole rest of what I got if you're interested."

"Lemme think about it, bro." Something about the man seemed strange. He had a nervous, jittery energy.

The man who hung back joined his compatriot. "We'll take a large," he said.

"Okay." Travis rummaged in his pickup bed for a nice large bundle.

When he turned around, the man pointed a gun at him. "Gimme your money, bro. Hurry your ass up. All your cash."

Travis's heart began pounding. His mouth went dry. His legs felt rubbery beneath him. He raised his hands. "Okay, okay, okay. No problem. No problem. Just take whatever." He handed over his wallet.

The man seemed even more nervous and jittery than the first man Travis had spoken to. "What you got in the truck?"

Travis opened the cab door. He reached for his zipper

pouch on the floorboard, where he kept most of his fire-wood earnings for the night. It was wedged under his staff. He picked up his staff to move it out of the way.

He heard a deafening crack and simultaneously felt a sledgehammer blow to his ribs. It knocked him into the doorframe.

"Shit, dude! Why'd you shoot him?" the other man screamed. *"Come on, we gotta move."*

The man who shot Travis yanked the zipper pouch from his hand. The two men dashed to the Maxima, jumped in, and screeched away. Travis watched their tail-lights disappear over the rise. His brain told him that he should have gotten the license plate number, but it was too late.

He managed to stay standing, but gripped the door of his truck for support. He didn't feel well at all. He couldn't feel his legs or arms. His face was numb. His heart was working too hard. He couldn't breathe. He had a coppery taste in his mouth. He was suddenly thirsty. And cold. He began to shiver uncontrollably.

He didn't think he could drive and decided to try to flag down a car. His legs failed him so he crawled toward the road, fumbling in his jacket pocket for his phone. He dropped it in front of him and dialed 911.

"Nine-one-one, what is your emergency?"

"I think someone shot me."

"All right sir, what is your location?"

"River Road. Is my mom there?"

"Okay, River Road. Can you tell me where exactly on River Road?"

"East of the bridge. I'm thirsty. Is my mom there?"

"Sir, I've got units heading your way right now, okay? I need you to stay with me. What's your name?"

"Travis Bohannon. Is my mom there?"

"Travis, hang in there with me. We'll try to get your mom. I need you to keep talking to me."

"I need some water. I need some water. Can't breathe."

"Keep talking to me, Travis. Travis. Travis? Travis? Travis? Hang in there with me, Travis. Can you talk to me? Travis?"

• • •

Some fall in glorious ways. On green fields of battle as old warriors, surrounded by friends, fighting for their homes, fighting cruelty.

Some fall crawling in the dirt of Forrestville, Tennessee, in the dark, impossibly young and alone, for no good reason at all.

29

DILL

"I feel bad Travis's not finding out the same time as me," Dill said.

"Do you know where he is?" Lydia asked.

"He mentioned River Road."

"Well, there aren't that many places he could be. Here." Lydia handed Dill her phone while she drove. "Text him. Find out where he is."

Dill texted him. No response. Tried calling. Nothing.

"He texted me earlier. Maybe he ran out of battery," Lydia said.

"He never runs out of battery."

"Not in the pre-Amelia days."

"Excellent point. Let's drive River Road for a while. I don't have to be home yet."

"Maybe we can help him sell firewood," Lydia said. "I can show some leg."

"Yeah, but then people would stop to buy firewood and get a lecture about objectifying women."

"So?" She turned onto River Road and drove a short distance before coming around a bend to see a wall of flashing blue lights. Forrestville police, White County sheriff. She slowed. "Oh wow," she murmured. "Maybe someone had an accident."

Dill craned to see. "Hope it wasn't Trav."

They neared. An officer stood in the road, wearing a reflective vest. He directed Lydia around the scene. A camera flashed.

Then they were able to see past the wall of flashing lights.

"Dill . . . is that Travis's truck?" Lydia said, a rising alarm in her voice.

Dill squinted through the glare. He couldn't discern the color of the truck with all the blue light. Another camera flash. Red. He felt a surge of adrenaline and dark dread. "Oh shit. Oh please, Jesus, no. No no no no no no no *no no no no no*. Lydia, stop."

She stopped in the middle of the road. They jumped out and ran to the officer directing traffic. He didn't look much older than them.

"Miss, I'm going to need you to move your car," he said.

Lydia's voice trembled. "Officer, this is our friend's truck. Can you please tell us what happened?"

"Miss, I can't at this time. There's been a situation out

here. I don't know what information the family has yet so I'm not at liberty to say."

Lydia fought tears, frantic and despondent. "Officer, please. I'm begging you."

"Miss, I am sincerely sorry. I can't give you any more information at this time. I apologize."

Lydia broke down.

"Please," Dill said, also starting to lose composure. "Please tell us where he is."

The young officer had a pained expression. He glanced from side to side. His fellow officers were putting up crime scene tape. An officer took a photo of a bloodstain on the pavement.

The officer leaned in close. "County."

They didn't even stick around long enough to thank the officer. They tore away.

They drove in deathly silence. The engine whined as Lydia pushed it, going twice the speed limit most of the way.

Please God. Please God. Please let him be okay.

They squealed up to the hospital, parked haphazardly, and bolted inside.

Time seemed to slow for Dill as he looked around the garishly lit emergency room. There was a strange disconnect between what he saw and the way his mind processed it—or rather, didn't process it.

Travis's father, sitting in a corner, beating the sides of his head with his fists and weeping, two police officers standing next to him, looking uncomfortable.

Travis's mom, lying on the floor, sobbing, three nurses stroking her back and trying to comfort her.

Something broke loose inside Dill's mind. Something that had been moored against the roaring tumult. It came untethered and crashed around with reckless abandon— burning, shattering, consuming. He stopped seeing color and all became a swirling, howling, leaden gray desolation. But the pain hadn't arrived. The way the sea recedes before a tsunami, so every part of him receded. And then the pain struck.

Dill had never manifested the gift of tongues. The Holy Spirit had never moved in him that way, just as it had never permitted him to take up the deadly serpent. But on the floor of White County Hospital, he screamed in some anguished and alien language of bereavement. He was unaware that Lydia knelt beside him, gripping his arm like she would plummet off the Earth if she let go, doing the same.

• • •

His mother's tone was sharp when he finally walked in. "Where were you?" But when she saw his eyes, his face, her tone became guarded concern. "Dillard? What's the matter?"

He already loathed the words, and he hadn't actually spoken them aloud to anybody. As if they were some terrible incantation that made it more real. They felt like thorns on his tongue. "Travis is dead."

"You don't mean your friend Travis do you? Bohannon?"

He sat and put his head in his hands. He stared at the kitchen table. Numb. "Yes."

Dill's mom gasped and covered her mouth with her hand. "Sweet merciful Jesus," she whispered. "Poor Anne Marie. What happened?"

Dill shook his head.

"Was . . . he saved?"

Dill expected the question and still had to think about how exactly to answer. "He had his salvation."

30

Lydia

"I have news," Lydia said as Dill climbed her porch steps. "Let's sit down."

Lydia's porch swing creaked as they swung slowly. "They caught the guys who did it," Lydia said. "My dad heard about it from one of his patients who works for the sheriff's department."

"Are you serious?" Dill asked.

"Yes."

"It's only been three days."

"Yeah. Seems like longer."

"I know."

"Do they know what happened?" Dill asked.

"Two asshole idiot meth heads were at a party in Cookeville. They wanted to score some meth, but they didn't have money. One of them saw Travis selling firewood when he went to visit his grandma earlier. So he went *'I've got an idea where we can get some quick cash.'*"

"But why did they shoot him?"

"When they caught the guys, it turned out they barely knew each other. They'd met that night. They didn't even know each other's last names. So the one who didn't do the shooting immediately snitched on the one who did. He said that as they were driving away, the shooter guy said that he shot Travis because he thought Travis was grabbing for a stick or a baseball bat."

"The staff."

"Yeah," Lydia said. "They killed our friend for one hundred and twenty-three dollars." Even saying the words wounded her. *They killed our friend.* The phrase was a bright, sharp pang, ringing through the white noise humming in her brain.

"I hope they burn in hell. Forever."

"Me too. And I hope they do it with a case of poison ivy on the inside of their skin." Lydia knew she could muster contempt for people she despised. But she surprised even herself with how much she wanted misfortune to befall Travis's killers.

It was unseasonably warm for February. Birds were singing that they usually didn't hear until later in the spring. Lydia wore a simple black dress. Dill wore a cheap black suit that had belonged to his father. It fit him poorly, but not as poorly as it would have had Lydia not made some hasty alterations. They swung for a while without speaking. They sat with their legs touching, as if to remind each other that they were there.

"I haven't been sleeping," Dill said. Not that he needed to say it. His face showed more than he could ever reveal in words.

"Me neither. Maybe ten hours in the last three days." Not that she needed to say it either.

"Every time I start to drift off to sleep, I remember. And it jerks me awake."

"The few times I have been able to sleep, there's about ten seconds when I first wake up that I don't remember. Then I remember. So I guess I've spent maybe forty seconds not thinking about it."

"I can't see myself ever feeling completely right again. The way I did before."

"Me neither." Lydia sighed and looked at her phone. "We should probably go."

"I really don't want to."

"Me neither."

"I mean, I want to be there for him. I just don't want to be going to a funeral for Travis."

"I know."

They got up and began walking. The funeral home was barely two blocks away. As they walked, Lydia worried about what would become of Dill. As soon as the numbness wore off, that's what would replace it—concern. Guilt over leaving Dill behind. Alone. Without a plan. Without backup. Without direction. Lost. Adrift.

When they arrived at the funeral home, they stood

outside for a moment, gathering their strength to go inside. "Let's wait until my mom and dad get here," Lydia said.

While they waited, a short, red-haired girl about their age in a black velvet dress arrived alone. She was crying.

Dill leaned in close to Lydia. "I think that's Amelia. Travis showed me a picture of her one night while he was staying with me."

"Travis was staying with you?"

"Yeah. I guess it's safe to tell you now. His dad beat him up the night he met G. M. Pennington and kicked him out. He tried to rip up his book, but Travis fought for it and won. He didn't want you to know because he was afraid you'd call the cops on his dad."

Lydia's face took on a grim cast. "He was right. I would have."

"We should say something to her in case it is Amelia. Travis was pretty crazy about her."

They approached her awkwardly.

"Are you Amelia?" Lydia asked.

Amelia looked surprised to be recognized. "Yeah . . . are you guys Lydia and Dill?"

"Yes," Lydia said. "Nice to meet you. We heard good things. How did you know to come?"

"The police got in touch with me. I was one of the last people he talked to before he died." Amelia wiped her eyes. "The funny thing is that I heard so much about you guys from Travis. And now I'm meeting you before meeting him." She paused. "I guess it's not really very funny. But you know what I mean."

"We do," Lydia said.

"We were supposed to meet up and read *Deathstorm* together. We were also going to go to the Renaissance festival. I guess we had a lot of plans."

"Travis and I were going to get a place together and be roommates after we graduated," Dill said.

"I was critiquing Travis's first story," Lydia said.

"You were the one who made it so that Travis could meet G. M. Pennington. He said that was the best night of his life. Will you send me that story Travis was working on?" Amelia asked.

"Of course."

They were silent for a moment as they thought about all that died with Travis.

Dr. and Mrs. Blankenship, dressed in black, walked up. Dr. Blankenship, looking uncharacteristically grim, kissed Lydia on the cheek and shook Dill's hand. Dill and Lydia introduced her parents to Amelia. Dr. Blankenship sighed and looked at his watch. "Well, I think the hour is upon us. Shall we?"

They went inside. The funeral home smelled of old hardwood, lemon furniture polish, and white lilies and gardenias. Hippie Joe was there. He and Travis weren't close, but he went to all students' funerals. A couple of Travis's shop teachers came. A few people Dill said he recognized from church. Then, to Lydia's considerable annoyance, there was a pack of classmates from Forrestville High, none of whom had ever known or cared about Travis particularly when he was alive, but in death saw a grand opportunity for drama and pathos.

Travis's father sat ashen-faced and stoic at the front of the room. He looked behind him, saw Lydia and Dill, and turned immediately back forward. *He knows we know.*

Travis's mother came up to Lydia, Dill, and Amelia. Lydia didn't think it was possible for anyone to look more ravaged over Travis's death than her and Dill, but Travis's mom did.

"Thank y'all so much for coming." Her voice cracked. "You were good friends to my Travis and he'd have wanted you here."

"We loved him," Dill said, tearful.

"Yes, we did," Lydia said.

"My mom sends her apologies that she couldn't come. She couldn't get off work," Dill said.

At the front of the room sat a plain pine casket. Inside lay what appeared to be a wax sculpture of Travis in a cheap blue suit—plastic and unreal somehow. They approached with trepidation.

"I love you, Travis," Dill whispered, tears pattering on Travis's lapel.

"Dill," Lydia said, tears streaming down her face. "Cover me. Hug me."

As Dill embraced her, Lydia pretended she was holding onto the casket for support. Then she reached in and tucked a tiny package into Travis's suit jacket, where it made a slight bulge.

Amelia followed behind them, weeping. She spent a long time looking at Travis's face.

Before taking their seats, a particularly elaborate and beautiful flower arrangement caught Lydia's eye. She read the card, which was from Gary M. Kozlowski:

Rest, O Knight, proud in victory, proud in death. Let your name evermore be a light to those who loved you. Let white flowers grow upon this place that you rest. Yours was a life well lived, and now you dine in the halls of the Elders at their eternal feast.

31

DILL

Dill and Lydia stood at Travis's grave gazing at the fresh brown dirt covering it, long after everyone else had gone home. The sky was incongruously, callously blue.

"He's got his signed page from G. M. Pennington and dragon necklace," Lydia said, not looking up.

"That's what you put in there with him? How did you get them?"

"I went to his mom. They released his personal stuff to her, and his signed copy of *Bloodfall* was with it. I cut the signed page out of the book and got his dragon necklace. The staff wouldn't have fit, or I would have put that in there too. But I've got it. I'm going to give it to you later to hold on to. I don't deserve to keep it because I gave him so much grief about it."

"We'll figure out the right thing to do with it. I wonder how Gary knew to send that card and flowers."

"I called his agent. I told her what happened and I told her to convey to Mr. Kozlowski how much what he did meant to Travis. That it was probably the best thing that ever happened in his life before he died."

"I wonder if that would have been Travis someday. A rich and famous writer, taking the time to meet with kids who were like him."

"If Trav ever became rich and famous, there's no question he would have. He gave me one of his stories to read on the day he died."

"Did you read it?"

"Yes."

"Was it—"

She laugh-cried. "It sucked."

Dill laugh-cried with her. "But he'd have gotten better, right? He planned to take writing classes."

"Of course he'd have gotten better. It was his first try. If he'd had forty more years, like Gary, he'd have been great."

They let themselves cry for a few minutes.

Lydia sighed and wiped her eyes. "He was brave."

"One of the bravest people I ever knew."

They stood there a moment or two longer. "Let's go somewhere," Lydia said. "Someplace that feels like being alive and together and happy."

• • •

The Column soaked up the warmth of the afternoon sun. Dill ran his fingers over what Travis had written—it seemed like years ago. *We leave so little behind.* They sat with their backs against it. Dill loosened his tie.

"You'd have learned more about Jesus than about Travis in that eulogy," Lydia said.

Travis and Dill's preacher had given the eulogy, and it was long on the light and the life and the resurrection and short on actual details about Travis's life.

"I guess to be fair, though, he didn't know Travis very well. And what do you say about someone who's only lived seventeen years?" Dill said.

"You can't really talk about all his grandkids, huh," Lydia said.

"Travis loved Bloodfall, Krystal burgers, and his staff, but he'd never kissed a girl."

"Travis never kissed a girl?"

"Did you ever hear him mention it? Who would he have kissed?"

"Yeah, good point. He was headed that way, though, it looked like."

"Not that you'd be able to say that much about me at my funeral," Dill said. *Hadn't kissed a girl either. Never worked up the courage to tell the girl he wanted to kiss how he felt about her. Didn't even like Krystal. Won a school talent competition. Recorded a few videos of his songs that were generally well received by the people who saw them online. Did laudable work at Floyd's Foods; rarely missed spots while mopping; was up for night manager. Had a couple of close friends. Maybe put his dad in prison, or at least his mom thought so. Did just so-so on the whole faith thing. The end.*

"I think lives are more than the sum of their parts," Lydia said. "I don't think it's fair to measure them in accomplishments. Especially not with Trav."

They listened to the river. Dill wondered if it existed before any humans had lived and died at its banks. He wondered if it sounded the same then. He wondered what it would sound like when the last human died. *Rivers have no memory; neither does the soil, or the air.*

"Where do you think he is?" Lydia asked quietly.

Dill pondered. "I want to say heaven. Truth is I'm not sure. I hope someplace better than this."

"When I think about it, sometimes I drive myself into a complete panic. Wondering if he's falling through space right now. Falling and falling and falling and it never ends. This empty black void, but he's aware. Of it. Of himself. He still has all of his memories."

"As long as he has his imagination."

"Yeah. I also wonder if heaven is maybe whatever you most wanted it to be. Maybe Muslims get up there and Allah's waiting for them. And they're like *'See? Right all along.'* Or Travis gets up there and he gets to drink mead out of a horn or something."

"I hope that's true," Dill said. "I have a hard time believing that all of Travis's memories—everything he loved, all that he was—don't exist anymore somewhere. Why would God make such a universe in someone and then destroy it?"

"Do you still believe in God?"

He fiddled with his shirt cuff before answering. "Yeah. But I think maybe he made all this and got in over his head a little. Like he can't keep track of all the bad stuff that happens or stop it." He reflected for a moment on what he'd said. "How about you?"

"I don't know. I want to. Sometimes I do. Sometimes I don't."

A humid gust of wind mussed their hair. "Do you ever wonder how many springtimes you have left?" Dill asked, brushing hair from his eyes. "We're seventeen now, so we get sixty-three more springtimes if we're lucky. Like that?"

"I hadn't. But I will now."

"I guess the answer is always one more, until it's zero more. And you never know when the answer will be zero more."

They watched a vulture turn lazy circles in the distance, floating on updrafts, gliding. "Nothing stops when we're gone," Lydia said. "The seasons don't stop. This river doesn't stop. Vultures will keep flying in circles. The lives of the people we love won't stop. Time keeps unspooling. Stories keep getting written."

"Lydia?"

She turned, tilting her head, seeking Dill's face. "Are you okay?"

He studied his feet. "I'm not sure. I'm numb right now. But I can feel the darkness coming. The way you can see a storm coming. I can hear voices in the darkness." He paused, gathering his strength. "I need to tell you something about myself."

He told her the story of the Serpent King. She clearly

made a great effort to remain neutral, which Dill appreciated, but her face betrayed her horror.

And now you know who I am. Now you've seen the tracks that have been laid for me. Maybe the force of my destiny is so great that Travis had to die to bring it into being. Run. Run from me the way people did from my grandpa, the Serpent King.

Lydia sat confounded and speechless for several minutes after he finished. "Just because grief ruined your grandfather doesn't mean it'll ruin you," she finally said. Dill detected the trace of uncertainty in her voice, much as she may have tried to mask it.

He put his face in his hands and wept. "It's in my blood. It's like each of my cells has this poison inside it, and the grief chemical from my brain dissolved whatever kept the poison bound up. So now it's starting to flow free and poison me. Like it did my grandpa and dad."

Lydia took Dill's hand and pulled it to her. "I want you to listen to me. They surrendered to their darkness. You don't have to, and I want you to promise me that you never will."

"I can't promise that."

"Promise me that if you ever feel like surrendering, you'll tell me." She put her hand on his cheek, turned his face to hers, and stared him dead in the eyes. "Dill, promise me."

"You're leaving. You won't be around."

Her eyes welled with tears, and they began streaming down her face and dropping onto the concrete. She pointed and spoke with greater resolve. "Dill, I will spend my life savings and charter a private jet if I have to. I will literally tie you up with duct tape and kidnap your ass and take you home with me. Now *promise me.*"

Dill took a deep, shuddering breath and turned his gaze away, but he said nothing.

"Dill?" She reached over and turned his face back to hers.

"I promise," he whispered finally. *I don't know if I can promise what I've just promised.*

"Say the words."

"I promise I will tell you if I feel like surrendering."

"At least promise me that before you consider surrender, not only will you tell me, but you'll at least try something completely unexpected with your life instead, since you'll have nothing to lose."

"What?"

"Anything. Go to college. Join the circus. Live naked in a tepee. Whatever. Just nothing involving snakes or poison, though."

"I promise."

· · ·

They sat their vigil like some sacrament. Until sundown and the blood-orange winter light of the dying day cast long shadows. Dill watched Lydia out of the corner of his eye. The breeze blew her hair across her face. She wore the sunset as a flaming crown. Young and beautiful and luminous and alive, keeping the darkness at bay if only for that brief moment.

32

lydia

When she arrived home, her dad was sitting on the couch, looking at a photo album. He still wore his suit and tie from the funeral. She sat down beside him and laid her head on his shoulder. He put his arm around her and kissed the top of her head.

"Are you looking at baby pictures of me?" she asked.

"Yes."

"Have you been doing this since the funeral?"

"With a break here and there. Are you okay, sweetie?"

"I miss him."

"I bet. Do you want to talk about it?"

"Not really. My heart hurts, Daddy." She wiped a tear from her cheek before it could reach her dad's shoulder.

"Mine does too. We're here for you if and when you feel

like talking." He drew Lydia closer to him and she buried her face in his chest. "We raised you here precisely so you'd never have to deal with something like seeing one of your friends get hurt. And then this happens. I'm an idiot. We should have moved right to the middle of Manhattan to raise you."

"Dad. You didn't know."

"We made the wrong trade-offs. We made the wrong choices. We tried. You need to know that. We tried to raise you the best we could. I'm sorry."

"I know that. If you hadn't raised me here, I'd never have gotten to know Travis at all. Like you said that time."

"I don't know what would happen if I ever lost you. It would destroy me."

"You won't."

"I want you to be careful in this world. My heart is wrapped up in you."

"I will."

After a long while, Lydia stood to go upstairs.

She hadn't made it more than a few feet when her dad called after her. "Lydia?"

She turned around.

"If I had bought all of Travis's wood that day, would he still be alive?" His voice sounded hollow and far away, like he was asking the question under great duress on behalf of someone who didn't want to know the answer.

"Are you asking me if you killed Travis?"

"Yes."

"No. I don't think you killed Travis. I think it was the two men who killed Travis who killed Travis. And I don't think you should absolve them even a little bit by accepting any responsibility."

He tried to smile, mostly without success. "Thank you," he said softly. He went back to looking at the photo album, and Lydia went upstairs.

• • •

She was sapped. She lay on her bed and stared up at the ceiling. Her phone buzzed.

Ugh, drama with Patrick. So over high school boys, Dahlia texted.

Lydia felt actual physical revulsion at the banality of Dahlia's problems in the great scope of things. Not that it was Dahlia's fault. Lydia realized she hadn't told her. Not telling anyone about Travis was just a reflex.

Can't talk right now. Lost a friend, she texted.

OMG, as in died?

Yes.

OMG, so sorry, love. You ok?

Don't know.

What happened?

Well, Dahlia, not that I ever mentioned him to you (or anyone else, really), Lydia thought, *but I had a friend named Travis Bohannon who sold firewood to make extra money to pay for writing classes and a new computer so he could write fantasy novels. And someone killed him for one hundred and twenty-three dollars.*

But he didn't dress right, so I was embarrassed by him. And that hurts on top of all of the pain of losing him. Then Lydia felt a compulsion.

Check Dollywould in a bit, she texted Dahlia.

She went to her desk and began typing. She balked for a moment. She knew she was venturing into the belly of the beast. But that's where she needed to go.

This is both a eulogy and a confession. But first, the eulogy.

I had a friend. His name was Travis Bohannon. A couple of days ago, while he was selling firewood, two men shot him and left him to die while stealing his money to buy drugs.

Travis was utterly comfortable in his own skin. He was who he was, and he was never afraid of what anyone would say or think. When the world wasn't big enough for him, he expanded it with the force of his imagination. He was one of the bravest people I ever knew. One of the kindest. One of the most generous. One of the most loyal. You probably didn't wake up this morning sensing that the world is poorer, but it is.

He deserves to be remembered. Please look at his face. Know that he lived and he was beautiful. And that I will miss him.

And now for my confession. I am a fraud. I pretend to be all of the things Travis was: comfortable in my own skin. Brave. The anonymity and disconnectedness of the Internet allows me to present that persona to you. But the reason you're only now finding out that I had a friend named Travis Bohannon is that I was a coward. Travis wasn't "cool" in the conventional sense. He didn't wear stylish clothes or listen to cool music. He loved fantasy novels. He wore a cheap dragon necklace and carried around a staff. I thought it would be bad for my blog if you knew about him. I thought it would make me seem less cool if you knew that he was my friend, so I kept him a secret. But no more. I would rather live authentically and take whatever consequences may come of it than live a lie. Travis, please forgive me. You deserved better.

She clenched her fists and wept. When she finished, she went through the photos of Travis from their school-shopping trip to Nashville. She found one of him gazing into the distance, leaning on his staff.

At the time, she thought he looked ridiculous. A child playing dress-up. As she posted it, she thought he appeared majestic. Noble. Kingly.

She completed the post and closed her computer. It wasn't that she was afraid of a bad reaction. She knew she'd get an outpouring of love and support. People would line up to offer absolution. And it was that mercy she feared most. She didn't feel worthy of it. She couldn't bear being told she'd done nothing wrong.

Deathstorm came out three weeks after Travis died, to nearly universal rave reviews. The *New York Times* said:

> G. M. Pennington faced a daunting task in tying to-gether the dozens of disparate threads in the Bloodfall series to bring things to a satisfying conclusion. With his 1,228-page opus, *Deathstorm,* he has succeeded in a manner that should satisfy even his most critical and de-manding fans. Epic in scope, violence, and imagination, *Deathstorm* is a new benchmark in the fantasy genre and cements forever G. M. Pennington's status as the Ameri-can Tolkien.

• • •

Dr. Blankenship hired a private grief counselor to come to their house to meet with Lydia and Dill. After one of their meetings, Lydia and Dill set out the few blocks to River-bank Books. It was warm, and the sickly sweet rot from winter's thaw and a coming storm perfumed the air.

"Are these meetings helping you?" Lydia asked. Dill looked gutted and spectral. Sleep-deprived. His eyes had retreated into his skull. He seemed much, much older than he was.

"A little bit. More than if we weren't having them, I guess."

They walked for a while in silence.

"Lydia?"

"Yeah?"

"Do you think I'm the reason Travis is dead? Like my name is so poisonous that bad stuff happens to anyone who gets close to it?"

"No, Dill. I do not think that. Not even a little bit. I take it you do?"

"Sometimes."

"I want you to stop, then. Right now."

They passed budding trees shading lush green lawns behind black wrought-iron fences. Crocuses, daffodils, pansies, and hyacinths sprouted from beds. Whirring, humming life everywhere.

Lydia tucked a lock of her hair behind her ear. "How's . . . the darkness?"

On cue, the faraway peal of thunder.

"You planned that," Dill said, with a faint smile.

Even that cheered her heart for a moment. "You overestimate my abilities, but only slightly. And you didn't answer my question."

"It's there."

"You remember your promise?"

"Yes."

They got to Riverbank and entered, the doorbell jangling. Mr. Burson didn't look up from his book as he stroked a cat.

"Welcome, welcome, make yourself at home, browse at your leisure. We're not a library, but feel free to pull up a chair and read as if we are."

Then he saw Lydia and Dill. His face fell. "Oh. Oh dear," he murmured, putting down his book. "I'm—I'm so sorry. I was devastated to hear of Travis's passing. He was a wonderful young man."

"Yes, he was," Lydia said.

"How could anyone do what those men did? To kill a boy over money." He stared off. His jowls quivered as he shook his head. "We are a fallen species, spitting on the gift of salvation. Humanity is irredeemable."

"We came to pick up Travis's special order of *Deathstorm*," Dill said.

"Yes. Yes, of course." Mr. Burson sounded hollow and distant. He got off his stool and waddled to his stock room. He returned a moment later, hefting the thick book. "I wish he'd gotten to read this. I don't have anyone left anymore to talk about Bloodfall with."

Lydia pulled her wallet out of her bag. Mr. Burson raised his hand. "Are you doing with this what I think you'll be doing?"

"Yes," Lydia said.

"Then take it. It's on me. I hate that I missed Travis's funeral. I was on a book-buying trip to Johnson City."

"That's sweet," Lydia said. "But Travis loved this store and would have wanted to support it. So please let him support it this last time."

Mr. Burson sat still for a moment, contemplating. "I suppose, then," he said finally.

They paid for the book and went to leave.

"I'm tired of many things," Mr. Burson said, fighting for composure. They turned. "I'm tired of watching children perish. I'm tired of watching the world grind up gentle people. I'm tired of outliving those I shouldn't be outliving. I've made books my life because they let me escape this world of cruelty and savagery. I needed to say that out loud to somebody other than my cats. Please take care of yourselves, my young friends."

"We will," Lydia said. *Or at least we'll try. The world sometimes has different ideas.* And they left.

Outside, Dill appeared even more wan and pale than usual under the blackening sky. Something about him seemed ethereal. As if he were disappearing right in front of her. Declining. Diminishing. Eroding. And she was watching it happen—bound and impotent.

• • •

They walked to the cemetery to leave Travis his book. The warm wind from the gathering storm blew white blossoms onto the road, where they lay, fallen and lovely.

33

DILL

The grief counselor suggested that he try to channel his grief through writing songs. So he tried. He sat on the couch, with an almost-blank page in front of him. The music felt buried in him. He strummed listlessly. The same chord over and over. He banged away in frustration, as though he could knock the music in him loose. As though he could disinter it by force.

One of his strings snapped with a scraping, rattling *sproink*. He hadn't changed them since the talent competition. He stared at the broken string blankly for a moment before tossing his guitar onto the couch beside him. He leaned back and stared out the window at the darkening twilit sky. He thought about texting Lydia but it seemed like too much work. *Plus, I guess I need to get used to her not being around on nights like this.*

Instead he sat and tried to visualize his life in a year. He tried to envision being happy or hopeful about anything. He tried to imagine feeling any color but muted gray. He did this for a while before he decided he might as well go to bed, where he at least stood a chance of not dreaming about anything.

As he stood, he saw a car pull up to his house. It was Travis's mom's Ford. He watched as Mrs. Bohannon got out and walked unsteadily up to the house, clutching her coat around her, looking from side to side.

Dill couldn't remember Mrs. Bohannon ever coming by. This was strange.

He turned on the porch light and opened the door before she had a chance to knock. She stood in the open doorway, her mouth slightly agape, as though Dill had robbed her of the last few seconds she needed to figure out what she'd say.

"Dill."

"Hey, Mrs. Bohannon. Do you . . . wanna come in?"

She smiled awkwardly. Unconvincingly. She looked like she was wearing a lot of makeup—more than usual—and her eyes were red. "Could I? Is your mom here?"

Dill stepped aside and motioned for her to enter. "She's still at work. She won't be home for a half hour or so. Did you want to see her?"

Mrs. Bohannon stepped inside and smoothed her hair as Dill closed the door behind her. "No—no, actually it was you I came to see."

"Oh. Okay. You wanna sit down?" Dill hurried to the couch and moved his guitar.

"Maybe just for a minute. I really can't stay long." She sat down and took a deep breath. "How are you, Dill?"

"I'm . . ." Dill started to say that he was okay. But he couldn't. There was something in Mrs. Bohannon's eyes that was too raw and wounded to lie to. "I'm not okay. I'm not good. I haven't been good for . . . since Travis."

Tears welled in her eyes. She gazed off while she blinked fast. She looked back at Dill. "Me neither. I just needed to talk to someone tonight who knew him. And I wanted to see how you were. And I wanted to thank you again for being such a good friend to him. I know he didn't have very many friends. Children are cruel to people who are different, and he was different. I'm rambling. I'm sorry."

"Don't be sorry." Dill began to choke up.

Mrs. Bohannon let out an involuntary sob and covered her mouth. "I did the best I could to be a good mother to him."

"I know. He said you were a good mother."

She bowed her head and covered her eyes with her hand while she gathered herself. When she lifted her head, mascara ran in inky streaks down her face. "One time—Travis must have been about six—we drove to visit my sister in Louisville. And we passed a shoe lying on the highway. Travis goes *'Mama, won't that shoe be lonely?'* He got himself so worked up about it, he started to cry. Well, of course Clint and Matt thought that was just the funniest thing they'd ever heard. They laughed and laughed. Not in an ugly way. Clint was nicer then. They just didn't understand. But that was my Travis. I have so many stories like that living in me." She pulled a tissue from her pocket and wiped her eyes.

"That sounds like Travis."

"I always thought Matt was the brave and strong one and Travis was the sweet and gentle one. In the end, it turned out that Travis was sweet, gentle, brave, and strong." She paused. "But they're both gone now. I'm not a mother anymore."

Dill and Mrs. Bohannon gazed at each other silently. Then they hugged for what seemed like an hour while they both cried some more.

Mrs. Bohannon took a deep breath and wiped her eyes. She glanced at her watch. "I'd better go. Thank you, Dill. For tonight. And for everything. I figure this is where Travis stayed for the time that—"

Dill nodded. "You're welcome." He walked her to the door.

Mrs. Bohannon started down the front walk. In the porch light, Dill noticed that her car was filled haphazardly with bags, clothes, and belongings. And he understood.

"Mrs. Bohannon?"

She turned, tears streaming down her face.

"I'm not going to see you again, am I?" he asked.

She shook her head.

"Then there's something you need." Dill went back inside, went to his room, and grabbed Travis's staff.

Mrs. Bohannon was still wiping away tears when he got back outside. Enough of her makeup had smeared away that he could see the bruises.

He handed her Travis's staff. She hefted it and smiled through her tears. She tried to thank him, but she couldn't speak. She touched his face and then put her hand over her heart.

"Good luck, Mrs. Bohannon."

"Thank you, Dill," she whispered. "Good luck to you too." She carefully laid the staff across the front passenger seat, got in, and drove away.

• • •

Dill lay awake that night, thinking about exits and escape from pain. He envied Mrs. Bohannon.

The next morning, Dill couldn't get out of bed. Not that he tried.

• • •

He heard the knock at his door, but he couldn't summon the energy to speak. A moment or two later, his mother pushed her way in.

"Dillard?"

"What?"

"Why aren't you up yet? You have school."

"I'm not going today."

"Are you sick?"

"I just don't feel like going."

"You should go."

"Why? What do you care? You didn't even want me to go this year." He rolled onto his side, facing away from her.

She came and sat on the edge of his bed. "No, I didn't. But you insisted. You committed. So I want you to honor your commitment. We honor commitments in this house. We're not rich but we have our word."

"Not today. Today's a bad day for honoring anything."

Her voice became uncharacteristically gentle. "Is this about Travis?"

Dill rolled onto his back to look up at her. "No, it's about my life. And Travis is part of that sad story. People leave me. It's what they do."

"Not Jesus. He's always with you. We're too blessed to be depressed."

Dill laughed bitterly. "Oh yeah. Blessed is the first thing that comes to mind when I think of our life."

"I know. We have trials. Don't think I haven't asked God, 'Why me?' But the answer is always the same. Why *not* me? Why should my life be free from pain and suffering when Christ suffered all things for us?"

"I'm glad that works for you."

"I'm worried about you, Dillard. More than I've ever been. I've never seen you like this, even when your father got taken from us."

Dill said nothing in response.

"Imagine how things'd be for us if I just decided not to get out of bed one day," his mother said.

"I wouldn't blame you. Maybe neither of us has much reason to get out of bed."

His mother was quiet for a moment. "I get out of bed every day because I never know where I'll meet with one of God's small graces. Maybe I'll be cleaning a room and find a dollar bill. Maybe I'll be at the gas station on a slow night, and I'll get to sit and be paid to watch the sun set. Or maybe I just won't hurt much that day. What a miracle each day is. To see the spirit of God move across the face of our lives like he did the waters in the darkness of creation."

"God's abandoned me."

"He hasn't. I promise."

"Today he has."

"Will you pray with me, Dillard?"

"No."

"Then I'll pray for both of us."

"You do that."

"Jesus knows our sorrows. He tasted them. He drank from the bitter cup."

"Then he knows already that I'm not getting out of bed today."

34

Lydia

Lydia sat in her car and tried calling Dill again. It was her fifth unsuccessful attempt. She shook her head and stared at Dill's ramshackle house, looking for movement inside. Nothing. His mother's car was gone. But the house didn't feel empty to her. She looked at her watch. School started in fifteen minutes.

Where are you, Dill? Somehow I doubt you decided to get up bright and early and walk to school.

She sighed, started her car, and went to put it in gear. Then she abruptly stopped.

Maybe another time. Maybe I'd just drive away. Catch up with Dill tomorrow. Maybe chew his ass out for making me come to his house for nothing. But these aren't normal times. You were oblivious while Travis's dad was knocking his front teeth out. You're not going to let Dill bleed to death or choke on his own vomit in there.

Her heart beating fast, she got out and walked quickly to Dill's front door. She knocked and listened for some sign of life. Nothing. She pounded again, louder. Still nothing. She turned and started to walk back to her car.

These aren't normal times. These aren't normal times.

Her heart pulsed. She steeled herself and turned back. She looked from side to side at the neighbors' unfortunate, decaying houses. It seemed unlikely that their inhabitants would care much if someone waltzed uninvited into the Early home.

She tried the loose, rattling doorknob. It turned and the front door creaked open. A puff of air smelling of mildewed carpet and stale bread hit her nostrils.

This is what despair smells like. She had never been inside Dill's house. He'd never invited her in. In fact, he'd always taken great pains to ensure that she never even saw inside. It was easy to understand why. It was worse than she imagined—not that she ever particularly enjoyed imagining how Dill lived.

"Dill?" she called. Her voice died, muffled in the closeness of Dill's sagging, dusty living room. She stepped inside, picking her way along in the gray light, as though the floor might collapse beneath her feet.

"Dill?" She looked into a spartan bedroom with a neatly made bed, a cross-stitch with a Bible verse above the bed, a Bible on the nightstand, and almost nothing else.

She turned to the closed door behind her, the floor creaking. She heard a buzzing in her ears. Her insides burned with adrenaline. She felt acid fear in the back of her throat. Cold panic rising.

She reached out, hesitated, and knocked softly. "Dill? Hey, dude. School. Dill?" Silence. She tried to sound casual and brave. "Hey, Dill, if you're in there cranking it, you better stop, because I'm coming in. And that would be very awkward for both of us." Silence.

Please. Please. Please. Just be okay in there. Please. You cannot die in this awful place.

She turned the doorknob and pushed. The door fell on its broken hinge and caught on the carpet. "Dill?" Lydia pushed a couple of times before she figured out that she needed to lift the door by the knob while pushing.

She looked around in the gloom. A bit of light crept in around the edges of the closed blinds, illuminating the shape in the bed. Dill lay shirtless and still, his back to the door. Lydia could see every bone in his back. He looked so small. Lydia's heart rate slowed a bit when she saw him breathe.

"Dill?" She slowly approached, catching herself as she almost tripped on one of Dill's boots. She sat on a corner of the bed beside him, reached out, and gingerly touched his shoulder. He felt warm. That was good.

"What," Dill said. His voice was stony and lackluster.

"I was worried about you. I *am* worried about you. You okay?"

Dill kept staring at the opposite wall. "Never better."

Lydia forced a laugh. "Ask a dumb question, right?"

"Yeah."

Lydia looked around the room as her eyes adjusted to the dark. Dill's few clothes—the ones she had helped pick out—lay strewn on the floor and hanging from half-open dresser drawers. A layer of wadded-up balls of paper, maybe torn from one of Dill's songwriting notebooks, covered the floor. His guitar leaned haphazardly in the corner, one of the strings broken and dangling.

Step one: get Dill to leave this room, because it's making me want to kill myself and I'm only moderately depressed.

Lydia touched his shoulder again and shook him slightly. "Hey. Hey. Let's go somewhere. Doesn't have to be school. Let's ditch and go watch trains or go to the Column or something."

"No."

"Let's go on a road trip somewhere. Where do you wanna go? Nashville? Atlanta? Let's go to Memphis and go see Graceland."

"No."

"Okay, you suggest something."

"Lay here."

"That's kind of a bummer of a party."

"Yeah, probably."

This isn't going anywhere. Lydia rested her hand on Dill's shoulder while she considered her next move.

"I saw Travis's mom last night," Dill said.

"How's she holding up?"

"Not good. She was leaving."

"Like . . . *leaving* leaving?"

"Yeah."

"But not with Travis's gross dad."

"Nope."

"Wow. Good for her. Did she say where she was going?"

"Nope. And I didn't ask. I sent Travis's staff with her."

"Good."

Another long silence while the house creaked and popped around them.

"I miss Travis too, Dill. Every day."

"It's not just about Travis."

"I know."

Dill rolled onto his back and stared up at Lydia. "Stay," he said softly.

"Okay, but I seriously think you'll feel better if you get out of bed and let me take you somewhere."

"That's not what I mean. I mean *stay*. Please."

She felt a fist grip her stomach as she understood. "Dill. I—"

"You're going to say you can't. But that's not true. You can. You just won't."

Not this. Not now. You promised. I mean, you didn't promise exactly this. But it was inherent in the promise. She looked him in the eyes. They were glassy and vacant. "I won't. I won't because I can't."

"You can do anything you want. You could stay."

"Dill, please don't. This is not fair. I'm not staying. *You* leave. Leave like me. Leave like Travis's mom."

"I—"

"Yeah, yeah, I know. You can't. But that's crap. You can. You just won't."

"I can't. I can't even get out of bed."

"Come with me. Come to New York. You can sleep on my couch. We'll find you a job. I'll hassle you about the Bible and give you guilt trips to make you feel at home."

"No." His voice had a bleak resolve to it.

"I'm not going to give up on you."

Dill rolled back onto his side. She grabbed his arm and gently tried to turn him back toward her. "Dill—"

He threw off her hand. "Just go," he whispered. "I want to be alone."

"You don't need to be alone right now."

"The hell I don't. I might as well get used to it. GO." Dill had never been so sharp with her before.

"No." She tried not to sound as frightened and helpless as she felt.

"Go!" he shouted. *"Leave me alone!"*

She stood, grabbed his arm, and spun him onto his back. She tried to will her voice not to quaver, but was mostly unsuccessful. She jabbed her index finger into his bare chest. "Okay. You know what? You're being shitty. You're being unfair and it sucks. And if you think I'm going to just let you drown and not try to do anything about it, you're dead wrong. So I'm going to let you wallow today, because sometimes people need to wallow, but believe me: I'm going to hold you to the promise you made me. And we're going to fix that broken string on your guitar. Got it?"

"Fine. Just go."

"You know how bad you hurt right now? I would feel that times a hundred—times a million if anything happened to you."

Dill didn't answer. He turned back on his side. Lydia stared down at him, pitching around for one last thing to say. Something that could fix everything. The perfect joke. The witty rejoinder. The insightful quip. And for once her mind was barren.

She turned and walked out. She stood for a second in the living room, clenching and unclenching her fists. Taking deep breaths, trying not to cry.

As she closed Dill's front door behind her, it felt like rolling a stone over the entrance of a tomb.

• • •

She lay on her bed in complete, leaden exhaustion. School was shitty. Everything was shitty. She was about to put on her favorite music for calming herself down—Dill's videos—when she remembered that all was not yet well there.

Lydia knew Dill hated texting because it was so cumbersome on his ancient flip phone. But she texted him anyway because the sound of his gray voice hurt her heart. *I've had the worst day and I need to know right now that at least you're ok or I'm going to scream and break things.*

A few seconds later. I'm ok I guess.

35

DILL

But he wasn't okay. Despite everything, the darkness encroached. Day by day, the poison spread, strangling him.

Sleeping didn't help. It never left him feeling rested. He had dreams of serpents. Visions of handling them, allowing them to twist around his arms and neck. Of wearing their skins and skulls and fangs; unkempt, bearded, and reeking of decay; a derelict hull. Of passing Lydia, home from college, on the street, where he stared at her with dead eyes but with no words between them.

Travis came to him in dreams, and they would make plans to live in a house together and have desks side by side and then he would wake up and for several seconds, he couldn't tell whether it had been a dream. He dreamed that Lydia announced she was staying and not abandoning him after all. And he'd wake up and he was a day closer to losing the only thing he had left.

Lydia looked at him with eyes that said she knew he was slipping away, disappearing before her like fog in the morning sun. And there was nothing she could do about it. And so he spent a lot of time alone. He wouldn't return Lydia's calls. Being around her—aware that the seconds were ticking away to her leaving too—made things worse. When they were together, she would take him to watch trains, but he couldn't bear their life and energy. He had no space for it.

His mom tried to reach him through scripture, by reminding him of Jesus's travails. It didn't work. And she didn't have the time to do much anyway.

Everything seemed muted and colorless. Every sound reached his ears as though through a thick wool blanket. He had no music in him. On the few occasions when he would sit to write, he ended up with a blank page in front of him. His fingers couldn't form chords on his guitar strings. His voice left him. Lydia would show him the mounting likes and views of his videos in an effort to break through, but it never worked.

Food had no flavor. All he could taste was the pervasive and consuming despair, like soot on his tongue. He stopped going to appointments with the grief counselor.

He walked through his days like an apparition. The act of living felt wrong and harsh and uncomfortable. Nails on a chalkboard. A machine running without oil. Gears grinding and gnashing on each other, breaking teeth, disintegrating. Burning up. Wearing out.

He would get up and go to school with Lydia, their rides mostly quiet, with Lydia trying to get him to talk. He would count the minutes until school let out, unable to focus or concentrate. He would go to work and perform his tasks in a somnolent haze. Then he would return home and go to sleep as soon as humanly possible, so that he wouldn't have to interact with his mother. She also knew she was losing him. He could see it on her face, and that was just one more thing that hurt. He knew she was praying for him and he didn't want to become one more unanswered prayer.

And most of all, there was the crushing weight of destiny. The ossifying conviction that he was living out some ancient and preordained plan, encoded in his blood, built into the architecture of his name. Something horrible and inevitable.

• • •

One day at the end of March, he woke up and wondered if he'd ever be happy again. It was a sunny day at least. The world was verdant, in contrast to the desolation inside him.

He went to Bertram Park to watch a train. He had to wait a long time. Then he walked alone to the Column and climbed up it. He wore his favorite clothes. Ones Lydia had picked out for him.

He sat with his back resting on his handwritten list of the things that he once loved. He closed his eyes and felt the sun on his face as he watched the light patterns behind his eyelids and thought about whether he had anything left to lose—if he had any reason left to stay. No.

Would Lydia miss him the way he'd miss her? Probably not. Would she at least forgive him for breaking his promise? He hoped so.

He wondered if he'd see Travis again. He hoped so.

He wondered if his parents would miss him. Maybe his paycheck, but probably not him.

He wondered how things might have turned out differently for him if he'd had more faith, a different name, or been born to different circumstances. He didn't know.

He wondered why it seemed like God had abandoned him. There was no answer to that question. Would God notice enough to be offended by what he was thinking about doing? He didn't care.

He looked down at the river and remembered the day of his baptism there.

• • •

He's eight years old and dressed in a white dress shirt and black dress slacks that are both too big for him. His father's told him that he's following in the footsteps of Jesus, who was baptized in the River Jordan by John the Baptist. And Dill's happy to be following Jesus, but even happier to have so pleased his father.

His father tells him that baptism symbolizes a death, burial, and rebirth as a disciple of Christ. That it will wash away his sins. And this sounds pretty good to Dill even though part of him realizes he hasn't had very much time to sin.

The congregants line the banks and sing "Amazing Grace" as Dill wades unsteadily into the river, sinking into its mucky bottom as he tries to reach where his father stands, smiling. The river writhes around his calves, knees, thighs, and then waist. It feels alive, like a snake.

His father takes his hand and holds him while he immerses him completely in the muddy water and quickly pulls him back up, dripping. Dill wipes the water from his face and the sound of applause from the riverbank becomes sharper as the water drains from his ears. His father hugs him. Dill wades back, singing "What a Friend We Have in Jesus" in his high, clear voice.

He feels cleansed. Like the river's flow has swept away his every burden and worry.

• • •

And as he gazed down, he longed for that feeling once more. He wondered if the turbid water gliding past could again carry away his burdens. Then he remembered the other time he had felt so free and clean. Standing on stage at the talent competition, looking into Lydia's eyes.

He waited for the indigo gradient of the sky as the sun went down, until the first star of the evening.

Then he stood, gathered his courage, and decided to end this life and take his chances on the next.

36

lydia

The knocking on the door grew more insistent.

"Hang on," Lydia called. "Just a second."

Knocking.

"Chill already, jeez," she called.

She got to the door and opened it, and her pulse quickened.

"Is everything okay?" she asked.

Dill stood on the doorstep. Tears streaked his face. "I'm here because I made you a promise. I need to leave and go to college or I'm going to die. I can't do it without your help."

She fell on him and embraced him harder than she ever had. She almost broke her glasses against his cheekbone. Her own tears of joy fell on his neck.

"Sweetie? Is everything okay here?" Dr. Blankenship said, coming to the door. "Dill?"

Lydia broke the hug and exhaled quickly, fanning herself with her hand while she composed herself. "Yes, everything's fine. Dad, I think we'll be pulling an all-nighter. Dill is going to college, and because his decision is coming a bit late in the game, we're in a hurry."

"You'll need coffee. The primo stuff. And lots of it," Dr. Blankenship said, starting for the kitchen.

"And Pizza Garden. With bacon and jalapeño cream cheese. Stat!"

"You hate Pizza Garden."

"I don't *love* Pizza Garden. There's a difference."

"What about Dill's mom? She probably frowns on all-nighters at girls' houses," Dr. Blankenship said.

"Correct," Dill said.

"And we can't mention college to her," Lydia said. "We need a solid lie."

"I'm officially required to tell you that I don't approve of lying to parents," Dr. Blankenship said.

"I'm officially required to tell you who cares and let's get cracking on that Pizza Garden," Lydia said.

"Touché."

"Okay. Lies," Lydia said. "You're not feeling well and you're going to sleep on our couch?"

"Not even close," Dill said. "We need to go full Bible . . . I'm reading the New Testament out loud and witnessing for Jesus to your whole family, and everyone is caught up in the Spirit, and you all keep demanding to hear more and more."

"She'll buy that?" Lydia asked, awestruck.

"Wanting to believe something is powerful." Dill smiled. A genuine one. The first Lydia had seen from him in weeks. Since before. They texted Dill's mom with the story. She was pleased. Besides the Jesus angle, she was probably happy to believe that Dill was excited about something again.

They spread out over Lydia's room. They kept her printer hot with college, student loan, and financial aid applications. Dill, fortunately and unfortunately, knew all of his family's relevant financial information, down to his mom's social security number.

"Dad?" Lydia called down at one point.

"Yes, sweetie?"

"Start writing Dill a letter of recommendation for college."

"Coming right up."

They worked through the night. They quickly determined that Dill would apply to Middle Tennessee State University, the University of Tennessee at Knoxville, and the University of Tennessee at Chattanooga. Middle Tennessee State was Dill's first choice, because of their music recording programs and Lydia's sense of where Dill might thrive. She Googled it and discovered that seventy percent of the MTSU student body were first-generation college students.

By dawn, Dill was ready to apply for college, complete with admission essay and financial aid documents. He and Lydia lay on her bed, side by side, staring at the ceiling, exhausted, quiet. Like marathoners who had just crossed the finish line.

"Dill?" A long pause. "Can I ask you something?"

Another prolonged silence. "Yes."

"How close did you come?"

He drew a deep breath and held it before releasing it. "Really, really close."

"What stopped you?"

"My promise. And remembering the talent competition."

She turned to him, lying on her right side, and put her hand on his cheek. "Thank you for keeping your promise. A world without you would break my heart."

He put his hand over hers and held it there for a while. Then he began slowly stroking her hand, running his fingers along hers.

37

DILL

He thought he could hear her heartbeat. Or maybe it was his own, thrumming in his ears. *Are you still afraid? Even now? Even as you listen to your own heart beating in death's shadow?* His hand moved more insistently on hers. She didn't move her hand from his face. He slowly slid his fingers between her long and delicate fingers. The way he'd wanted to for a very long time. His heartbeat grew louder in his ears.

38

lydia

Every part of her felt warm and liquid and flushed as Dill's guitar-callused fingertips stroked the webs of her fingers. She spread them to let his in between hers. *Whatever this is, I like it. However reckless, however unwise this is, I don't care. I'd rather lose him this way than any other way.* This was the most coherent translation of her incoherent thoughts. The wild delirium she felt might have been lack of sleep combined with too much coffee. But she didn't think so. She'd been sleep-deprived and overcaffeinated before, and it didn't make her desire her best friend's hands doing all over her body what they were currently doing to her hand.

39

DILL

The fingers intertwined and they clinched hands. *And here you thought that just deciding to keep living was the bravest thing you'd do this week.* He went to the secret vault where he kept his talent show feeling. He opened it for the second time in twenty-four hours. He hoped it would sustain him one more time.

With a quick motion, Dill turned onto his side and raised himself up on his left elbow, his face about a foot from Lydia's. They looked each other in the eyes. He could hear her breathe and then stop. For a second Dill feared she would start laughing. But she didn't. Instead, she parted her lips as if about to say something. But she didn't. He thought the most alive he could feel was in the moment after he'd done something incredibly brave. Turned out, he also felt pretty damn alive in the moment just before.

Dill discovered that there was another thing that came as naturally to him as making music.

40

lydia

Dillard Early's lips were on hers, and it was her first kiss just like it was his. But they acclimated quickly and after a few hesitant moments, the kissing really began. Face. Neck. Fingers. There was a lust and hunger to it that went even beyond sex. More primal and vital. The weight of years of longing for it.

It is a very bad idea to take this sort of plunge with your best friend two and a half months before you leave for New York City. It is a really good way to have both your hearts broken. It is a really good way to be distracted in your new life. It is.

It is.

It is.

It is.

. . .

"Lydia?" Mrs. Blankenship called out, thumping up the stairs.

Dill spun off Lydia like she was radioactive. They lay side by side, staring up at the ceiling, trying to catch their breath and stifling laughter.

Mrs. Blankenship appeared in the doorway, mug of coffee in hand, dressed for work. "Well. You kids had quite the busy night, didn't you?"

"And morning," Lydia said. She could feel Dill shaking next to her, trying desperately not to laugh. *Don't do it, Dill. Don't do it. Keep it together.*

Dill let out an involuntary snort from the back of his throat. He tried to cover it with a cough. And that did it. Gales of laughter. Floods. Lydia turned to Dill and buried her face in his arm.

Mrs. Blankenship studied them with a suspicious expression. "Ooooookay . . . I feel like I'm missing something."

"Nothing, Mom," Lydia said, trying to gather herself, her voice muffled in Dill's sleeve. "We were just laughing about a joke."

Mrs. Blankenship raised her eyebrows and leaned against the doorframe. "I like jokes. Tell me."

"Tell her, Lydia," Dill said, pushing Lydia to face her mom.

Lydia backhanded Dill in the chest and wiped away tears. She cleared her throat. "Okay, okay. All right. Okay. Knock knock." She and Dill both seized up again, giggling.

"Who's there?" Mrs. Blankenship took a sip of coffee.

"To."

"To who?"

"To *whom*." Lydia could barely finish the joke. She and Dill were in hysterics. Tears streamed down their faces and dripped on her bedcover. Lydia started hiccuping.

"Mmmhmmm," Mrs. Blankenship said. "Very, very funny, Lydia. But you know what? I think you two might need some sleep."

"Yeah," Lydia said. "We have definitely been having some trouble thinking straight this morning."

"All right. Have a good day, sweetie. Dill, you too. And congratulations on college. You made a smart choice. I'm excited for you."

"Thank you, ma'am. I've been making lots of good choices lately."

Mrs. Blankenship smiled and walked away. "Get some sleep. I'm serious," she called back over her shoulder.

• • •

Lydia waited for her mom's footsteps to fade and turned back to Dill. "We just made out on my bed."

"Yep."

"A genuine make-out sesh. Like a grass-fed, free-range, organic make-out sesh."

"A Grade A make-out sesh."

"I feel like I'm blabbing. Blah blah blah."

"No."

"But I'm not *not* blabbing." Lydia snuggled up to Dill.

He put his arm around her. "No. Or yes. I don't know. Whichever one means I don't mind. I'm too tired to think through a double negative."

"You were supposed to be witnessing for Jesus to me," Lydia murmured.

"That was the story."

"I feel like there's a really inappropriate joke in here somewhere."

"You'll think of it. I trust you."

Lydia turned, planted her elbows on Dill's chest, and rested her chin on her crossed arms. "So you know from now on, 'witnessing for Jesus' is going to be our euphemism for making out, right?" *From now on???*

"Yep."

"Just wanted to get that out of the way."

"Okay."

"So let's just review the last twenty-four hours. One, you did not kill yourself. Two, you applied for college. Three, we made out. Those are three, like, really good things."

"The only thing that would be better is if I became a famous musician too."

"Did I not tell you that every single one of your videos has over a hundred thousand views now?"

"Are you serious?"

"Dead serious."

"Wow."

"Yeah. You have it all, Dillard Early."

"Except like a TV and a dad who's not in prison."

"Touché. So what do we do now? Where do we go from here?"

"I don't know. I haven't thought that far ahead." Dill reached over and stroked her cheek.

"Should we make out some more?"

"Probably. Yes."

So they did.

"This complicates things," Lydia said when they were done.

"Our lives *were* pretty complicated."

"Yeah, but this further complicates our complicated lives."

"Yeah. I know."

41

DILL

There were rules, explicit and implicit. Mostly Lydia's.

Explicit: they kept things a secret. They didn't need hassling from Dill's mom or classmates. Also, it helped Lydia promote Dearly's music on her blog—so that she didn't look like she was plugging her own boyfriend. Closely related to this was a strict rule against public displays of affection. And referring to each other as boyfriend and girlfriend.

Implicit: no losing themselves too completely. They were still going their separate ways in a couple months. They didn't forget.

Dill began his long, slow climb out of the abyss. He had good days and bad days. He quit his job at Floyd's Foods and Dr. Blankenship hired him to work twenty hours a week filing and cleaning his office. He made more money (which mollified his mother), and better yet, all of Dr. Blankenship's employees, even the part-timers, were on the group health plan. Dill finally had health insurance and was able to see a real therapist and get on a good antidepressant medication. Those things helped a lot. His music started to come back, bit by bit. The good days began to outnumber the bad.

And then one warm day in late April, Dill came home from school to find an acceptance letter from MTSU. He called Lydia, who turned her car around and insisted they make an immediate random road trip to the MTSU campus so that Dill could see where he'd be studying.

Lydia queued up a mix for the drive. "So when are you going to tell your mom you got into college?"

"What day is the day before fall semester starts at MTSU? Then."

"I recommend doing so sooner, since, you know, she's your mom."

"We'll see."

Dill sang along with the music as they entered the city limits of Murfreesboro, with its strip malls and chain restaurants. It felt huge to him. They rolled down the windows and let the sun-scented wind buffet their faces. His heart beat with the richness of potential.

Lydia parked in a neighborhood near MTSU. Dill's pulse quickened as they walked the couple of blocks to campus.

The four-story brick-and-glass library loomed. He stared at it in awe. He had seen larger buildings, but never one that had any connection to his own life.

Lydia turned to him. "That alone would be the biggest building in Forrestville by a wide margin. You getting excited yet?"

"Yes. I can't believe how many people there are."

The campus bustled with activity. Young people were everywhere. They walked past three people sitting on a bench, speaking what sounded like Arabic. A girl with purple hair, talking to a boy with numerous facial piercings. Students on skateboards and riding bikes. Assemblies composed of wildly differing social groups held animated discussions. Of course, there were plenty of the sort of people who probably would have tormented Dill and Lydia at Forrestville High, but they didn't seem to enjoy any special status.

They passed two tattooed girls—one with a shaved head—strolling and holding hands. "There's a decent sign that college will be a lot different from Forrestville High," Lydia said.

"I couldn't be happier about that." He was trying to play it cool and not stare, but.

"You should see the look on your face. You look like a kid at Disneyland."

"I've never been on a college campus before."

"Seriously?"

"Seriously. It's amazing."

Lydia stopped walking and smacked her forehead. "Are you saying that I could have convinced you much sooner if only I'd dragged you out here?"

Dill half-smiled. "Maybe."

Lydia rolled her eyes. "Come on."

"Where are we going?"

She grabbed his wrist. "Campus bookstore. You need an MTSU hoodie as an I-got-into-college-and-will-be-escaping-the-oppressive-smallness-of-where-I-grew-up present."

After buying the hoodie, they passed a bulletin board covered with announcements for various activities. "Hey, Dill, check it out." Lydia pointed to a flyer for an open mic night at the student union. "I think you'll make a lot of friends fast here."

Dill pointed. "Here's one for a band that needs a guitarist."

Lydia took a picture of Dill standing in front of the bulletin board. "When you get here, don't wait around. Jump in. Start doing stuff and meeting people."

"That thought makes me nervous."

"Remember the talent competition? You've played in front of the shitlords of Forrestville High. Plus you finally put the moves on me. Nothing should make you nervous anymore."

"Good point."

They turned to leave. "I know what you're thinking," Lydia said. "You're whoever you say you are here. You get a new start. No baggage."

"But anyone who Googles my name will see a bunch of stuff about my dad."

"So? Cool people will get that you're not your father. You won't be living in a shitty small town anymore, where people try to make themselves feel better by making other people feel smaller."

"You think?"

"Of course I do. Don't get me wrong, there'll always be a few lame people who make your father's sins your sins. But for the most part? Clean slate."

They walked out of the bookstore and sat on a low brick wall, where Lydia snapped a selfie of the two of them. "I mean, you might even find people who think it's romantic. You can go 'Yeah, babe. I've had it rough. Dad in the state pen,'" Lydia said in a tough-guy voice. Dill laughed.

She thumbed around on her phone. "Okay . . . this way." She pointed. "Let's go see where the music recording nerds like future-you hang out."

They strolled the short distance to the mass communication building. It was dark and cool inside. Plaques, awards, and photos covered the walls. The sheer amount of glittering visual information overwhelmed Dill. Everywhere there were groups of the sort of people who probably weren't popular in high school. *My kind of people.*

"This place looks really fun, Dill. I'm actually a little jealous."

He gave her hand a quick squeeze, rules be damned. "You could probably get in here." *Worth a try.*

"Don't get carried away."

They explored the building before getting hungry. As they left to head toward the student union and grab a bite, they passed a pretty girl in sunglasses with shaggy blond hair, a nose ring, and sleeve tattoos. She sat cross-legged on a low brick wall with her flip-flops on the ground in front of her. She glanced up from her phone and made brief eye contact with Dill. She smiled, looked down, and smoothed her hair. Dill smiled back. Lydia saw the exchange. He might have imagined it, but he could have sworn that Lydia gave the girl a subtle "step off" look. *That's new. Never seen that before.*

Then the girl looked back up. "Hey, excuse me. Not to be a weirdo, but I recognize you."

"Oh, yeah, I run a—" Lydia started to say.

"Sorry, no, I meant you." The girl pointed at Dill. "Do you play music?"

A beat passed before Dill realized the girl was talking to him. "Uh . . . yeah."

"Okay, are you Dearly?"

"Yeah."

"So, one of my friends posted one of your videos the other day. It was awesome. You have an amazing voice." The girl smoothed her hair again, twisting a lock of it.

"Oh . . . wow. Thanks. Tell your friend thanks."

"So what are you doing here? Just hanging out?"

"Sort of, yeah. I'm going here next year."

"Awesome! I hope I see you around."

"Yeah, me too."

"Are you going to be playing shows around town?"

"I hadn't really thought about it."

The girl flipped her hair. "You should. My friends and I would totally come. Your video had a lot of good comments on it."

"Oh, right on—"

"Anyway," Lydia said loudly. "We better keep going on the tour. It was nice to meet you . . ."

"Marissa."

"Nice to meet you, Marissa. I'm Lydia, Dearly's manager. Say goodbye, Dearly."

"Bye."

Once they walked out of earshot of Marissa, Dill turned to Lydia, glowing. "That girl totally recognized me."

"Yeah, I noticed. I'm not surprised, dude. Your videos keep getting passed around. They have a *lot* of views. You're really good."

"Maybe when I get to college, that's all people will know about me—that I do music."

"Your life is going to be better in so many ways." Lydia stopped. "Speaking of, there's something else we need to talk about."

"Okay." Dill's heart abruptly switched from racing over being treated like a small celebrity to racing in its much more familiar "there's something we need to talk about" way.

Lydia pondered for a moment. "So, not that high school

taught you this—and don't get a big head—but you're weirdly handsome in this brooding, dark, intense way that a certain type of girl finds very intriguing. Plus, you sing and play guitar like the incarnation of Orpheus, as you just saw."

"Thanks, that's—"

"Hush. I'm not giving you compliments; I'm stating facts. And I wasn't finished. This 'certain type of girl' is often nuts. What I'm telling you is you'll have lots of opportunities to hook up with nutty girls in college, but you'll regret it."

Dill smirked. "Maybe I could have a special huge fly-swatter made for me for swatting all the crazy girls away."

Lydia grabbed his arm. "Dill, I'm serious."

"Okay." Lydia was usually emphatic in getting her way, but Dill had rarely seen her this emphatic. *Or territorial.*

"I hate the thought of you hooking up with anyone, nutty or otherwise." Lydia maintained her grip on Dill's arm and gave the stink eye to a guy who glanced over as he walked past.

Dill looked her in the eyes. "You can call yourself whatever you want. But I call myself your boyfriend. And as such, I don't intend to be hooking up with anyone. Nutty or otherwise. Okay?"

"Okay. Just FYI, I don't intend to hook up with any dumb, gross boys either."

"That makes me very happy."

"Or even nondumb, nongross boys."

"Good."

Lydia seemed immersed in thought for the rest of the walk to the student union. For as far as they could see, there were huge 1950s-era buildings surrounded by tall trees. The aroma of warm cut grass, woodchips, and grilling hamburgers hung in the air.

And then, out of nowhere, as if it were the most normal thing imaginable, Lydia reached out and took Dill's hand. And there they were, walking down the sidewalk, holding hands. In public.

"This is a blatant violation of the rules," Dill said.

Lydia was unruffled. "Yes, but so is Marissa hitting on you in front of your girlfriend, so I'm declaring a moratorium on the rules. MTSU is a lawless, anarchic no-man's-land."

Dill intertwined his fingers with hers. "If that's true, then there's no rule against me just kissing you right here, in front of everyone."

"I guess not."

"You said anything goes."

"I did."

"All right then."

"All right."

"I'm doing it." Dill abruptly stopped, pulling Lydia backward.

"Why are we still talking?"

"Okay." He drew her close, put his hand on her cheek, and kissed her. Long and slow. Like they were completely alone instead of in the middle of the sidewalk while students streamed around them, hurrying to class.

"Dearly's first performance at MTSU gets excellent reviews," Lydia murmured, with her eyes still closed.

"Oh yeah?" Dill's lips barely brushed hers.

"Yeah. Maybe we should repeat it for Marissa and her friends."

"I'm down. Let's go find her."

Lydia broke away and grabbed Dill's hand again, pulling him toward the student union, almost yanking him off-balance. "Let's grab some food. I'm starving. Come on, rock star."

They got sandwiches in the cavernous food court. Dill set down the bag with his new MTSU hoodie, surveyed the room, and felt something blooming inside him. Nobody could replace Travis. Nobody could replace Lydia. But at least he wasn't facing the crushing aloneness any more. Now his life had the sun and the soil to keep growing. He imagined long talks with Lydia in which they both discussed classes and new friends. That'd be a lot better than listening to Lydia go on about classes and new friends while he talked about what a great night they'd had at Floyd's. Without warning, a mixture of joy and melancholy and hope and nostalgia overwhelmed him. He fought back tears.

It was almost as though Lydia could read his mind. "Hey, Dill."

He coughed and cleared his throat. "Yeah?"

She patted the MTSU hoodie in the bag on the table. "You did it."

• • •

It was dark when they got back to Dill's house. His mom would be home in about an hour. Lydia leaned over her seat to kiss him goodnight.

"Hang on," Dill said. "Come in with me. I have something for you." He hadn't planned on this. It wasn't quite ready yet. But he'd realized that day that there was no better time for it.

Lydia followed Dill inside for the second time ever. Dill motioned for her to sit on his sagging, tragic sofa.

"Do you want me to turn on the lamp?" she asked.

"No. I like the dark." He went to his room and grabbed his guitar. He stood in front of Lydia, blushing. He hoped she couldn't see.

He quickly checked his tuning. "Um . . . okay. So, this is a song I wrote for you. It's called 'Lydia.'" He made one last tweak to his tuning. "I guess I could've just told you that the song was called 'Lydia' and you'd probably have figured out that I wrote it for you."

"Probably."

He played "Lydia" for her. It was a song that was somehow soaring and quiet at the same time—the way his heart felt when he was with her. He heard her start sniffling about thirty seconds in, and saw her take off her glasses. It was messy and imperfect. But he was never prouder of how it sounded.

"Anyway, I hope you like it," Dill said when he finished, still blushing. "I'm not doing a video of that one. That one's just for you. I mean if you want—"

But Lydia stood and cut him off with a kiss that felt like a summer storm.

42

lydia

When Lydia got home, her dad was playing his electric guitar (he wasn't faring well compared with the performance she'd just heard) while her mom sat on one of the porch rockers, reading, with a glass of wine.

"Hey," her mom said. "You're home late."

Lydia flopped down in the rocker next to her mom. "I took Dill to tour MTSU. He got in today."

Her mom set down her book on her thigh. "Really? That's wonderful. I gather that'll be healthy for Dill to get out of here."

"No kidding," Lydia said.

They rocked for a while, not saying much. Lydia sat cross-legged in the rocker. "So . . . out of curiosity, tell me more about how you and Dad ended up getting together."

She tried to sound nonchalant. *Just shooting the shit about something I've never once cared about. No big deal.*

Her mom gave her a canny squint. "Just curious, huh?"

Mental note: be more slick. Lydia refused eye contact. "Can't I be interested in the process that led to my existence?"

Her mom set down her wine glass. "Honey, I was born in the morning, but not yesterday morning."

"Fine. Busted. Good job," Lydia muttered.

"Hey, it didn't take a master detective."

The electric guitar fell silent. A few seconds later, her dad opened the front door and poked his head out. "There're my girls. What are—"

"In," Lydia commanded, pointing. "Back inside."

He gave Lydia a wounded look. "That's a nice way to—"

"In. Side."

"Denny, darling," her mom said gently. "Girl talk."

Her dad raised both hands in surrender and backtracked. "Okay, okay. I'm retreating. I'm making no sudden movements. Don't hurt me. Glad you made it home safe, Lyd."

Her mom waited until she was sure Lydia's dad was gone. "So? How long?"

Lydia picked at the chipped polish on her toes. "About a month. Since Dill's all-nighter applying to college."

"I knew it. You two thought you were being *so* sly with your knock-knock jokes."

"Well."

"You have some timing."

Lydia sighed. "No shit."

Her mother made a little sound of disgust. "Lydia. Come on with the language. At least try."

"Sorry. Anyway, back to the subject at hand. Yeah. Timing. Bad. I know," Lydia said. "It's not like we planned this. It just sorta seemed like the right thing to do. I mean, I don't regret it, but leaving was supposed to be easier than this. I don't know what to do."

Her mom picked up her glass of wine and took a sip. "What can you do? Enjoy your time together. Let it—whatever it is—be beautiful while you have it. Maybe you won't end up together forever and that's okay. But the heart wants what the heart wants. When it wants it."

"The heart sucks."

"He's your first boyfriend, isn't he?"

"Of course. Who else was I going to date here?"

They rocked for a while. "Dill's a good first boyfriend. He's liked you as more than a friend for a long time," her mom said.

"Really? How do you know?"

"Oh sweetie. It was plain as day. Did you really not know?"

"I had my suspicions I guess. But I knew I was leaving so I never really thought about it as a thing that could happen. I just . . . couldn't." Lydia slumped down in the rocker. "What if you'd known that you and Dad would be separated? Would you have jumped in anyway?"

"Of course. Life is short, sweetie. I'm sorry you've had to see that firsthand. You can't live with your heart locked up in a safe."

43

DILL

He was still ringing with the day's excitement when his mother arrived home. He had told himself that he would wait until closer to the start of school to tell her, but as he made dinner, he began to doubt his resolve.

He drained the spaghetti and put some on a plate. He spooned some of the canned sauce heating on a saucepan on the stove over it. He handed his mother the plate.

"Thanks. You seem to be in a good mood."

He served himself some spaghetti. "I am."

"I'm glad you're doing better lately," she said between bites. "The Lord hears prayers."

"Yeah, he does."

"How was work today?"

"Fine." A stab of guilt. *You have to tell her.*

"When do you—"

"No, wait. Hang on a sec, Mom. I didn't go to work today. There's something I need to tell you."

She put down her fork and fixed her exhausted eyes on him. The air grew still.

"I visited MTSU today with Lydia."

Her face hardened. "Why?"

Tell her you just did it for fun. Harmless fun. But then he saw himself standing on the stage at the talent competition. He saw himself kissing Lydia. And he knew he couldn't betray who he was now. He was more now. "Because I'm going there next year. I got in."

"We agreed you weren't going to do that." Her voice was soft, but not like a pillow. Like a pile of fine metal shavings or powdered glass.

"*You* agreed. I didn't. I just didn't *disagree*. But now I do. I'm going."

"We cannot afford this, Dillard. You will bankrupt us." She spoke slowly and carefully, like she was explaining to a toddler not to touch a hot stove.

"I got need-based financial aid. I'll get loans that I'm responsible for to take care of the rest. But I'm doing this."

She shook her head. "No."

"I'm not asking you for permission. I'm telling you because I love you. This is happening. Maybe someday I'll explain exactly why this needed to happen. But not now. Now all you need to know is that it's happening."

She breathed deeply, deliberately. The air rattled in her

throat. She looked away and closed her eyes as if praying. *Not as if. Of course she's praying. For what? The words to persuade me? The grace to accept my decision?*

She stood and pushed away her half-eaten plate of spaghetti, almost daintily. She turned and walked to her bedroom. She shut the door carefully, slowly. As if she knew Dill wished she would slam it.

Dill sat in the hush, listening to their clattering refrigerator. It felt like the moment between when he finished his song at the talent competition and the lukewarm applause that followed; like when he first kissed Lydia—like every time he kissed Lydia; when he knew he had done something painful, brave, and beautiful. *And if you're going to live, you might as well do painful, brave, and beautiful things.*

44

lydia

Lydia and Dill sat in their corner of the cafeteria, which was abuzz with talk about prom in a week, at the beginning of May. Nobody bothered them anymore. Not after Travis died. But whether that was the product of some sense of decency or their classmates simply having moved on after so long, Lydia couldn't say.

Dill had out his laptop and was reading up on which classes to take at MTSU next year. "So are we hanging out on prom night?" he asked while typing.

Lydia didn't look up from her Djuna Barnes novel. "Sorry, Dill, I'm going to senior prom in a yellow Hummer H2 limo with my hunky football player boyfriend. We'll have seven seconds of frenzied, grunting sex in the backseat. I'll get pregnant and we'll get married. He'll get a job selling used cars and—okay, this joke is starting to depress me."

Dill closed his computer. "No, seriously."

"Seriously. Sure." She snapped into a hummus-covered carrot, still not looking up.

"I think you should go to prom with me." He said it with his alluring new confidence.

She finally set down her book and gave Dill a coy eyebrow raise. "Oh you do?"

"Yes. And I have an idea of how we can make it not suck."

"I'm all ears."

He leaned in. "Pathetic Prom. We set out to intentionally have the most pathetic prom night imaginable."

Lydia let the idea sink in. "The kind that anyone who thinks about us would expect us to have."

"Exactly. We throw this high school a big middle finger." He extended his middle finger at the cafeteria for emphasis. No one noticed.

"The sort of thing that not only we'd have let Travis take his staff to, we'd have insisted on it."

"Exactly."

Lydia raised her hand for a high five. "I'm so mad I didn't think of this first."

• • •

Dill wore the suit he had worn to Travis's funeral (it wasn't like he had many to choose from). Lydia pulled up and honked. Dill jumped off his porch.

"Okay, I didn't get you a corsage, as you insisted," Dill said as he got in the car.

"Excellent," she said, handing him a dead rose and a

binder clip. "Clip this on my dress." She wore a gaudy, red-sequined, 1980s vintage prom dress.

Dill complied, and Lydia binder-clipped a dandelion to Dill's lapel.

"Wait," she said. "Hop out. We need lots of selfies. And by the way, you've gotten enough mileage out of my pretending not to know you on my blog. After your hundreds of thousands of video views, you'll be fine if people think I'm being nepotistic. So this is all going on the blog. Pretend you're having fun with me."

Dill laughed when he saw Lydia standing. She had gotten just her right leg and just her left arm spray tanned.

Lydia struck a pose. "They didn't want to do it at first. They finally caved after I paid for a whole-body spray tan."

She also had ridiculous, garish makeup caked on her face, and an elaborate, upswept hairdo. She had long, neon-pink fake nails.

"You look insane," Dill said.

"I was going for pageant contestant made over by a truck-stop prostitute. Or vice versa."

"Nailed it. You do actually look pretty, though."

Don't blush. "Oh shut up. Come stand over here."

They took a bunch of pictures, individually and together. As Lydia tweeted and Instagrammed them, Dill smiling in each one, she basked in her relief. *Dill is alive. He's happy. He has a future.*

"Okay, time for our Pathetic Prom dinner," Lydia said. "Which I will be paying for, to make things more pathetic."

"Nope. Sorry." Dill reached into his wallet and pulled out a crisp fifty-dollar bill.

"Is that from the talent competition?"

"Yep."

"Dude. Taking a girl out for a night on the town with your rock-star earnings is like the least pathetic thing ever."

"Guess I can't even get Pathetic Prom right; that's how pathetic I am," Dill said breezily.

They drove about a half hour to Cookeville. They listened to a positive affirmations self-help CD on the drive. Lydia found herself enjoying it unironically, such was the lightness of her mood. She also found herself unironically enjoying Dill's hungry glances at her. She might have thrown Dill a few longing glances herself.

"Where are we going?" Dill asked.

"Cracker Barrel."

"But I like Cracker Barrel."

"I know. I'm cheating a little here," Lydia said. "Technically, Krystal would be the most pathetic, followed closely by Waffle House. But remember? We're so pathetic that we can't even do Pathetic Prom right, so we're eating decent food." The mention of Krystal reminded Lydia of Travis. *It doesn't feel quite right without him.*

They drew stares as they walked in. Lydia flipped her hair and flounced past the gawkers. Their matronly server was unfazed both by their getups and the attention they drew.

"Don't y'all look nice all dressed up. Is it y'all's prom tonight?" she asked.

"Yes ma'am it is," Lydia said, with a markedly thicker Southern accent than normal. She trotted it out for special occasions.

Their server bent in close. "Well, I'll take great care of y'all on your special night."

Dill played the little peg game at the table while they waited for their Diet Sprites (the most pathetic of all beverages, according to Lydia). Dill was about to win the game when Lydia casually reached out and flicked it onto the floor, scattering the pegs.

"Sorry, Dill," Lydia said as Dill scrabbled around on the floor to gather the pegs. "Winning the Cracker Barrel peg game is *not* pathetic. It's a triumph of the human spirit. Come on. You invented this idea."

The server returned with their Diet Sprites. "Have y'all decided?"

"Yes," Lydia said. "I'll have a bowl of fried chicken livers; a stack of blueberry pancakes with a scoop of vanilla ice cream on top; and a piece of Double Chocolate Fudge Coca-Cola Cake, also with vanilla ice cream on top."

Dill started to speak. "And I'll have—"

"He'll have what I'm having."

The server looked from Dill to Lydia and back.

"I'll have what she's having," Dill said, with happy resignation.

The server gave Lydia an admiring look. "Yes, ma'am. Coming right up." She shuttled off.

"Look me in the eyes and tell me that isn't objectively the world's most pathetic meal I ordered us," Lydia said.

"What if you got a scoop of ice cream on the chicken livers?"

"Yeah, then we're entering postfood, performance art territory. Which is not pathetic. I appreciate the thought, but please, follow my lead tonight."

"This all was my idea."

"I don't care."

"Got it." He sipped his soda and pointed at one of the pictures hanging on the wall. "You ever think about how many pictures of dead people there are on the walls of Cracker Barrels?"

"I think you're supposed to say 'Crackers Barrel' if you want to be grammatically correct. What if when they hang your photo up at Cracker Barrel, your ghost has to forever haunt Cracker Barrel?"

"We should sneak a framed photo of Travis into a Cracker Barrel and hang it, just in case," Dill said. "I think Travis would enjoy haunting a Cracker Barrel."

He and Lydia laughed. She felt a sharp, fleeting twinge. "I miss Travis," she said. "I wish he were here."

Dill looked down and toyed with the peg game, suddenly less cheery. "He'd have had a lot of fun tonight. He would've asked Amelia."

"What do you think Travis would have thought of . . . our current situation?"

"He'd have approved. I know for a fact. We talked about

it. He tried to get me to make a move with you before he . . ." Dill's voice trailed off.

Tears flooded Lydia's eyes and began to fall. It wasn't only because of Travis. Yes, mainly Travis. But it was Dill too. Specifically, the impending lack of him. It was even a bit that there were no Crackers Barrel in New York City. *There's no way I could have played this night straight. I'm a mess even with the jokey premise.*

She reached out her hand. Dill took it. He'd started crying too, right as their server walked up with their food.

She eyed them with concern. "Are y'all okay here? Everything all right?"

"Yes ma'am," Lydia said, wiping at her eyes gingerly with her ring fingers, taking care not to poke herself with her fake nails. "It's that we both keep losing the peg game and we're emotionally fragile."

"Well, honey, I don't believe I've ever seen the game make someone this upset. Maybe y'all should just let it be for a little while if it's upsetting you, okay?"

Lydia sniffled and laughed.

"Here we are on prom night, crying at a Cracker Barrel in Cookeville, Tennessee. I'd say we're getting the hang of this Pathetic Prom thing," Dill said, after the server left.

Lydia wiped her nose with a tissue. "Let's get a quick selfie while it still looks like we've been crying."

45

DILL

"Good thing it's a nice night," Lydia said as they pulled into her driveway.

"I'm afraid to ask," Dill said.

Lydia gave him a mischievous grin—the one Dill had come to know all too well. "You won't need to ask. You'll find out."

She opened her front door. "Dad?" she called. "Bring the limo around."

"Sweetie," he called. "Are you sure about this?"

"Pathetic Prom."

He sighed.

"We need to head to the dance. Come on."

"Sweetie, look, I'll drive you. Having your dad drive you to prom is pretty pathetic. I'll wear a goofy outfit."

"As opposed to your many outfits that *aren't* goofy? I said bring the limo around."

Dr. Blankenship shook his head and disappeared around the corner. He returned, wheeling a creaking, rusty, thrift-store Huffy mountain bike.

"Oh man," Dill said, laughing. "I haven't ridden a bike since I was a little kid. I'm not sure if I remember how."

"They say it's like riding a bike," Lydia said.

"Be careful!" Dr. Blankenship called after them as they tottered away with Lydia perched on the crossbar.

• • •

Dill peeked down at Lydia as they rode. She watched the street with a blissful air. She turned and reached up to brush an errant shock of hair from his eyes. *I'm really glad I'm here, now, and not lying at the bottom of the Steerkiller River.*

They could hear a lawnmower somewhere. The herbaceous smell of cut grass mingled with lilac. The combination smelled like honey in the warm early May air.

"Will any part of you miss this?" Dill asked, as they turned onto Main Street and passed Riverbank Books, waving at Mr. Burson.

"What? Hanging out with you? Or"—she made a sweeping gesture at the town—"this?"

Dill mirrored her gesture as they approached Good News Coffee, the town square with the gazebo, and Forrestville's abandoned 1920s-era downtown theatre. "This. Of course you'll miss hanging out with me."

"Flatter yourself much?" Her tone turned wistful. "Yeah," she said softly. "I'll miss this. Now that I can see the light at the end of the tunnel, this town doesn't seem so bad anymore. Good News made a halfway decent Luke Latte. And New York City may have a lot of bookstores, but it doesn't have Riverbank. How about you?"

"Yeah. A little bit. I'll miss our trains and the Column." He allowed a contemplative moment to pass while he pedaled. "I thought I'd live my whole life and die in this town. I don't know how I existed like that."

Lydia adjusted her position. "We're gonna be college kids, Dill."

"Yeah. We are."

"Like with classes and stuff."

"We'll both have lots of college classes." The thought of school had never made him excited. But that was Forrestville High.

"We'll be able to talk about them. Or we could talk about literally anything else that's more interesting, which is probably everything."

They laughed.

Lydia leaned back into the hollow of Dill's body, warm and snug against his chest. Dill leaned down and kissed her on the spot between her ear and her jaw.

"We made it, Dill."

"Yeah," Dill said softly. "We made it." *If only we were making it in the same direction and the same place.*

And their twoness made him think of Travis again. *Lying*

alone under the ground, in the dark, while Lydia and I live and move forward and laugh. What tempered his guilt was the hunch that if Travis was watching them from some lofty vantage point, he was happy for them. *Travis would have wanted us to be doing exactly what we're doing.*

They rode on a bit farther before Dill spoke again. "This part would have been hard to do with Travis."

"Even if we had him pedal, and you sitting on the cross-bar with me sitting on your lap, we wouldn't have had room for the staff."

"We'd have broken the bike. I think Travis weighed more than both of us combined."

Lydia gazed into the distance. "You're going to make me cry again. I'll smear my mascara." She turned back to Dill. "Oh wait."

46

lydia

They pulled up to the school as a PT Cruiser limo was leaving, having deposited its passengers. Jasmine Karnes and her date, Hunter Henry, stood a little ahead of Dill and Lydia in line to get into the high school gymnasium. Jasmine turned, saw them standing there, and scowled at Lydia in particular. *You two are trodding roughshod on the most important night of my life,* her heavily made-up face said. She leaned in to Hunter and whispered something. Hunter turned, looked them up and down, and laughed, but in a way more for them to hear than as a manifestation of actual mirth.

"Hunter's laughing because Jasmine pointed out the inherent futility of human existence and illusion of consciousness, and the only way he could emotionally process these ideas was through the incongruous reaction of laughter," Lydia whispered to Dill.

They entered the darkened gym. A DJ played some generic pop hit from four months ago. They could hear the scornful whispers and muttering and feel the stares.

"How awesome does it feel that in a few short weeks, neither of us will see any of these people on a regular basis ever again?" Lydia said.

"*You* won't. Some might be going to MTSU."

"But they'll never achieve the same critical mass of awfulness ever again. Even at MTSU."

"True. It feels amazing. What also feels great is to not care at all anymore what any of these people think of me."

On cue, Tyson Reed and Madison Lucas walked by. "Oh Lydia, honey," Madison said, her voice dripping with mock concern, "I think they missed a spot or two on your spray tan."

Lydia laughed breezily. "*Did they?* That is the *last* time I order the 'Madison Lucas brain activity MRI' spray tan package."

"Always so clever," Madison said, sneering.

"Always so not," Lydia said.

Dill stepped between Madison and Lydia. "Hey, Madison, Tyson. Do you guys not get it? You can't hurt us anymore. You can't do anything to us. You can't take anything from us. You're nothing now."

Madison's expression was as though she'd just farted during a prayer. Tyson got up in Dill's face. "You're lucky it's prom, Dildo. Otherwise I'd beat your ass. I don't give a shit that your friend died and everyone feels sorry for you."

Dill didn't blink. He smiled. "You think you can cause me pain after what I've lived through? Go on. Hit me with your little fist." He stared down Tyson until Tyson once more blustered about how fortunate Dill was that it was prom, grabbed Madison's hand, and stomped away.

"Sorry about the whole no-college-wanting-you-to-play-football-for-them thing," Lydia called after them.

Lydia turned to Dill, put the back of her hand to her forehead, and pretended to swoon. "My knight in shining armor!"

"Wouldn't getting a black eye on prom night be pathetic?"

"Unquestionably."

The DJ played a slow song. Lydia took Dill's hand. "Come on, Sir Galahad. Being the only people dancing at prom is also pathetic."

She led him to the middle of the dance floor, where they stood alone, people staring and snickering. Dill put his (shaking) hands on Lydia's hips. "We should probably dance too close together, for patheticness's sake," she said. "We might as well do this right." She drew in nearer to him. Near enough to feel his warmth. To see his (beautiful) jawline out of the corner of her eye and not the stares. To hear his (fast) heartbeat and not the snickers.

While they danced, swaying like two trees in the wind, she realized she wasn't doing a very good job of feeling pathetic.

47

DILL

They rode home to Lydia's under the moon and stars. Lydia sat on the crossbar, leaning her shoulder against Dill's chest.

"The prom photographer guy seemed pretty unamused," Dill said.

"I could not conceivably care less," Lydia said. "The irony is that everyone acted more concerned with us mocking their precious rite of passage than with drunk driving or girls getting roofied."

"I had the time of my life."

Lydia turned, looked up at him, and smiled. "That was pretty badass when you stood up to Tyson, by the way. It was—dare I say—rather sexy."

Sexy, huh? Dill took one hand off the handlebars and

flexed his arm, mugging. "What can I say, babe? Tyson bought a ticket to the gun show."

Lydia snorted, grabbed his wrist, and pulled it back down to the handlebars. "You are an irredeemable dork. Fortunately for our relationship's continued viability, you suck at acting like a dumb bro."

They passed Riverbank Books. Dill tried to concentrate on the road, but the geometry of Lydia's neck distracted him.

"I'll miss this," Dill said. *That was the understatement of the century.*

"This town?" Lydia gestured back at the town square. "Or *this*?" She gestured at the two of them.

"This. Being together." He loved the way the words *being together* felt on his tongue, like nectar.

Lydia reached up and pinched his cheek. "Aw. Look who's getting the hang of this evening."

Dill pulled away. "Is that pathetic? To miss you?"

"Of course not. I'm just giving you shit." She rested her head back against Dill's chest.

The floral night breeze blew a lock of Lydia's disarrayed hair against Dill's lips. It tickled, but he made no move to brush it away. They arrived at Lydia's house.

When Lydia jumped off the bike, Dill took a quick look to make sure the coast was clear. Then he grabbed her by the waist and drew her to him. "There's one more thing I'll miss." And he kissed her. The way she kissed him back left him doubtless that the rules were once more on hold.

"Anyway," Dill said at last. "We better stop before your dad sees."

"He deserves to see his daughter making out with the preacher's kid as punishment for making me grow up in this hick town. But come on." Lydia motioned for Dill to follow her into the backyard. She kicked off her shoes and walked over to the outside faucet. "Now we enter the final phase of Pathetic Prom. While our classmates are getting zongered at the Holiday Inn in Cookeville and getting pregnant, you and I will be playing in the sprinkler and looking up at the stars until your curfew. Yes?"

She didn't wait for Dill's answer before she turned on the water and the sprinkler *chick-chick-chicked* around the lawn in a circle.

"Come on, Dill." She jumped in the sprinkler's path and squealed and giggled like a child as it soaked her.

Dill put his hand over his face, laughed, and shook his head. Lydia was already a dripping mess. What remained of her mascara ran down her face in inky streaks. Her hair had come loose and fallen out of its elaborate style. It dangled sodden around her face. Water droplets coated her glasses. She cackled and picked up the sprinkler, chasing Dill with it.

He tried to run. "No! Get away!" He slipped and skidded on the wet grass and Lydia pounced. She tackled him (he didn't fight that part too vigorously, especially when she lay on top of him for longer than necessary) and left him drenched. They ran and jumped through the sprinkler for several minutes, yelping and giggling.

Lydia's parents stepped out onto the back porch. Lydia's mom folded her arms. "Lydia, are you sure Dill thinks this is as funny as you do?"

He stood up, rivulets of water pooling at his feet, a colossal grass stain up the side of his suit. "Yes ma'am, I do. At least I think I do. I don't always get what's in Lydia's head."

Mrs. Blankenship sighed. "Welcome to the club."

"All right, kids, we'll leave some towels by the back door if you want to come inside later," Dr. Blankenship said. "We'll be up watching TV."

Lydia gave them a "now scoot" gesture, and they went inside. Lydia grabbed Dill's hand. "Okay. Stargazing time." She pulled Dill out to the center of the lawn and they flopped onto the wet grass, lying on their backs side by side.

For a couple of hours, they talked and laughed incessantly about nothing in particular while they dried slowly. After that, they fell quiet and gazed up into the boundless starlit expanse while the owls and crickets sang their night hymns all around them.

Then, Lydia nestled up close to Dill and laid her head where his chest met his arm. Every nerve in his body suddenly felt like a rush of wind in long grass.

"Okay, Dill," she murmured. "I lied. *This* is the final phase of Pathetic Prom. Instead of getting laid, your prom date is falling asleep on you."

Lydia's hair cascaded across his chest, forming tributaries and estuaries. Her breathing slowed and her head became heavy. *What will become of this? Of us? No, don't ask. Just accept this gift, this moment, after all that life has taken from you.* He felt aglow, like his blood was fluorescing. Like you could see his pulsing, humming heart through his skin.

After a while, she stirred with a purring sound and snuggled in even closer, resting her lips on Dill's neck. He could feel her warm breath. She laid her leg across Dill's leg.

She's it. She's everything. She's the standard by which I'll judge beauty for the rest of my life. I'll measure every touch to her breath on my skin. Every voice to her voice. Every mind to her mind. My measure of perfection. The name carved into me. If I could, I would lie with her under these stars until my heart burst.

He slowly reached over to her hair with his free hand, and caressed it. He gently ran his hand along its course. And again.

Again.

Again.

If he could be still enough, all the world's motions would cease. The orbit of the Earth. The dance of tides. The march of rivers to sea. Blood in veins. And all would become nothing but her perfect and temporary thereness.

Hold this moment. Keep it. Until the next train whistle in the distance pierces the stillness.

48

lydia

The early June dusk was soft and green, not yet with the oppressive heat of summer. New grass grew on Travis's grave. They sat beside it and searched for what to say to each other and to Travis. Lydia no longer felt like she was abandoning Dill, but she did feel like she was abandoning Travis. Which was somehow worse at the same time as it was more irrational.

"How long is your drive?" Dill asked, picking at blades of grass.

"I think about ten hours," Lydia said, smacking a mosquito on her calf. She loathed making small talk in general—a thousand times more when it was with someone as important to her as Dill. But she understood why they had to do it.

"Are you doing it in one day?" Dill's demeanor conveyed that he wasn't enjoying making small talk any more than she was, but he also wasn't ready to fill the silence with anything else.

"Yeah."

"Damn. When are you leaving tomorrow morning?"

She sighed. "Probably around six."

"Ouch. And then your internship starts—" Dill carefully plucked a ladybug from his arm and held it in his palm so that it could fly away.

"Next week. June ninth."

"I wish you didn't have to leave so early."

"Me too, but I want to have some time to explore and get settled in before I start my internship."

"Are you nervous to be working for the *Chic* lady? You said she was scary."

Lydia laughed ruefully. "Yes, and she is."

A pensive stillness passed while they listened to the hushed chirr of insects in the trees that surrounded the cemetery like an embrace. The ten days or so they'd had since school ended flew by in a blur of work, watching trains, sitting at the Column, random road trips (Graceland was Dill's favorite), and lots and lots of lying under the stars and kissing.

Dill leaned back onto his hands. "Won't it be hard to park Al Gore in New York City?"

"Yeah. I'm selling him to one of Dahlia's friends from school. We're meeting in the city and he's driving Al to

Stanford." She felt a fleeting ache. *Oh come on. You're not seriously getting sentimental about inanimate objects now too, are you? You were not supposed to be this big of a mess. That was not in the plan.*

"You're selling Al Gore? I'll miss him." The wisp of betrayal in Dill's tone told her that he was in the same mindset. *Irrationality loves company.*

Lydia ran her hand along the top of the grass. "Me too."

"I hope you kept the bike from prom so I can give you rides when you come back to town."

"I bet I can convince my dad to let us use his car."

"Yeah, but the bike is pretty fun."

Yes it is, Dill. Yes it is.

Fireflies flickered among the headstones in the leaf-green failing light. The cemetery smelled of clean dirt and sun-washed stone.

"We should have planned some ceremony," Lydia finally said.

"Planning means we would have had to think about this, and I didn't want to think about this."

"Me neither."

Dill gazed at the ground. Lydia pretended to do the same, but instead peered at Dill's profile out of the corner of her eye, the glowing waltz of fireflies around his head. Her heart ached with the knowledge that every time it beat, it was counting away another second to her leaving and not seeing him anymore.

"Dill?" She put her hand on his knee.

He looked up. "Yeah?"

"I hope we're always a part of each other's lives, no matter where we go or what we do." *Let no one accuse me of not cheesing this up,* she thought with an inward cringe. *But I guess New York City's going to give me an abundance of opportunities to be cool and unsentimental.*

Dill scooted closer to Lydia and put his arm around her. "I'm committed if you are. You're going the farthest in life."

She rested her head on his shoulder. "Don't count on that. I think the future has a lot of great surprises for you."

"I hope."

"Do you regret us—" Lydia started to ask, in a hesitant murmur.

"No. Whatever you were about to ask. I don't regret anything about us."

She thought about the things she would miss. She loved the way he cocked his head when he talked to her, to keep his hair out of his eyes; the way he sat, cross-legged, leaning on his hands. He didn't always look at her when he talked, but when it was important, he looked her right in the eyes, and it made her tingle. And then there were his eyes; incandescent and dark all at the same time. Lightning illuminating a thunderhead.

It was strange to think about him existing beyond

her view. She wondered if he had a completely different vocabulary of private gestures. Perhaps he held his head at a different angle. Sat differently. Perhaps his eyes contained a different luminosity and intelligence.

Lydia gave a mournful sigh. "I guess I should say goodbye to Travis."

She and Dill stood by the grave. Dill put his hand on Lydia's shoulder. She began to say something, but stopped. Again. And stopped.

"Travis, I miss you." Her voice quavered. She took a deep breath. "And I'm glad that I got to have you as a friend. I talked about you at graduation in my salutatorian speech. About a month ago, Dill and I went to prom together, and we wished you were there. I hope that you're happy wherever you are. And you maybe have a cool cloak and a sweet sword or whatever. I'm sorry I don't read enough fantasy to even know what sort of stuff I should wish you have. I did finish *Bloodfall*, though, and it was really good. I wish we could talk about it. I'm sorry I gave you so much grief over your staff. I'm sorry I didn't tell more people sooner that we were friends. I'm sorry I didn't know how bad things were for you at home. And I'm sorry I don't have something more clever or profound to say."

She wiped away tears and turned and hugged Dill. "I feel guilty leaving him behind."

"Me too."

• • •

They went to the Column, where they stole a few more
quiet minutes together, listening to the river wear its way
deeper into the Earth, the way people wear grooves into
each other's hearts.

49

DILL

Lydia let him pick the music on the way home. He picked "Love Will Tear Us Apart" by Joy Division, because he remembered that it was her favorite song. They sang along loudly. In Dill's case, he sang because it felt like a more acceptable way of screaming in agony, which was what he wanted to do. The effort of trying to keep himself together was making him sick to his stomach.

They pulled up at Dill's house.

"Well," Lydia said, her eyes welling up. "I guess this is your stop."

"Yeah," Dill said, clearing his throat. "I guess it is."

He opened the door and got out. He went around the front of the car to Lydia's side and opened her door. She unbuckled her seat belt, jumped out, and hugged him. Tight. Tighter than she ever had before.

"I'll really, really, really miss you," Lydia said, and loosed the floodgates.

"I'll really, really, really, really miss you," Dill said, and broke down too.

They hugged that way for minutes, rocking gently, their tears mixing and falling, before either spoke again.

"Remember this, Dillard Early," Lydia whispered, her voice cracking. "You are you and you are magnificent and brilliant and talented. You're not your grandfather. You're not your father. Their serpents are not your serpents. Their poison is not your poison. Their darkness is not your darkness. Not even their name is your name."

Dill buried his face in her hair. He breathed in its smell—pear, vanilla, sandalwood—while he gathered his courage. *At least send her off with every secret treasure of your heart. Haven't you learned by now that you're completely naked? You've danced with death. What do you have left to fear? You can survive anything. Serpents. Deadly poison. This.*

"I love you," he whispered in her ear.

Lydia hugged him tighter, pressing her tear-stained cheek to his, but said nothing for several moments. She started to say something, but caught herself. And then she stood on her tiptoes, put both hands on the sides of Dill's face, and pulled him down to her.

50

lydia

She could taste her tears on Dill's lips. And she briefly remembered her trip to Nantucket at the end of summer last year and the salt of the ocean on her tongue. That was the taste on her lips at that moment, but like the end of a summer that had lasted her entire life.

A stillness came over her, a surrender, like she was falling from a great height but would never hit the ground. Like she was drowning and didn't mind. His trembling hands ran through her hair and stroked her back and neck. And they felt like fire coursing through her.

And.

And.

51

DILL

And.

After everything, this might be the thing that finally destroys you. But he didn't care. He wanted to be destroyed this way. He welcomed it. *But you still have to let her go. You have to watch her leave.*

They broke the kiss at last, but immediately locked in another ravenous embrace. He had no idea how much time had passed. Hours. Days. Seconds. His hand returned to the back of her head, and he stroked her hair one last time. "You saved me."

She put her lips to his ear. "You saved yourself." She had no voice left. He could barely hear her over the crickets.

Because he couldn't stand the torment of prolonging things, he broke their embrace. Then he remembered. He told her to wait and ran into his house, came back out with a CD, and handed it to her. "I recorded some of my songs for you. In case you feel like listening to something different on your drive. The song 'Lydia' is on it."

She clutched the CD to her heart. They gazed at each other for a second, wiping away tears. And because there was nothing left to say and everything left to say, they kissed one more time.

"Call me when you get there, okay? So I know you got there safe?" Dill asked, his words catching in his throat.

She nodded.

She got in her car. He returned her plaintive wave, stood in the street, and watched her taillights fade and disappear.

He walked up his steps, sat on his disintegrating stoop, and bowed his head as if in prayer. Through the blur of tears, he caught a glimpse of the church sign. WHEN JESUS COMES INTO A LIFE, HE CHANGES EVERYTHING.

After a while he opened the door, and started to go inside. But he couldn't. Only the expanse of the indifferent, infinite starry sky could contain his ferocious, surging hurt.

52

Lydia

She thought she'd done pretty well for herself the night before, not-completely-losing-her-shit-wise. All things considered, she was doing okay—riding a wave of excitement—as she pulled into the truck stop outside of Roanoke, Virginia. While she gassed up, she made dinner plans with Dahlia and Chloe (something low-key and out of the way, since Chloe tried to avoid attention; something that would accommodate Dahlia's gluten-free diet; something ethnic because Lydia was from Forrestville). She was documenting the trip for her Twitter and Instagram followers, so she took a few pictures while she waited.

She felt sleepy and went inside to get some strong trucker coffee. The truck stop was a wonderland of Southern kitsch. T-shirts emblazoned with stern eagles in Confederate uniforms and "American by Birth, Southern by the Grace of God." Aprons that said "Pitmaster" above a crude cartoon of an anthropomorphic pig, barbecuing (presumably) another pig. Tank tops with images of the Southern states as cast-iron skillets. She grabbed a Tennessee one. She took picture after picture.

Then, the ultimate prize: a porcelain cherub holding a Confederate flag with "Heritage Not, Hate" painted beneath. She laughed, took a picture, texted it to Dill, and then tweeted it to her 187,564 followers with the caption *Racists: not so good, with the, commas.*

She had a sudden memory. On their last school shopping trip to Nashville, Dill had pointed out a billboard that said VISIT DELLA TAZZA VINEYARD, THE FINEST WINERY IN MIDDLE TENNESSEE. He had a knack for pointing out things she'd find hilarious.

"Dahling, fetch my finest NASCAR jacket and airbrushed Confederate flag T-shirt. I've a hankering for a glass of fine Tennessee wine," she'd said.

And then it hit her. Like, well, a truck. The realization that the one person she most wanted to show the rebel flag cherub to, and laugh about it with, wasn't there. And wouldn't be there for most of the other things she'd ever see and do in her life. And with it, the realization that she already missed a life she was never supposed to miss and missed Dill a thousand times more deeply than she ever imagined.

She crumbled. Right in the middle of the aisle, the heritage-but-not-hate-loving cherubs observing her impassively with their lifeless, alabaster eyes. A good, ugly, makeup-smearing cry, with tears and snot running down her face. *And this is why I thought it would be a bad idea to try to listen to your CD while I drove. If you could see me now, Dill. If you could see me now.*

She managed to pull herself together after a minute or two and took her coffee and tank top to the front. The cashier was a careworn woman in her sixties.

"Now honey," she said. "Everything all right?"

Lydia nodded, but on came the faucet again. She shook her head. "I wish I'd told someone before I left that I love him too. That's all."

"Well, honey, even if you didn't tell him, did you show him?"

"I hope so," Lydia said, her voice shuddering and breaking.

"Then I think he knows. We ladies ain't so great at keeping things like that hid." The cashier gave an empathetic half-smile and reached under the counter. She came up with a teddy bear as careworn as her.

"This is a truck stop, honey, so we're no stranger to people missing people and people having regrets over stuff they wish they'd said before leaving. You need a hug with Chester here?"

Lydia reached out and accepted Chester the bear. She hugged him. He smelled like cigarettes and cheap trucker cologne. *And why shouldn't I begin my glamorous new life as a big city girl by crying in a truck stop, surrounded by racist cherubs, while hugging a stinky teddy bear.* Chester wasn't who she wished she were hugging, but he would have to do.

53

DILL

Dill stood as the guards led his father in. He caught Dill's eye with his ardent stare, but Dill met it and didn't look away. His father pulled out a chair roughly and started to sit, but he saw that Dill didn't intend to sit, so he stood. They looked at each other for what felt to Dill like a long time.

"So," his father said. "You must know that I know." His voice had a viperous calm.

"I do."

"Explain yourself."

Dill commanded his voice not to waver, and it didn't. "I'm going to college. I'm going to have a better life than this. That's all there is to explain."

"You are *abandoning* your mother." His father spat the word like it was profane.

"You're one to talk."

His father's poisonous calm began to vanish. "No. I did not abandon you and your mother. I was taken from you. You are abandoning us by choice, the way your grandfather abandoned me."

"No, I'm not. I almost abandoned you that way. But I didn't." Dill could tell from the look that passed over his father's face that he had broken through, just for a second.

And then the Pentecostal fire returned. "You flaunt the commandments of God by dishonoring your father and mother in this way. There is a place of eternal torment set aside for those who flaunt God's laws."

"I honored you enough to come tell you face to face. That's more honor than you deserve."

Dill's father leaned forward, hands on the table, his eyes boring into Dill. A look of surrender passed across his face. Dill knew his father must have had that look on prior occasions, but he had never seen it before. "This is the doing of the whore, isn't it? Your little Delilah. *Lydia.* Your mother told me about her. How she spoke in your ear."

Dill felt a swell of white-hot rage; it tasted like iron in his mouth. And then he understood. *Your rage is what he wants. Deny him it. Whatever he wants you to be—whomever he wants you to be—deny him it.*

"You don't know what you're talking about," Dill said quietly. "You have no clue. And I feel sorry for you. I hated you. When I thought I'd become you, I hated you so much. I was less afraid to die than to become you. But now that I know I'll never be you, I can finally feel sorry for you." And with that, Dill turned and walked away.

"You will fail," his father called after him. "You will fail and fall. Dillard? Dillard?"

But Dill did not look back.

• • •

Outside, Dr. Blankenship was waiting in the parking lot, the back of his Prius full of purchases from Trader Joe's.

"Hey, Dill," he said as Dill got in. "You ready to go?"

Dill nodded and smiled. "Yeah. Hey, Dr. Blankenship, while I'm thinking about it, could I trouble you in a couple months to give me a ride to MTSU? I looked into buses, but it'll be hard to do."

"You bet. No trouble whatsoever. I'd be glad to help you get settled in."

"That would be amazing. I would appreciate that so much."

"We can even swing up to Nashville if you want to come by here to visit your dad."

"No, that's okay."

• • •

The days of summer bled together in a haze of work and more work. Without a single friend left in town, Dill had little use for free time. He worked for Dr. Blankenship during the day and worked nights at his old job at Floyd's, and gave his mom as much money as he could while saving some for school. He spent what scarce downtime he had writing songs or talking with Lydia. They spoke every day.

Lydia kept busy at her internship during the day. At night, she worked on the expanded version of *Dollywould* that Dahlia and Chloe had put up the money to launch. She was bringing in outside writers for the first time and taking on broader issues of interest to young women. It was already getting favorable buzz and snagging high-profile interviews.

A month or so after Lydia left, Laydee saw one of Dill's videos in Lydia's Twitter feed. She retweeted it to her 1.9 million followers. That got things rolling for Dearly in a big way. A few weeks after that, Laydee's manager called to talk to Dill about Laydee's recording one of his songs on her next album. In a tone that suggested she was understating things greatly, she told Dill that he'd be able to buy a few textbooks with the royalties.

• • •

Dill sat in his living room, waiting for Dr. Blankenship, with everything he was taking to college surrounding him. Two thrift-store suitcases full of every piece of clothing he owned (including what had come in a box Lydia had sent him from New York), a set of sheets, and a towel. A backpack with his laptop inside. His guitar. His songwriting notebooks. He surveyed his meager possessions with wonder over the unexpected course of his life.

The night before, he'd had his own solitary goodbye

ceremony at Travis's grave. He left a Krystal burger. He was playing his first coffeehouse gig the next night. It promised to be a full house.

Dill's mother, dressed in her maid's uniform, walked in and looked around, her face grim. "I've seen God's plan for you, and this is not it," she said.

"How have you seen God's plan for me?" He pointedly banished any hint of rancor from his voice, even though he knew he wasn't going to like her answer. He didn't want a cloud over his leaving.

Dill's mother's stony aspect softened. "When I held you as a baby and looked into your face, the Spirit revealed it to me. Your place is here. Working hard, living simply. Living in a godly way."

Dill ran his fingers through his hair and looked away. "There was a time I would've believed that."

His mother recoiled. "You don't anymore?"

Dill studied the carpet for a moment, fixating on the discolored patch that sometimes caught his eye while he sat playing his guitar. "I have a memory too. When you were in the hospital, in a coma after your wreck. The doctor told me you might die. I held your hand for hours, listening to the machines beeping and breathing for you, and I asked God to heal you and to make my life better someday. And he has. He sent me people who made me feel brave and like I have choices. Now I believe God gives people lots of paths they can take. Not just one."

She raised her eyebrows. "And you think this is one of the paths he's given you?"

"Yes."

She shook her head. Not as though expressing disagreement—more as though trying to make her ears a moving target for what Dill was saying. So his words wouldn't make it in. "What you think is God might be Satan appearing as an angel of light."

Dill smiled wistfully. "Trust me, the angels I know would have told me if they were Satan."

"That's not funny." Dill's mother brushed a stray wisp of hair from her eyes. "You're different than you used to be."

"How was I?"

"Less prideful."

He looked her in the eyes. "What you call pride, I call courage."

She folded her arms. "Things are what they are. Doesn't matter what we call them." After a hesitant silence, she said, "I also have a memory from when I was in a coma. I remember seeing a beautiful light. It filled me with warmth and love. And I knew that I could follow it to a better place, where I'd kneel at my Savior's feet and nothing would hurt anymore. But I didn't. I came back to take care of you. I made the choice not to leave you, and I've suffered for that choice. But I don't regret it."

Dill stood and faced his mother. He had been taller than her for a long time, but he felt like he was towering over her. "I don't expect you to understand. This is the spirit of God moving in me. This is the sign of my faith. I did this to save myself."

"We don't save ourselves," she said with a tinge of scorn.

"I didn't say I didn't have help."

"I did what I could for you, Dillard." She sounded resigned and broken.

"I know. But this isn't the place or the life for me anymore." He started to tell her how close he came. How lucky she was that he was even still alive. But he couldn't. Some things she never needed to know.

Dill's mother smoothed her blouse, shaking her head.

"Is there any part of you that's proud of me?" Dill asked. *You already know the answer.*

"The girls at work tell me I ought to be."

"Are you?"

She looked at the ground. "I don't know," she said quietly.

Dill knew that he was supposed to feel hurt by that. Instead, he felt more of a residual, weary sadness. A fading bruise. Only the disappointment that her answer was exactly what he expected. *No, not exactly. You expected an outright no.*

His mother broke the silence by picking up her keys from beside the lamp. "I need to get to work." She started out the door.

"Mama?" Dill said it before he knew what he was going to say next.

She stopped with one hand on the doorknob, the other pinching the bridge of her nose, her head bowed. She didn't turn.

"I love you," he said to her back.

She turned slowly. Tears filled her eyes. "I'm afraid of being alone," she whispered, as though she were afraid that normal speaking would bring down some precarious barricade inside her.

"I know." *We all are.* Dill stepped forward tentatively and hugged her. He hadn't hugged her in a long time. He could feel the bones of her afflicted back and shoulders. She smelled like knockoff Ivory soap and powdered laundry detergent from a yellow box labeled "Laundry Detergent." She covered her face with her hands and didn't hug him back.

When Dill finished hugging her, she put her damp hand on his cheek. "I'll pray for you, Dillard." She sounded like she was leaving him to die in some wilderness. She tried to turn and leave before Dill saw the tears begin to stream down her cheeks in force, but she didn't quite make it in time.

He sat for a while, gazing at the wall. He plugged in the air conditioner, got out his guitar, and played over the clatter, until Dr. Blankenship pulled up in his Prius and honked.

Dill unplugged the air conditioner and put his guitar in the case. He slung on his backpack and carried his two suitcases and guitar with a precarious grasp. He walked into the bright morning, feeling lighter and freer than he had ever felt.

Acknowledgments

From the bottom of my heart, I wish to thank the following people who made this book possible:

My amazing agents: Charlie Olsen, Lyndsey Blessing, and Philippa Milnes-Smith. My brilliant editorial team: Emily Easton and Tara Walker. Isabel Warren-Lynch and her talented design staff—Alison Impey for her incredible artistic vision for the book jacket, and Trish Parcell for the amazing interior design. Phoebe Yeh, Samantha Gentry, and everyone at Crown Books for Young Readers, and Barbara Marcus, Judith Haut, John Adamo and his marketing team, and Dominique Cimina and her publicity team at Random House Children's Books.

My awesome readers: Joel Karpowitz, Shawn Kessler, Sean Leslie, Heather Shillace, Amy Saville, Jenny Downs, Sherry Berrett, Valerie Goates, Ben Ball, and Dr. Daniel Crosby.

SWAB.

The Bev boys: Jeremy Voros, Rob Hale, James Stewart.

My Guru: Fred Voros.

My fantastic bosses: Amy Tarkington and Rachel Willis.

Lindsay Reid Fitzgerald, for telling me I should write more.

David Arnold and Adam Silvera, for welcoming me into the brotherhood.

Dr. Małgorzata Büthner-Zawadzka, the first to call me a writer.

Jarrod and Stephanie Perkins, for always being there for me and for being such inspirations.

John Corey Whaley, for being all that I hope to be someday. The only thing rivaling your incredible talent is your generosity of spirit.

Natalie Lloyd, for constantly making me laugh and for Midnight Gulch and the magical worlds you'll yet create.

My real-life Lydias: Tracy Moore and Alli Marshall.

Denise Grollmus, I will ever be in your debt. This book would not exist without you.

My fourth-grade English teacher, Lynda Wheeler, who made me believe I might be a storyteller.

Joe Bolton, for your poetry.

Everyone at Tennessee Teen Rock Camp and Southern Girls Rock Camp.

Everyone who said, even sarcastically, that I should write a book someday, because I generally understand even sarcastic compliments to be sincere.

Everyone who ever listened to my music and supported me. This book would not exist without the stories that began as songs. Those songs would not have existed without you.

The city of Nashville, Tennessee, for welcoming us back. The Nashville Metro Transit Authority for making your buses such a great place to write. Most of this book was written on your buses.

The Nashville Public Library system, Parnassus Books and Rhino Booksellers in Nashville, and Riverbank Books in Sparta, for existing.

My mom and dad, who instilled in me a lifelong love of books. Who read to me. Who dropped me off at the library with a quarter for the pay phone so that I could call for a ride when I was done spending hours there. You made this book possible.

My beautiful wife and brilliant best friend, Sara. Without your encouragement and support, I could not have written this or anything else. You are my world. You bring music to my life. And to my beautiful son, Tennessee. Thank you for being the perfect son and making me so proud always. I'll never forget the mornings we spent both working on our books.

Love deserves monuments, and this is the only kind I know how to build. I'll keep building them as long as I have strength enough in my mind and hands. I love you both. Thank you.

About the Author

JEFF ZENTNER is a singer-songwriter and guitarist who has recorded with Iggy Pop, Nick Cave, and Debbie Harry. In addition to writing and recording his own music, Jeff works with young musicians at Tennessee Teen Rock Camp, which inspired him to write a novel for young adults. He lives in Nashville with his wife and son. *The Serpent King* is his first novel. You can follow him on Facebook and Instagram, and on Twitter at @jeffzentner.

About *The Serpent King,* Jeff says, "I wanted to write about young people who struggle to lead lives of dignity and find beauty in a forgotten, unglamorous place. Who wonder what becomes of dreams once they cross the county line. This book is my love letter to those young people and anyone who has ever felt like them, no matter how or where they grew up."